Scandalous Secrets

What would Lord Anthony Mortimer think, if he found out that young and beautiful Lady Lucinde Coldwell had committed a most shocking theft?

What would Lord Anthony say if he learned that Lucinde was involved in a circle where ruinous gambling was the rule and ladies made their own luck by dubious means?

What would Lord Anthony do if he discovered that Lucy's heart was his to do with what he would?

Even for someone as unafraid as Lucinde, these were fearful questions indeed . . .

A native of Yorkshire, England, IRENE SAUNDERS spent a number of years exploring London while working for the U.S. Air Force there. A love of travel brought her to New York City, where she met her husband, Ray, then settled in Miami, Florida. She now lives in Port St. Lucie, Florida, dividing her time between writing, bookkeeping, gardening, needlepoint, and travel.

SIGNET REGENCY ROMANCE

COMING IN DECEMBER 1990

Sandra Heath
A Christmas Courtship

Emma Lange
The Reforming of Lord Roth

Emily Hendrickson
Double Deceit

Lady Lucinde's Locket

by

Irene Saunders

A SIGNET BOOK

SIGNET
Published by the Penguin Group
Penguin Books USA Inc., 375 Hudson Street,
New York, New York 10014, U.S.A.
Penguin Books Ltd, 27 Wrights Lane,
London W8 5TZ, England
Penguin Books Australia Ltd, Ringwood,
Victoria, Australia
Penguin Books Canada Ltd, 2801 John Street,
Markham, Ontario, Canada L3R 1B4
Penguin Books (N.Z.) Ltd, 182-190 Wairau Road,
Auckland 10, New Zealand

Penguin Books Ltd, Registered Offices:
Harmondsworth, Middlesex, England

First published by Signet, an imprint of New American Library,
a division of Penguin Books USA Inc.

First Printing, November, 1990
10 9 8 7 6 5 4 3 2 1

Printed in the United States of America

Prologue

Vitoria, June 21, 1813

On the western hillside overlooking the town of Vitoria, Wellington and his staff officers gazed unhappily at a scene of complete devastation as the big French guns successfully held at bay the British infantry.

Colonel Anthony Mortimer reached inside his scarlet tunic and took out his watch. "Just five more minutes, sir," he said quietly, "and the guns will inflict no more damage, for they will be in our hands."

Wellington nodded. "The waiting is the worst. Are your men in position for the blockade?"

"Yes, sir," the colonel affirmed, "and if you will excuse me, I'll join them at once, for I'd not like to miss any of the fun."

At a nod from his commander he mounted his black gelding and set off down the hillside, then paused on a slope just above the battlefield. As he had predicted, the guns had finally stopped, but the heavy damage they had inflicted was even more obvious from this elevation.

Women were scurrying back and forth helping the wounded men to where, just out of range of the guns, a surgeon's tent had been set up. He noted that most of the wounded went first to a spot nearby, where two women appeared to be checking the extent of the injuries and either motioned them toward the surgeon or into a line rapidly forming to their rear.

One of the women, as tall and big-boned as a man, had her head down as she bent over a soldier, but the other glanced up in his direction. She was gowned in black and quite small, but obviously most competent. Even at this distance there was a surprising air of quiet authority about her.

There was something vaguely familiar about the way she carried herself, and he knew for a certainty that he had seen her before. It was a pity he was so far away, for he would have liked to get a closer look. Then the black shawl she wore over her head slipped, revealing a mass of curly red hair, and he knew at once who she was.

He had an immediate part to play, however, in what he was convinced would be an important British victory. Putting all thoughts of the little lady aside, he set off at a gallop to where he and his men had, earlier in the day, succeeded in completely blocking the Great Road, the enemy's main line of retreat.

Napoleon's fleeing soldiers, and the brother he had named King Joseph of Spain, would be forced to leave weapons and valuables behind them as they fled along the only other way of escape, the narrow road to Pamplona.

Lady Lucinde Coldwell had not missed the glance in her direction. She had recognized at once the black-haired colonel who sat tall in his saddle, but thought herself well enough disguised until she reached up a hand and realized that the shawl she always wore no longer concealed her hair.

She shrugged. If he had not already done so, it would be but a matter of time before he remembered her, for in the two and a half years she had been out here she had not met a single woman with hair the color of her own.

For the next four hours she had little time to worry about the colonel. Wives held their menfolk as she and her tall friend, Gussy Bradbury, the widow of a sergeant, prodded and poked to be sure that not the smallest piece of metal was left in a wound to cause festering, then cleansed and stitched it together, At first, stitching had been the part she hated most, but like everything else out here, she had gradually become inured to it and now thought only of doing it as neatly as possible.

She had told Gussy earlier that she had seen the colonel, and now, as the sun started to sink, she turned to her friend. "I believe it would be best if I disappear for now. If the good colonel comes asking questions, you could pretend not to know whom he is talking about," she suggested with a grin.

"P'raps 'e won't come, milady," Gussy murmured, bending low over a soldier as she reached for a piece of metal with her tweezers. There was a yelp as the fragment was removed. "Your shawl might not 'ave slipped until afterward. But I'll tell 'im nothing and I'll make sure t'other women don't say anything either. If you're going to t'camp followers you'll be busy tonight, for there's usually one or another of 'em needs a poultice or an ointment made up."

"I'll join the gypsies, I believe," Lucy decided, "for, should he come, they will enjoy themselves teasing such a serious English colonel. I almost hope he will, for they'll lead him a merry dance."

She chuckled at the thought. "You've no idea how stiff-rumped and top-lofty he used to be, Gussy. When we first arrived, there was little to do but wait for Massena to retreat, so we had to devise our own entertainment. Do you know, he actually told Henry it was not at all the thing for me to dance with anyone below the rank of lieutenant?" Her eyes sparkled with mischief. "Of course, after that we teased him unmercifully."

Gussy shook her head, knowing full well that the colonel had been right. "Sir Henry was a wild one, to be sure," she said. "With the pranks you two played, I swore you were brother and sister till my Bert told me you were wed. I don't wonder you're not anxious to see 'im. There's no knowin' what 'e might do. And you with no 'usband to protect you now."

"Oh, I think he realized it was all just fun," Lucy told her, laughing softly. "But it's strange you should say that, for Henry was like a brother to me much of the time, except, of course, at night.'' The last words were said in almost a whisper, and her sunburned cheeks showed a decided flush.

''I've been meaning to ask you. You're not still taking that stuff I told you about, are you, milady?'' Gussy's voice was gruff.

''Of course not, Gussy. I stopped it as soon as Henry died. What kind of an innocent do you think I am?'' she asked, looking even more embarrassed and glancing down at the young soldier whose arm Gussy was bandaging. To her relief she saw that he wore the uniform of the Spanish militia.

''A long way from the young newlywed who couldn't stand t'sight of blood when she first came out 'ere.'' There was warm affection in Gussy's eyes as she looked at the young lady who now knew more about healing than she did herself. ''You'll not take in London, y'know, if this colonel finds you and sends you back. From what I 'ear, freckles aren't fashionable there.''

''Don't even think such a thing,'' Lucy said sharply. ''I don't know what I shall do when the war is over, and it may not be long now. I can't go to Henry's mama and papa, nor to my own mama, for I have a letter informing me that she has married again and her husband does not know she has a twenty-year-old daughter.''

She made a face, then started to gather together her various belongings before striding off in a decidedly unladylike manner.

Gussy gave a snort to indicate her disgust at such a mother, then turned to the next injured soldier.

After sharing a meal with some of her gypsy friends, Lucy spent the next couple of hours treating the ailments of others, mostly children, for word of her presence had quickly spread. But one child was too sick to be moved, so she hurried across the camp to the tent where the little girl lay. After giving the mother some advice and a potion for the child, Lucy started back toward the gypsy camp.

As she stepped from the clearing into a wooded area, she

suddenly felt herself grasped from behind, then a hand covered her mouth, effectively stifling her scream.

"Don't be alarmed, my lady," a familiar voice murmured softly. "I've seen enough fighting this day without being set upon by a bunch of gypsies. If you'll promise not to scream, I'll take my hand away and escort you back to the army quarters."

Lucy nodded, temporarily relieved when she recognized the voice, for she had feared she was being attacked.

The hand was removed from her face, but she was still held firmly by her arm as Henry's old friend, Anthony, hurried her toward the military section of the camp.

"I'd like to think you were not avoiding me, my lady," the colonel went on quietly, "but your friends have given me so many false directions as to your whereabouts that I can only conclude you saw me and went into hiding."

"You flatter yourself, sir," Lucy snapped, digging her heels into the ground so that he was forced to come to an abrupt halt. "And I would appreciate not being dragged along at such a pace."

"I beg your pardon, my lady." There was a touch of amusement in his voice. "However, the sooner we reach the army camp, the less danger there is of someone trying to rescue you from my clutches."

"I should never have promised not to scream," she muttered to herself, then heard his soft chuckle.

"That was one of the things Henry told me about you. He said that, once given, you never broke your word no matter what happened," he remarked, loosening his tight grasp as they reached the military tents and placing her hand on his arm, much as if they were going for an evening stroll.

"Where are you taking me?" she asked as they passed the section where she and Gussy shared a tent.

"To the officers' quarters, of course," he said blandly. "Then you can explain to me what you are doing still out here when it is much more than a year since Henry was killed."

A few minutes later he escorted her to a house that was being used temporarily as headquarters for the regiment, and took her directly into a large office.

"You're not the new C.O., are you?" she asked, realizing with dismay that if he was he could order her home right away.

"Temporarily, I am." He held a chair for her to sit in front of the table, then took his place behind it. "And now, my lady, I want an answer to the question I just asked you. What are you still doing here?"

"I'm sure you saw for yourself what I am doing," she snapped. "I started helping in whatever way I could just after you were transferred. I couldn't just stand around when there was so much to be done, so I learned how to help the sick and wounded. Henry approved completely."

"But Henry isn't here now," he remarked mildly, "and he was fully aware, I am sure, that the battlefield was not a suitable place for a lady."

"What should I have been doing, then?" she asked sharply, her blue-green eyes flashing. "Organizing parties and picnics for the other officers' wives?"

"In my opinion, officers' wives should not be here at all, though I will admit that many of the enlisted men's wives out here are almost as valuable to the army as their husbands." He looked sternly at her and she glared back defiantly, knowing full well that it was not the wisest thing to do, but she was no simpering miss and she'd not beg him to let her stay.

"Early tomorrow morning I will have two of my most trustworthy men escort you to the coast and put you on the first available vessel leaving for England," he said calmly, then paused as Lucy told him in most unladylike terms just what she thought about him.

When she had finished, he went on as though he had not heard a word. "Mrs. Augusta Bradbury, who I understand is also a widow, will accompany you to your final destination."

"But Gussy's needed here," Lucy protested. "She's every bit as good as the surgeons are."

"As a lady, you cannot travel alone," the colonel said firmly, "and Mrs. Bradbury's position here is no more tenable than yours. Do you have any money?"

Lucy flushed. "No, I don't," she admitted, and added, "and I won't take any money from anyone."

"You have a mare here, I understand," Colonel Mortimer said quietly. "I can use her and will be glad to give you a fair price for her. That should be more than enough to cover your expenses to wherever in England you decide to go."

She glared angrily at him, even more infuriated by the fact that he seemed to have an immediate answer to her every objection. "I can see there's no talking to you," she said, looking with loathing at the man who had so calmly turned her whole life upside down in just a few hours.

"There's no talking me out of it, if that's what you mean," he told her, "and one day you may even thank me for insisting you return home while you're still in one piece."

She rose, and he was on his feet in an instant, taking her arm and leading her out to where a sergeant waited.

"This is Sergeant Morgan, who will escort you to your tent now and accompany you on your journey tomorrow to the coast. I wish you a good night and hope you have a safe and comfortable passage home, my lady." He took her hand and bowed low over it before leaving her in the sergeant's capable hands.

When she arose the following morning, it was to find that everything had been arranged and all she and Gussy had to do was say good-bye to the soldiers' wives who had prepared food for their journey, then mount the waiting horses.

As she started to do so, she felt a light hand on her arm and turned to find one of the camp followers whose little son she had made well some weeks before. The woman curtsied and thrust a small package into Lucy's hand, then ran off before she could even thank her for it.

From an upstairs window of the temporary headquarters, Anthony Mortimer watched, and he wondered what the woman, obviously a camp follower, had handed to Lady Lucinde. It was probably food for the journey, he decided, as he saw her slip it into the pocket of her black gown and turn to agilely mount her mare before Morgan could come close enough to assist her.

A part of him wished he was going with her, for he had felt a strong attraction to her from the moment they first met. But she had been Henry's wife then, and decidedly off-limits as far as he was concerned.

He had been surprised to find that yesterday, even as he and his handpicked men methodically accomplished the task of blocking the major departure route to France, his mind had kept drifting back to the young woman he had seen again for that brief moment. She had been tending the wounded in a spot where the battle could have recommenced at any moment, and his one thought had been to get her away from the danger, out of Spain altogether and back in England, where she belonged.

He was a handsome man, tall and broad-shouldered, with a thick head of unruly hair. His light-blue eyes followed her now as the two women and their escorts set off at a gallop and soon disappeared from view. If everything went according to plan, he might also be back in England very shortly, and if he was, then he certainly meant to look her up and find out how she was getting along.

As they rode away from the camp, Lucy had the strange feeling that they were being watched, but once on the road, there was little time to think of anything save getting to the coast before the ship sailed without them. Once aboard, however, when she was feeling more miserable than she had since Henry died, she saw the package the woman had thrust into her hand and she opened it. Inside was a gold, jeweled locket, obviously quite old and very valuable. It must have been part of the treasures that Napoleon's brother, King Joseph of Spain, had been forced to abandon at Vitoria, she decided.

Rumor had it that the king's carriages had been plundered by the French, Spanish, and British soldiers in turn, and Wellington had been furious. Though she felt a little uneasy about owning the locket, she decided to keep it as one of her few mementoes of the Peninsula.

1

Viewed from the side of the ship, London's dock area looked much the same to Lucinde as it had when she embarked for Portugal as Henry's bride. On that occasion, however, she had happily left the arrangements to him, and now she realized, to her dismay, that she had not the least idea of the proximity of the docks to London itself or, for that matter, to anywhere else in England. She had been barely eighteen when she left, and it had never occurred to her, of course, that she might return alone.

While waiting for the ship to dock, she pondered the question of where to go. Visiting her mama was not possible. Nor could she go to the family of her late husband, for Henry had married against his parents' wishes. She had learned, after they were wed, that he had rejected their choice of a suitable bride who would have brought with her lands adjoining their own estates.

There were, of course, numerous aunts and uncles on her mama's side of the family, but she could not even recall where most of them lived. So that left Grandpapa and Grandmama, Lord and Lady Amberley, and though she had not seen them for many years, she was sure they would not turn her and Gussy away.

Once the ship was tied up, Lucy reached for the small portmanteau that held all her worldly possessions except for the locket, which was in her reticule, but Gussy quickly grabbed the heavier bag from her.

"You'll not carry that while I've got two hands, milady," she said severely, walking toward the gangplank. "What would your family think?"

Lucy smiled and went over to the captain to thank him for his numerous kindnesses to the two of them. Then she joined Gussy on the dock and looked around to see if a hackney was in sight at this early hour of the morning.

"Where be ye going, missy?"

The gruff voice had come from behind her back. Lucy swung around and saw a ruddy-faced farmer walking along the dock carrying a heavy sack on his shoulders.

"There'll be no 'ackneys 'ere for an 'our or so, and this ain't no place for young ladies to wait around. As soon as I've put this'n aboard, I'll be right glad to give ye a ride to one o' them 'ackney stands," he told her. "I'm Willie Ramsbottom, an' anyone'll tell you you're safe wi' me."

He had the kind of friendly, open face that made Lucy feel sure she could trust him, and she jumped at the chance to get quickly away from the decidedly squalid docks.

Not five minutes later she and Gussy were nestled comfortably against the sacks on the back of the farmer's wagon. As luck would have it, he was going right through the heart of Mayfair, for his farm was to the west of London, so he volunteered to take them all the way.

They were fortunate to be arriving during the long days of summer, for it was quite light even at six in the morning, and it was a most interesting time to view the sights of London. An early-morning haze was just lifting, and Lucy gazed from side to side, feeling perfectly safe atop the wagon, but finding it hard to believe how large London was, for though the horses went at a steady clip, it still took them more than an hour to reach the elegant Mayfair area.

"If you're going to one o' them grand 'ouses in Berkeley Square, missy, p'raps I'd best let you off a street or so away an' you can tidy yerself up a bit afore they see you," the farmer called out, and pointed a finger to the right. "Berkeley

Street'd be best, jus' afore the Duke of Devenshire's 'ouse over there."

"That would be perfect, Willie," Lucy told him, reaching for her purse, for though he'd not asked a fare, she was sure he could always make use of some extra money. After he helped them down and pointed out the square, she thanked him and pressed the coins into his hand. Though he protested, she insisted, for she knew that a hackney would have cost a great deal more.

It was just after seven o'clock when Lucy ran up the steps of Number Fourteen Berkeley Square, a perfectly respectable hour, she thought as she swung the knocker loudly enough to waken the dead.

"Lady Lucinde Coldwell and Mrs. Augusta Bradbury to see Lady Amberley," Lucy told a rather sleepy-looking footman.

Then, as he mumbled something about waiting and made to close the door, Lucy gave it a sharp push and stepped inside, Gussy at her heels.

"Don't you dare close the door on me, young man," Lucy snapped, sounding for a moment so very much like her grandmama that the elderly butler, who had been standing in the hall, listening, came hurrying forward.

"Duffield, isn't it?" Lucy inquired. "You may show us into the drawing room until Grandmama can receive us, and please send in a fresh pot of tea."

The usually austere butler, who had been with the Amberleys since he was a young man, was trying hard not to show his surprise.

"Of course, my lady," he murmured as he opened the drawing-room doors to reveal a couple of maids busily polishing the furniture. At a sharp turn of his head they scurried out through a side door as Lucy and Gussy went in.

Much to Lucy's pleasure, the pot of tea she had ordered was accompanied by a plate of scones fresh from the oven, a dish of strawberry jam, thick cream, and butter. After what they had been used to in Spain, this was indeed a feast, if served at an unusual hour of day. Lucy had just finished and was wiping away the traces of jam from her lips when Duffield returned.

"Lady Amberley will see you at once in her upstairs sitting room, my lady. Mrs. Bradbury is to wait here," he intoned solemnly. "I will show you the way."

Lucy grinned. "Unless it's been moved, I know exactly where it is, so you can save your legs, Duffield," she said cheerfully, already halfway across the room. "I may be quite a while, Gussy, so just make yourself comfortable here until I return."

The old servant watched as she ran lightly up the wide staircase and took the passage to the right, then he turned back toward the kitchen, shaking his head slightly in bewilderment.

Out of consideration for her grandmama, Lucy knocked on the sitting-room door and waited until she heard a faint response before entering. She paused and looked at the expression of wonder on the old lady's face, then hurled herself across the room and into the outstretched arms.

After a moment she realized she must be crushing both their gowns, though her own was already beyond redemption, and she stepped back. Lady Amberley looked into the face that was so much like her own had been many, many years ago, gave her granddaughter another hug, then motioned for her to take the chair next to her.

"Did your governess not teach you to write, young lady?" she asked, her voice gruff with emotion she was trying hard to conceal.

"There was no time to ask if I might come to stay," Lucy explained apologetically. "You see, the decision to return was made one evening, and by the following morning I was on my way to the ship. It docked a few hours ago."

"You need never ask if you can stay here, my dear. Our home is yours at any time and for as long as you wish. Who is the female traveling with you, and where is that husband of yours?" Lady Amberley asked, her eagle eyes taking in the poor cut and inferior quality of the black gown Lucinde was wearing.

"Henry was killed in action, and my companion is Mrs. Augusta Bradbury, who is also widowed." Lucy hoped her grandmama would not ask any more questions about when Henry had died. After the life she had led on the Peninsula, she had no desire to enter the giddy, partygoing whirl of the *ton*, which was why she had hesitated to stay in London. But where else could she have gone?

"Am I correct in assuming that she is not a lady of gentle birth?" Lady Amberley's eyebrows were raised, but her bright eyes twinkled.

"She is not a lady of rank, if that is what you mean," Lucy said sharply, "but she is the best friend I have ever known, and she only came to England because it was not thought proper for me to travel alone."

Her grandmama did not ask who had not thought it proper, but gave silent thanks for that person's sound judgment. "Assuming you wish her to stay here, have you decided what her position would be?" she asked quietly.

Lucy sighed heavily. "Grandmama, Gussy is an exceptionally capable nurse, and if I were ill, I would much rather have her than any doctor. She is extremely knowledgeable about herbs and potions to use, and is a stickler for cleanliness. It would be a terrible waste of her talents were she forced to seek work as a scullery maid for the rest of her life."

"Humph," Lady Amberley grunted. More than eager to meet this paragon, she preferred to have her position in the household clear before she did so. "If she also has a talent with hair, clothes, and such, perhaps she could become your abigail," she suggested hopefully.

Lucy's face lit with pleasure. "I knew you'd think of something. I can't wait to tell her. But I am concerned about leaving her so long alone, for if she thought herself not wanted and went away, I would never find her again."

Lady Amberley reached for the bellpull and gave it a couple of tugs, and a moment later a middle-aged woman dressed in a plain black dress appeared.

"Peters, this is my granddaughter, Lady Lucinde," she said, and the woman gave a little bob in Lucy's direction. "There is a Mrs. Bradbury waiting in the drawing room. I want her brought up here at once."

The woman gave her mistress another bob and hurried from the room.

"Peters is my abigail, companion, maid-of-all-work," Lady Amberley explained, then added, "it will be up to you to decide whether you want Mrs. Bradbury to do all that bobbing up and down. I've always thought it a vast waste of time, but the older servants seem to feel it denotes respect."

Lucy did not believe one word of her grandmama's pronouncement, but vowed that, if Gussy started to work for her, she would definitely not allow it. While her grandmama spoke to her abigail, Lucy noticed for the first time how much older Lady Amberley had grown. When last they met her grandmama's hair, once as red as her own, had been streaked with silver. Now it was almost pure white. The deep blue-green of her eyes was fading, also, but her skin, though starting to wrinkle, still had the creamy color and soft texture that she remembered.

There was a knock on the door and Gussy was ushered into the room.

For more than a year now, Lucy had rarely glanced at a gown when she donned it on a morning, but in this elegant sitting room, hung in the same soft-green velvet as it had been when she was a child, the comparison between her grandmama's gown and the ones she and Gussy were wearing was quite ludicrous. She flushed as she realized that they looked no better than a couple of Spanish peasants.

She suddenly became aware that Lady Amberley was waiting for her to make the introductions.

"Grandmama," she said quietly, "I'd like to present my friend and companion, Mrs. Augusta Bradbury. Gussy, this is Lady Amberley, Countess of Pemberton."

Gussy curtsied and Lady Amberley motioned for her to take a seat, noticing how careful she was to select a wooden chair, for her black gown was still quite obviously dusty.

"I think I'd best call you Gussy, also," Lady Amberley began, "and first, I must thank you for all that you have done to bring my granddaughter safely home."

Gussy flushed and muttered something quite indistinguishable.

"Lady Lucinde tells me that she would like you to stay here and work for her as her abigail/companion." Lady Amberley did not miss the woman's perplexed frown as she looked across at her granddaughter. "You would be required to look after her wardrobe, wash, iron, and mend her clothes, help her dress on a morning, change gowns during the day, arrange her hair becomingly, and wait up each night to help her out of her gown and into her night attire. Do you think you could do this? I am aware that you are an outstanding nurse, and we would all be happy to use those talents if and when they were needed, but I sincerely hope that will not be for some time."

"I've done me share of washin', ironin' and sewin', m'lady," Gussy told her, "but I've never done anybody else's 'air but me own, so I might be a bit slow at first. I'd 'ave duties in the kitchen as well, of course, wouldn't I?"

Lady Amberley smiled and shook her head. "No, your duties would lie only with the care of my granddaughter. However, as a lady cannot go out unaccompanied," she explained kindly, "you would, on occasion, be required to go with her on shopping expeditions, walks in the park, and so on. Would that be satisfactory?"

Gussy swallowed hard and nodded. "It just seems too good to be true, milady, and I give you my word that I'll take good care of 'er," she promised.

Lady Amberley was more pleased with the arrangement

than she would have admitted, for she had taken a strong liking to this large, angular woman and felt that her granddaughter would be in the best of hands. She gave the bellpull several sharp tugs and turned back to Lucinde.

"When we go to the modiste I'll procure a couple of lengths of fabric so that Gussy can make herself some new gowns in her spare time. I'm afraid you both look as though you brought half the dust of Spain back with you on your clothes," she said dryly.

"I assure you we left much more there, Grandmama," Lucy said with a laugh, "but you have the right of it. There were times when we felt that we ate, drank, and slept in dust. But I had not realized just how worn this gown looks until just now when I compared it with yours."

There was the sound of footsteps along the corridor and Lady Amberley said, "Ah, this must be Mrs. Waterhouse, my housekeeper. I don't believe she was with us when you were here last, Lucinde, but that must be all of six years since, I should think."

"Six and a half, I believe," Lucy told her, and looked toward the door as a short, stout woman knocked and came bustling in.

After introducing Lucinde, Lady Amberley said, "I want you to meet Mrs. Bradbury, who has been with my granddaughter in Spain and will work for her now as her abigail/companion. I'm sure you'll make her as comfortable as you can, and probably what she needs most at the moment is something to eat and a hot bath."

The two women seemed to take to each other at once, and when they had left, Lady Amberley said, "Now, give me your arm, my dear, and we'll go down to breakfast. Your grandpapa will, by now, have finished his, but I am sure he'll be waiting impatiently to see you again."

For all her rather brusque manner, Lucy realized that her grandmama really was happy to see her, and she, in turn, was now more than glad to be here. They both had the same tiny bones, but while Lucy's arms were firmly fleshed out, her grandmama's were extremely thin, and the one Lucy was holding felt as fragile as a piece of delicate bone china. Lady Amberley had always had an iron will, however, and there was no question but that it was as strong as ever.

Lord Amberley rose and came forward as they entered the breakfast room. He took one of Lucy's hands in each of his own and just stood looking at her for a moment. Then he pulled her toward him and clasped her in his arms, swallowing hard. "It's good to see you home safe and sound again, my dear," he murmured huskily. "At times, we were extremely worried."

When Duffield had served them and left the room, Lucy started to appease her still-quite-considerable hunger, while Lord Amberley looked astutely at his granddaughter, noting her dark complexion and quite pitiful attire.

"Lucinde's husband was killed in action, my dear," Lady Amberley murmured. "She will stay with us for as long as she wishes."

"Of course she will," Lord Amberley said sharply. "She can hardly stay with her bird-witted mother, can she?"

Lucy looked up and grinned ruefully. "I'm afraid you're right, Grandpapa, for my mama wrote that she had married someone younger than herself and just could not let her husband know that she had a twenty-year-old daughter."

Lord Amberley made a loud "humph," and his face turned a reddish-purple hue. After a worried glance in his direction, Lady Amberley quickly changed the subject.

"How did Sir Henry's parents take the news of his death, my dear? You wrote them, of course?" she asked her granddaughter.

"They took it in much the same way as they did our marriage. They did not approve of their son marrying me, for they wanted him to wed someone of their choice," Lucy said quietly. "When I notified them of his death, they asked me to send his body home. I made arrangements for a lady from the north who wished to return there to deliver it safely to them."

"Then you have never met them?" Lady Amberley asked in surprise.

"No. We were married from Mama's house. They absolutely refused to see me, and then, within two weeks we were sent to Portugal," Lucy said matter-of-factly.

"You mean to tell me that a Coldwell had the absolute gall to turn down my granddaughter?" Lord Amberley growled, glaring fiercely.

"I had but a very small dowry from Papa. And the Coldwells had hoped Henry would do what they wished, for they were land-poor," Lucy explained apologetically then, as much to change the subject as anything, she asked, "Do you think I might help myself to just a little more of that quite delicious kedgeree, for this is the first I have had since I left England?"

"Allow me, my dear," Lord Amberley said, getting to his feet and going over to the sideboard. "And how about a little more kidney while I'm at it?"

"No, thank you, Grandpapa, for I shouldn't even be having the kedgeree, but I simply couldn't resist," Lucy confessed.

"Now don't skimp yourself. You could use a little meat on your bones, my dear," her grandfather said gruffly. "I'd heard that food was not plentiful on the Peninsula."

"We often had to forage for what we could," Lucy admitted, "and sometimes, when the army was on the march, the womenfolk would go ahead to the small villages and get most of what there was to spare." She laughed. "They sometimes beat the headquarters' staff to it, and then there was hell to pay."

Lord Amberley tried hard to suppress a chuckle, but his wife's brows drew together in a heavy frown and Lucy realized at once what she had said.

"I do beg your pardon, Grandmama," she murmured contritely, reaching out a hand to touch the older lady's arm. "I'm afraid I have spent too many years in the rough-and-tumble life of the army. I promise to watch my tongue more carefully in the future and not make you ashamed of me."

Putting a small white hand on the sunbronzed one of her granddaughter, Lady Amberley gave a little sigh and shook her head, but her eyes had softened once more.

"Just so long as you don't use such language in front of Lady Jersey or, worse still, Mrs. Drummond Burrell, my dear," she said. "You're a little old to be branded as a hoyden, but much too young to be able to say what you like and get away with it."

Lucy looked curious. "Who are these obviously very influential ladies?" she asked. "Am I likely to meet them often?"

When her grandpapa started to laugh and her grandmama looked shocked, she realized they thought her either an innocent or an ignoramus. She waited for one of them to explain.

"Oh dear," Lady Amberley moaned. "Your entry into society is going to be much more difficult than I had anticipated, Lucinde. But, of course, you were still a little girl when last you visited London. How could that daughter of mine have been so grossly negligent?"

"Now, my dear," Lord Amberley said firmly, "I have not the slightest doubt that our Lucinde knows a lot more about the things that really matter in the world today than do any of the patronesses of Almack's."

"Of course she does," his wife readily agreed, "but if she is to feel comfortable around my friends and able to converse with them intelligently, then I will have to spend some time each day, I think, explaining just how one goes on in society."

Lucy groaned inwardly, but said nothing, for she had suddenly realized that deep down she had always loved her only two living grandparents, though she had seldom seen them. She would never willingly do anything to hurt or upset them, and if Grandmama wanted to teach her the ways of the *ton*, then for that reason alone, she was willing.

She had forgotten until she stepped into the breakfast room

this morning what a big cuddly bear her grandpapa really was, and she intended to spend as much time with him as he would allow, for she was more than a little interested in what went on in the Houses of Parliament.

2

By late afternoon of the following day, Lucy was near to regretting her decision to stay in London.

In the company of Lady Amberley, who seemed amazingly tireless for a lady of her advanced years, she had spent more than two hours at the modiste's. She had stood or turned around while assistants draped and pinned fabric over her until both her grandmama and Madame were satisfied as to the style best suited to her small, slender figure.

Guilt played a not insignificant role in her lowness of spirit, for her grandmama had assumed that Henry had been killed recently. As Lucy had no wish to take part in the London Season that both Henry and her mama had frequently expounded upon, she had not corrected Lady Amberley's assumption.

The beautiful satins, laces, brocades, bombazines, and muslins brought out for approval were, therefore, all in the deepest black, but it was, of course, a color that admirably suited her red hair. It did nothing, however, for her brown complexion, which her grandmama so deplored and upon which she insisted a special preparation be applied nightly in an attempt to lighten it.

Two gowns and a pelisse had been brought out and fitted shortly after they arrived at the elegant establishment, and Lucy could easily picture in her mind the girls in the back workshop at this moment, crouching over the garments, their needles flying in and out of the fabric, as they hastened to alter them to fit her, for they had been promised for early tomorrow morning.

Lady Amberley finally arose from the comfortable armchair Madame had provided.

"I think that will be all for now, my dear," she said to Lucy. "Madame will send a selection of gloves, reticules, and such to the house for our perusal, but we must visit with milliners next to see for ourselves what best suits you. After that comes the shoemaker, for you simply cannot be seen walking about town in those heavy boots."

Lucy looked down at the now shabby but still serviceable high boots that Sir Henry had ordered for her, and thought of the miles of Spanish countryside they had taken her safely across. She was determined not to part with them no matter how many pairs of shoes her grandmama might buy.

When they returned to Berkeley Square another two hours later, Lucy sank gratefully into a chair in the drawing room and sipped the fragrant tea her grandmama had poured.

"Thank goodness that is over with," she murmured, then looked across at Lady Amberley's amused expression. "Oh, no, you can't mean we haven't finished, Grandmama?"

The old lady now laughed aloud. "That is only a start, my dear Lucinde. All we succeeded in doing today was to make you presentable enough to appear in public. You cannot really mean that you do not enjoy shopping? It is known to be a lady's favorite occupation."

But it was definitely not to Lucy's liking, and in the days ahead, although she was forced to admit that she made a much better appearance than she had ever done in her life, she became increasingly bored with not only the shopping trips, but with the interminable visits back and forth between her grandmama and her friends.

She had committed to memory the names of all the patronesses of Almack's, although, to her relief, she had not met them as yet, and she could recite by heart exactly what she might and might not do at that establishment. It was her profound hope that she would never need to pass through its portals and put her newly acquired knowledge to the test.

She had not worn more than half the new gowns that had been delivered thus far, yet more arrived every day, and for one person to own so many seemed to her to be the height of extravagance and a shameful waste of money that might have been put to better use.

One morning, when Gussy brought up her hot chocolate and was pulling back the yellow rose-patterned curtains, she determined that today she was going to rebel.

"Don't you think I look a trifle pulled this morning, Gussy?" she asked, trying hard to hide a grin.

"Can't say as I'd noticed, milady," her old friend told her, "but if you'd only use that lemon concoction 'er ladyship 'ad me make up for you, it might 'elp."

Lucy put down her cup at once. "You're quite right. That's just the thing. Could you go and get it and help me put it on right away, Gussy? Lady Amberley won't be up for a couple of hours yet, and if we use the lemon stuff and then dust on some flour, I'm bound to look as though I'm sickening for something."

Gussy started to laugh. "T'old lady's finally worn you out, 'as she?"

"It's not Grandmama. She's bright as a button, Gussy, but I don't know how she can stand seeing those same women day after day, and chattering like magpies about nothing of the slightest importance," Lucy complained in exasperation. "There is a war going on in Europe. Our men are being killed in France right this minute, and no one here seems to know very much about it, or even care."

"D'you think stayin' 'ome, pretendin' to be sick will do any good?" Gussy asked bluntly as she took some of the cream and applied it to her mistress's face.

"It will do *me* good, for as soon as Grandmama goes out, I'm going to go down to the study to talk to Grandpapa and find out what is going on over there, and what Parliament is doing to help," Lucy said quite decidedly.

Gussy smiled. "All this 'asn't changed you one bit, milady, 'as it? An' I doubt that it ever will."

Everything went according to their plans. Lucy did look a little pale, and her grandmama insisted that she should stay in bed or, if not, then indoors all day.

"You can keep Lord Amberley company this morning, Lucinde, if you feel up to it," she said. "He'll be delighted, for he was complaining that he's seen little of you since you arrived, but don't let him tire you out."

"I won't," Lucy promised, then, as soon as Gussy told her the coast was clear, she jumped out of bed and hurriedly dressed.

Lord Amberley was in the study at this hour of the morning, but as her grandmama had suggested she keep him company, she felt sure she would not be intruding on his privacy. She knocked loudly on the study door and waited until he called for her to come in.

He rose to his feet as soon as he saw who it was, and came around the desk to greet her.

"I was hoping you might feel well enough to visit with me, my dear," he told her, placing an arm around her shoulders and drawing her over to where two large wing chairs faced each other in front of the fireplace. "Did you have breakfast? Would you like a cup of tea?"

"No, thank you, Grandpapa, I'm quite all right," Lucy assured him as she sank into one of the chairs. "I have seen so little of you since I first arrived that I thought this might be a good opportunity for us to get to know each other again."

Lord Amberley settled himself comfortably in the other chair, then smiled warmly at her. "Delighted as I am to see you, my dear, I have the feeling there is a little more to it than you're admitting. Perhaps, despite everything London has to offer, you miss the army life in Spain. Is that it?"

Lucy nodded. "I was doing something there that was very worthwhile, and I'm not accustomed to having nothing to do," she said, frowning a little.

His face became grave. "There's something I've been waiting to ask you, my dear, as soon as we had a moment alone. Why did you stay on there for such a long time after Sir Henry was killed?"

She could not conceal a little gasp of surprise, then felt suddenly relieved that he knew. "Because I had already been helping with the sick and wounded for quite some time. I was needed. And I did not feel I had anywhere to come back to. But how did you know?"

"I saw Colonel Henry Coldwell's name on the list of fatalities more than a year ago, but I did not want to say anything to your grandmama until we had some word from you. I even had inquiries made as to your whereabouts, but you seemed to have disappeared without a trace. My worst fear was that you had been killed also," he said quietly.

Tears filled her eyes as she realized the anxiety she must have caused him. "I'm truly sorry. The last thing I wanted was to worry you and Grandmama. It never once occurred to me that anyone over here, except Henry's mother and father, would have received news of his death."

He had watched her expressive face as surprise and then regret at the sorrow she had caused passed over it. She was so very much like her grandmama had been at the same age.

"Why didn't you tell us, when you arrived, that you had been a widow for so long? Lady Amberley would never have put you in black, had she realized." Though he sounded very serious, there was a twinkle in his light-gray eyes.

She nibbled on her lower lip for a moment, attempting to find the best way to explain herself, and finally said, "It seemed so difficult trying to make someone like Grandmama, who has always led this kind of a life"—she made a sweeping gesture with her hands to indicate the opulence of even the study—"understand how important it was for me to feel I was doing something useful, to make her realize that was my reason for staying on for as long as I could."

Her grandpapa nodded understandingly. "I can see how you would feel the army was your family after a while," he said. "But what happened to cause you to return when you did?"

An expression of disgust came over Lucy's face. "Colonel Anthony Mortimer is what happened," she said bitterly. "He was an old friend of Henry's, but was transferred not long after I came on the scene, and I didn't see him for a couple of years. Then he saw me helping the wounded at Vitoria. He'd been made acting commander of the regiment, and when he ordered me home, there was nothing I could do about it."

Lord Amberley was secretly amused, for he knew the young man in question quite well. His mother was a dear friend of Lady Amberley's, and if the fellow came home on leave, he was sure to meet up with Lucy again. He decided that silence was the better part of valor.

"Can you tell me what is happening over there now, Grandpapa? I've been so worried that the French would make a stand once they were over the border and into their own country, and this time Gussy and I would not be there to help." She looked appealingly at him, hoping he could give her some information.

"There's talk of peace going on right now, but no one has yet decided to have a cease-fire," he told her. "These things always take forever to arrange and it will probably be the spring before anything is definite."

She breathed a sigh of relief, for the one thing better than being out there with them was to know that peace might not be far away.

"I really felt most ashamed of myself when Grandmama bought all these new gowns for me in the belief that I would still be in official mourning for some time," Lucy said. "But I much prefer it this way, for I'm not eager to go to parties and such and dress in the height of fashion. Must you tell her?"

He shrugged. "I'll not tell her anything at this stage, for she would now wonder why I kept it from her. You'll have to wait and see what happens. But I must warn you, young lady, that truth has a way of coming to the fore, so she may find out yet,'' he cautioned.

''I'll face that when the time comes,'' she told him philosophically. ''But I was wondering if you would do me a favor, Grandpapa. Would you let me know what is going on over there, as word comes through, and tell me what the House decides on matters of importance? I am extremely interested, you know.''

His old eyes twinkled. ''I didn't know, but I might very well have guessed. If you'd like to come down to breakfast at about eight o'clock of a morning, when I'm usually reading *The Times*, you can take a look at it also. I'll be glad to give you my own opinions and those of the House—when it is in session, of course—and pass along any other news that reaches me from France.''

She jumped up quickly and bent to kiss his cheek. ''You've no idea how much good you've done me, Grandpapa,'' she told him gratefully. ''I feel so much better now that I can find out the important things that are happening in the world. I know that you must be eager to get on with your own work, so I'll not disturb you further but will see you at breakfast tomorrow, eight o'clock sharp.''

He watched her run lightly out of the room, closing the door quietly behind her, and he silently thanked God for bringing her safely back to them. She was like a breath of spring in the autumn of their lives, and he meant to cherish and protect her until such time as a truly worthy suitor came along.

After her day of rest, Lucy participated once more in her grandmama's daily activities until, one afternoon, just ten days after her arrival in London, an old friend of Lady Amberley's came to call.

In his sonorous voice, Duffield announced the arrival of the dowager Lady Mortimer and Lord Mortimer, Earl of Grassington.

Lucy was about to pour tea for one of her grandmama's guests when she heard the announcement, and the empty cup slipped out of her hand and dropped harmlessly into her lap. Fortunately, no one noticed and she quickly retrieved it; then, with but the merest glance toward the door, she continued the task she had been assigned. That glance had been sufficient, however, to confirm her worst fear.

She watched him covertly as he bowed low over her grandmama's hand and then Lady Amberley was coming toward her, bringing the two newcomers over to meet her.

"Josie, this is my granddaughter, Lucinde. She's Penelope's girl, but is not at all like her, thank goodness. Lucinde dear, this is Lady Mortimer, one of my bosom bows, and her son, Lord Mortimer, the present Earl of Grassington. You and Lucinde should have much in common, Anthony, for she has also just returned from the wars on the Peninsula." Lady Amberley was so delighted to finally have someone visit who was nearer her granddaughter's own age that she failed to notice the strained expression on that young lady's face.

After greeting Lady Mortimer, Lucy looked up at Anthony and found, to her amazement, that he was actually smiling at her.

"We have already met, Lady Amberley," he said, "for Sir Henry Coldwell was an old friend of mine." He turned toward Lucy. "I am delighted to find you at last, my lady, for I already journeyed north to the Coldwells', expecting to find you there."

"As a friend of their son's I'm sure you were received more kindly than I would have been, my lord," Lucy said bluntly.

"For some reason they do seem to have taken you in aversion," he said, frowning, "and they have obviously mellowed little in the year and more since Henry was killed. They did, however, tell me that you were related to the Amberleys."

Glancing quickly toward Lady Amberley, Lucy saw that the two older ladies seemed to be busy catching up on gossip. Perhaps her grandmama had not heard. All she could do was pray that they had been discussing something extremely interesting when Anthony mentioned Henry's death.

"It is of no consequence," she told him, then added, "but I am surprised to see you here in London and not with Wellington, pushing the French toward Paris."

He grinned somewhat ruefully. "The day after you left, a new commander was appointed to the regiment, so I reported back to headquarters. Once there, however, I persuaded Wellington to release me from overseas duties. My father died shortly after I joined the army, but this was the first time I could reasonably request a leave of absence to take care of things here."

"Do you mean to tell me that if I had stayed hidden for a couple of days, Gussy and I would still be over there?" In her indignation, she forgot to lower her voice, and her grandmama frowned and then came across to them.

"I could not help but hear one of your remarks, Anthony, and my granddaughter's strange question," she said, her smile deceptively benign. "Exactly when was Sir Henry Coldwell killed?"

He looked first at Lucy, who appeared to be staring intently at something on the other side of the room, then he turned back to Lady Amberley. "He was killed in action at Salamanca in July last year," he said, frowning suddenly, for though he had noticed how elegantly Lucy was gowned, and that she did, in fact, look completely different from the widow he had seen in Vitoria, it had not occurred to him that she should not still have been in black.

Once she had left Spain and he had been riding to join Wellington at headquarters, he had tried to honestly analyze his motives in sending her back to England.

After much deliberation, he was forced to admit to himself that, had she been anyone else, he would not have been so insistent. But he had seen her out there on the battlefield helping the wounded, and it had not taken much imagination to picture her being injured, or even killed.

Perhaps it was because she was such a little thing that he had felt so protective where she was concerned. Or perhaps it was something else that he did not wish to even consider just yet.

"I think you and I will have much to talk about later, my girl," Lady Amberley said sharply, then turned away to greet some new arrivals.

Lucy's cheeks had turned a rosy pink.

Lord Mortimer looked apologetic. "I don't suppose you will believe me when I tell you how sorry I am to seemingly interfere once more in your affairs, but I assure you that was not my intent," he murmured softly. "I can only assume that you did not wish to explain what you had been doing over there for the last year. If it would be of help, I'll gladly tell Lady Amberley of the high esteem in which you were held, and—"

"I don't need any more of your kind of help," she snapped. "Don't you think you've done enough harm already?"

"Won't you at least permit me to call on you and take you for a ride in the park tomorrow afternoon?" he asked, a glint of amusement in his blue eyes. "It would give you an opportunity to tell me exactly what you think of me, as you did once before, if I recall?"

She knew he was referring to the things she had called him in Vitoria when she had realized that no amount of pleading to be allowed to stay with the army would have any effect.

By the time she had taken a severe scolding from her grandmama, she would be more than ready to rail at him, she decided, so she accepted his invitation.

When he moved away to greet some of his mother's friends, Lady Mortimer, who had been watching them with considerable interest, came over and took a seat beside Lucy. "It seems strange that I have known your grandmama all these years, but have never met you until today, my dear," she remarked. "My son was extremely worried about you when he found that the Coldwells were so inhospitable toward you. I cannot imagine behaving in that way to the wife of one of my sons."

"You have other sons besides Anthony?" Lucy sounded surprised. She had thought him to be an only child.

"Oh, yes. Anthony is, of course, the oldest, but I have two younger sons and a daughter. And a daughter-in-law and a son-in-law, both of whom I love dearly. I always felt our family was just a nice size," she said, trying not to sound smug.

"I wished I had brothers and sisters when I was little, but Mama said she wanted no more children, and I suppose it would have been much more difficult to go, as we did, from one relative to another if she'd had several children in tow." Lucy chuckled. "We had a home, of course, but once Papa died, Mama did not wish to live there anymore."

"I remember her as being a pretty child," Lady Mortimer remarked, "but not at all like you and your grandmama. Yours are the kind of looks that last, you know."

"That's what Henry used to say," Lucy told her, reminiscing a little. "He also said that the nicest things always come in small packages."

"You must miss him a great deal, my dear, as I miss my dear husband. It was a tragic loss for you," the older lady remarked feelingly.

"I'm afraid it was inevitable, Lady Mortimer." Lucy had come to this conclusion some time ago, but rarely expressed it in words. "He was the best of companions, but I'm afraid he never quite grew up. Perhaps he would have done, had he lived, but I doubt it. He was quite a daredevil and volunteered for every dangerous mission there was, and took terrible chances. I did not stop caring, but I had to stop worrying about him or I could not have borne it."

Lady Mortimer nodded understandingly. "Anthony said as much to me just the other day. He was very fond of him, you know."

Lucy looked up and saw that the last of the callers were

leaving. Lord Mortimer came over to collect his mother and asked Lucy softly, "Will two o'clock tomorrow be all right?"

She nodded and walked with them to the door, where her grandmama was saying good-bye to her guests. She dreaded the moment when they would be alone, for the old lady had a sharp tongue and there was nothing she could say in her own defense. But she had brought it upon herself, so she stepped back a little and waited until the Mortimers left and Lady Amberley closed the drawing-room doors.

3

Lady Amberley turned around and walked over to where Lucinde stood by the side of the handsome Adam fireplace, and faced her with a look in her eyes that Lucy had never seen before and hoped never to see again.

"Would you care to give me an explanation, Lucinde, for deliberately lying to me about the date of your husband's death?"

Although Lady Amberley was irate, her voice also held a hint of the pain she felt at Lucy's deception, and this was Lucy's undoing.

She blinked back the tears that threatened to spill over, and swallowed hard before saying huskily, "I had not thought to deceive you, Grandmama, and I did not actually lie, but when you assumed that Henry's death had been recent, I did not correct you."

When Lucy hesitated for a moment, seeking the right words, Lady Amberley snapped, "That is every bit as bad as lying, in my book."

"I know, and I'm not making excuses but trying to explain. You see, I did not think you would understand why I had not come back to England right away, but stayed there for another twelve months," she said. Even to her own ears, however, she sounded to be prevaricating.

"And why did you?" The question was undoubtedly much sterner now than it would have been when she first arrived in London.

"First of all, I had used up all the money Henry had left by paying for the return of his body to his family. I had none remaining for my own passage home," she began.

But her grandmama interrupted once more. "Then what have you been living on for the past year?" she asked grimly.

"Believe it or not, I found it quite possible to live there without money. You see, I already knew Gussy, and when she realized my position, she took me under her wing. We occasionally had to forage for food, but more often than not were given a chicken, a piece of pork, or any number of things in return for treating the sick and wounded." Lucy saw from her grandmama's expression that she was beginning to understand, if not condone.

"So when you told me that Gussy was an excellent nurse, you omitted to mention that you were also." It was a statement rather than a question. "If you preferred to do that than come back here, what made you suddenly change your mind?"

"A certain colonel who was appointed temporary commander of the regiment just after the Battle of Vitoria," Lucy said sharply.

Lady Amberley's lips began to twitch and the twinkle came back into her eyes. "It was Anthony Mortimer who sent you back, wasn't it?" she said, enjoying a good laugh at Lucy's expense. "What a turn of events! And he didn't know who you were?"

Lucy shook her head, smiling ruefully. "He knew I was Henry's wife, that's all, and he didn't approve of a lady being out there alone, or tending the sick and wounded on the battlefields."

"Thank goodness he had some sense, if you did not. I can't imagine what the previous commander was thinking of allowing you to remain," the old lady said sharply.

"He had come up through the ranks and would not have been considered a gentleman in your estimation, though he was a fine soldier," Lucy explained somewhat dryly.

They had both been standing all this time, and now Lady

Amberley sank gratefully into a green velvet chair near the window. "Give a tug on that bellpull for Duffield," she instructed Lucy, "I think we both need a glass of sherry after this."

Lucy did as she was told, then took the chair opposite her grandmama, noticing how tired the old lady suddenly looked.

"Can you understand at least a little, Grandmama?" she asked quietly.

"Oh, I understand, all right, though I still don't approve. First thing in the morning all those new widow's weeds are going back to the modiste and we're going to dress you the way you should have been from the start," she said firmly, "and I'll brook no arguments, missie."

Lucy sighed and gladly accepted a small glass of sherry from Duffield, noting that he left the crystal decanter on a side table. If she was to go through all that poking and prodding again, she would need more than one glass of sherry to sustain her.

"I accepted Lord Mortimer's invitation to a drive in the park tomorrow afternoon," she remarked. "Will we be back in time or should I send him a note?"

"You'll be back in plenty of time, for all we'll have to do is select new fabrics for each of the black gowns. There's no need to do all that measuring and picking out styles again. And if we start out early enough, we may find something that can be altered in time for your drive." Lady Amberley gave her a warning glance. "And don't you go quarreling with that nice young man. He had no idea that he was letting the cat out of the bag."

Lucy could not help but smile at the stern and unyielding Colonel Mortimer being described as a "nice young man," but she had to admit that he had presented a completely different side of himself this afternoon. She was not likely to forget, however, that it had taken all the courage she possessed to stand up to him at their previous meeting in Spain.

"You know that half of London will be talking, don't

you?" Lady Amberley went on. "For you to appear for one week in mourning, and then come out of it right away, will seem odd, to say the least."

Lucy wanted to suggest that they leave things as they were, but knew better than to do so. "I haven't met very many people," she said, "but I do realize they were all your friends. By all means tell them the truth if you wish."

"I'll do no such thing," Lady Amberley said firmly. "It will do no harm to give the busybodies something to gossip and speculate about. And don't you tell any of them either. It's always best to brazen things out and then they're never quite sure of what is and is not the truth."

That evening Lucy insisted on helping Gussy pack up the gowns and other articles of black clothing that were to go back to the modiste.

"It's such a pity that these plainer ones would not fit you," Lucy said, "for I'm sure that Madame will not give my grandmama all of her money back on them."

"Nay, she'll not need to, milady, for your grandmama won't 'ave paid for 'em yet, nor for many a month," Gussy said flatly. "Didn't y'know that them that 'as money are t'last to pay their bills?"

"I knew that Mama never paid ours, but I thought that was because she didn't have much money once Papa died," Lucy said thoughtfully. "I wonder if Henry owed anyone anything when he died?"

"If 'e did, you'd 'ave 'eard from 'em by now, mark my words," Gussy said firmly. "But with this new gown and the other when I make it up, I'll 'ave plenty to wear, an' better stuff than I've ever worn before."

Lucy sat on the four-poster bed for a moment thinking as she swung her slippered toes back and forth above the rich green-and-gold carpet. Like Gussy, she had never worn any gowns of such quality, nor had she ever had such a luxurious bedchamber to herself.

"You know, Gussy," she said softly, "I feel quite relieved that Grandmama now knows everything. I felt very guilty allowing her to think of me as newly widowed. She said she would tell Grandpapa tonight, but though he knows all about it, he'll not tell her so, I'm sure.

"Even after all this time I still miss Henry quite often, though. Mostly at night, I suppose. Do you miss Sergeant Bradbury sometimes, Gussy?"

The abigail was bending over one of the boxes and a low chuckle escaped her. "Of course I do, particularly in cold weather, for 'e 'ad the warmest feet of anyone I ever 'eard of. I was never cold in bed when 'e was around," she said gruffly.

Lucy gave an embarrassed laugh. "Oh, Gussy, you know I didn't mean that."

"Didn't you?" Gussy asked with a slight smile. "And if you didn't, why not? It's only natural."

Lucy's cheeks went a bright shade of pink. "It was for Henry and me, but Mama told me I shouldn't let him realize even if I did like it."

Gussy stopped what she was doing and came over to where Lucy sat on the bed packing another box.

"Now, you just listen to me an' never mind wot she said. Your grandma is goin' to look for a 'usband for you, mark my words, an' if it's someone you like, you'll be married afore long. The only way you'll keep 'im from 'aving a mistress is to let 'im see you like wot 'e does to you. Then, after a bit, try putting the shoe on t'other foot. You touch 'im an' stroke 'im an' see 'ow 'e likes it." She smiled knowingly. "I promise you 'e'll want nobody else to come anywhere near 'im."

Lucy started to laugh. "What a good thing it is that these walls are not thin, for Grandmama would probably have a fit of the vapors. My mama certainly would. But I will remember, Gussy, if the time ever comes, for I couldn't bear to love someone and then find that he preferred other women to me."

Gussy had a sudden thought. "So you're goin' out with your grandma in the mornin' to buy more gowns? What do you want to wear? The one you 'ave on now? You can't wear the one you came 'ere in, or she'd make you ride with the coachman."

Lucy started to giggle. "Did we pack everything else away?" she asked, still laughing.

"That we did, except for that riding outfit you like so well," the maid confirmed with a grin. "If you're only going to see Madame, as you call 'er, it surely won't matter if you wear the same gown as today."

"But what if she doesn't have anything she can alter right away? I forgot to tell you that I'm going for a drive with Lord Mortimer in the afternoon, and he might even refuse to take me if I'm wearing the same gown two days in a row," Lucy said in mock horror.

Gussy was smiling broadly. "So it's Lord Mortimer now, is it? A week ago it was 'that abominable colonel.' "

"He's going to feel abominable, Gussy, by the time I've finished with him, for I'm not going to let him get away with causing me all this trouble," Lucy vowed. "He didn't have to go and tell Grandmama that Henry died twelve months ago."

"Yes, 'e did, milady. When 'e was asked a direct question, 'e'd no call to tell an outright lie for you, now, 'ad 'e?" Gussy asked.

Lucy frowned as though debating the point, then she sighed heavily. "You're right as usual, Gussy. I had no reason to expect him to lie for me, or even prevaricate, for I wouldn't have lied for him. But I suppose we'd better pull out one of the gowns we've packed just in case I've nothing else to wear."

"If I were you, milady, I'd also keep back that black lace shawl, evenin' bag, and gloves, for there might be some strong color in a gown that they'd look just right with." As she spoke, the maid bent down and took out one of the pairs of black evening slippers. "An' these, too, don't you think?"

Lucy nodded in agreement. "It all seems such a ridiculous fuss, though, Gussy, doesn't it? A month ago we didn't have to think twice about what we put on each morning, and here I am now having to change clothes twice a day, and it will be three times when we start going out in the evenings. And all because, as the colonel said, I'm a lady by birth."

"Just be grateful for what you've got and what you are, milady," the older woman advised. "We could be in a lot worse straits than we are now."

To Lucy's surprise, the modiste was not at all put out by having to take back so many gowns and replace them with ones in greens, blues, yellows, and whites. There must be no pinks, reds or lavenders, for these all clashed with "that glorious hair."

She also found a gown that did not require too much alteration, in a lovely apple green, and promised to have it finished and delivered to Berkeley Square not later than one o'clock.

Lucy was quite elated at this latter piece of luck, but tried not to show it. She had wanted to look her best for her first drive in the park with a gentleman, even if she did still mean to ring a peal over him.

Her grandmama was as kind and helpful as ever, and behaved as though there had never been any words between them. To Lucy's relief, it seemed that she was still the type of person who said her piece and then did not bring up the matter again.

The only place they visited that morning besides the modiste's was the milliner's, and they took with them a length of the same fabric as the gown she would wear this afternoon, for Lucy must have a bonnet to match.

In no time at all, a pretty straw poke bonnet had been trimmed with the piece of fabric, and a parasol in the same shade had been selected and added to the order. Now they could go home and have a leisurely luncheon before it was time for Lucy to change for her drive in the park.

She was a little cross with herself, though, for she was not a young girl going out with a gentleman for the first time; she was an old married lady—yet there was no doubt about it, she felt an unusual excitement at just the prospect of a ride in the park with Anthony Mortimer.

She gave Lady Amberley a warm hug before they stepped out of the carriage, and when she went upstairs to take off her bonnet, she found that the gown had already arrived and Gussy was ironing out the few small creases.

"It's just right for you, milady," Gussy told her. " 'Er ladyship 'as good taste."

Lucy was forced to agree with her, and would have liked to don the gown at once, but knew that her grandmama would be ready for luncheon. She had no wish to keep her waiting, so she hurried down the stairs and into the dining room. But suddenly it seemed that her stomach was tied in knots as she thought of being alone with Anthony. Would he be gentle, as he was yesterday or, once they were alone, would he be the severe colonel again? She made a pretense of eating her food, though she was really just pushing it around on her plate and taking an occasional nibble, while making polite conversation.

"I think you'd best run upstairs and get changed, my dear," Lady Amberley said at last, "for it does not seem that you are at all hungry. Try not to be long, though, for I'm almost as anxious to see you in that gown as you must be, after hiding yourself in black for so long."

She was still sitting there, sipping her coffee, when Lucy came down some twenty minutes later, and the expression on her face as she looked her granddaughter up and down told Lucy all she needed to know even before Lady Amberley spoke.

"You should be spanked soundly for trying to stay in widow's weeds, Lucinde," she pronounced. "That color is so perfect with your curls, for it turns the red to auburn. Now, I want to watch Anthony's face when he sees you."

It was not just the color of the gown, however. There was a flush to Lucy's cheeks that had not come out of a pot, and her eyes, now appearing more green than blue, had an added sparkle.

As she had expected, he was prompt, and a quick peek out of the window as the doorbell sounded revealed what looked like a shiny new curricle in black with gold trim, drawn by a beautifully matched pair of grays. They seemed most eager to be off and tugged impatiently on their reins as a short person in black livery walked them around the square.

Her grandmama made a hissing sound and Lucy quickly released the lace curtain and slid into a chair as the drawing-room door opened and Lord Mortimer was announced.

He bowed low over Lady Amberley's hand and she beamed up at him and said, "It's good to see you again, Anthony, and I do believe your dear mama looks five years younger since your return."

"That's nice to hear, my lady, for she's been through too much pain and anxiety in the years I've been away," he said softly.

Then he turned to where Lucy sat, quietly watching and noting his good manners. He paused for a moment as though not quite believing it was the same person, then he was beside her, taking her hand in his and bowing once more. "Are you ready to leave?" he inquired.

"I am, and so are those magnificent grays, by the look of it," she told him, not caring in the slightest that he would know she had been watching. "That young man looks as if he can scarcely hold them back."

"He'd better," Anthony said with a grin, "or he'll be looking for another position tomorrow."

As Lucy rose, her grandmama did also, and warned, "Now, just you take good care of her, young man, and if the two of you mean to squabble, just be sure none of my friends hears you."

"Grandmama," Lucy started to protest, but Anthony quickly took her arm and steered her out of the room before she could say anything further.

After helping her into the curricle, he took the reins from

his tiger and they set off slowly at first, turning along Mount Street rather than toward Piccadilly, which was quite busy at this hour of the day.

Once they were proceeding at a leisurely pace toward the park, he turned to Lucy and asked, with a grin, "Are we going to squabble? If so, I'd best take the quieter route."

It was difficult to glare at him when he was being so charming, but there were some things Lucy intended to get off of her chest now that she had him to herself.

Before she could start, he put in quickly, "Judging by your expression, I see a strong possibility of words, so we'd best take the northerly route until you've had your say—and I've had mine."

She turned to look at him, all her nervousness gone. "No matter what you say, you cannot deny that you overstepped your position by ordering me home and sending me to the ship under armed guard," she said heatedly.

"You weren't sent to the ship under 'armed guard,' as you put it. The escort was simply to make sure you arrived there safely. They were armed only for your protection, and I'd have had their hides if they had hurt you in any way," he assured her.

"If you'd only waited a few days until the new commander was appointed, we'd still be with the regiment," she protested.

He looked at her and slowly shook his head, a hint of laughter in his eyes. "You would have been forced to come home eventually, for the war will not go on forever, Lucy," he said, as though reasoning with an obstreperous child, "and I was acting in your best interests, whether you liked it or not. Are you finding London so very unpleasant?"

"How would you like to either serve tea or go out to tea every single day, and make foolish conversation with a lot of ladies who have not a thought in their heads beyond which gowns they will wear the next morning, afternoon, and evening? They celebrated Vitoria just after I arrived by illuminating London for two nights, and not one of the ladies I talked to knew what Vitoria was,'' she protested vehemently.

Lord Mortimer was sure that few men could have looked at her expressive face and flashing eyes, and listened to the passion in her voice, without wanting to take her in his arms, if not his bed. But right now he had to address her problem.

''Don't make the mistake of taking everyone at their face value, Lucy, and certainly not some of the ladies you meet over tea. There are some very intelligent women here in London who, though they officially have no say in what goes on in Parliament, have considerable influence on the way their husbands vote,'' he quietly informed her. ''Your grandmama does not, I am sure, completely influence Lord Amberley, for he is an astute gentleman, but she is no one's fool, either, and neither is my mama.''

Though he had not agreed with her, he had taken her seriously, and this Lucy appreciated. She would think about what he had just said and look at some of the ladies differently, she knew. But there was something else that bothered her.

''Then there's the waste of money. No one could possibly wear the number of gowns Grandmama has just ordered for me.'' She looked a little sheepish as she added, ''And, of course, there were just as many made for me in black that have been returned. Spending money like that is criminal when you can see people starving on the streets.''

''There would be even more people starving if she left the money in a vault and didn't spend it,'' he remarked. ''That money bought both goods and services. The dressmaker pays girls to fit and sew the garments. A mill-owner pays the spinners and the weavers who made the fabric. Others were employed to make the buttons, deliver the material to London, and so on. I'm not saying that the money they receive is equitable, but that's something you've not even thought of yet and I, for one, don't wish to be around when you do,'' he said with a grin.

"You think I'm being foolish, don't you?" Lucy felt a little crestfallen, for his argument made a great deal of sense.

"Not at all," he said firmly, "but you're jumping to conclusions too quickly. You're not giving yourself time to understand a different way of life. To change the subject for a moment, what happened to Mrs. Bradbury? Did she return to family in the North of England?"

Lucy's face broke into a smile. "Oh, no. She had nowhere to go either, so Grandmama said she could be my abigail. She's still my friend, though, and I'm sure she always will be."

He grinned. "Of course. Do you remember Morgan, who went with you to the ship?" When Lucy nodded, he continued, "He's still with me, for he was my batman. He took a strong liking to Gussy. I think I'll let him know where she is, and they'll probably get together from time to time."

"I never would have thought of you as a matchmaker, Anthony," she said, laughing merrily at the idea. "But then, I didn't know you very well at all, did I? I thought a ride in the park always meant going slowly through, as Grandmama and I sometimes do in her carriage, smiling and waving to the people she knows, and stopping to chat with a few of them."

"We may do just that one day," Anthony said, smiling at her complete frankness, "and if so, I shall expect you to do exactly what everyone else does. But when everything gets bottled up inside of you and needs to come out, then we'll do just what we did today. And we can truthfully tell Lady Amberley that we didn't squabble, can't we?"

He squeezed her hand as he helped her down outside the house, but he refused to come in for tea, saying that he had an appointment. He did, however, promise to stay home the next afternoon when his mother was receiving and she and her grandmama were expected.

4

Lady Amberley was quite consciously emulating her granddaughter, for when she heard the curricle return, she moved quickly over to the same window Lucy had peeked through earlier in the day, and watched as Anthony helped Lucinde down.

Resuming her seat near the fire, she permitted herself a nod of satisfaction. Things must have gone well, for both their faces wore that comfortable look that comes only with understanding. She must be turning into an inquisitive old lady, she decided impatiently, for she could not help but wonder how he had managed to achieve such a transformation. Lucinde had looked decidedly aggressive as they left. Perhaps her own parting shot had helped pave the way.

There was no doubt about it, the girl had the looks to carry anything off, and whether red hair was currently fashionable in London or not would make no difference as far as suitors were concerned. Even if Josephine's boy did not come up to scratch, there would be little difficulty in finding Lucinde a suitable husband, for she still did not look a day older than eighteen.

She heard her hurrying through the hall and up the stairs to take off her bonnet and gloves, and suddenly a dreadful thought occurred to her. Lucinde and Henry had been married for a year and a half and her husband had been with her most of the time, but no children had come of the union. Even if it was not Lucy who was at fault, eligible men would consider it a clear indication that she was barren and give her a wide berth. At the very first opportunity she must have a word with Gussy. They were very close, and she would be sure to know if she had ever miscarried.

Lucinde almost collided with the tea tray as she came hurrying into the room, but she stopped just in time and held the door wide so that the girl could get through. Then she followed her closely, peering over her shoulder to make sure there were plenty of her favorite maid-of-honor tarts, for now her appetite had returned.

When the girl left the room, Lady Amberley asked, "Did you have a pleasant drive, my dear?"

Lucy smiled warmly. "Very pleasant indeed, Grandmama, and we didn't squabble at all. In fact, I found him to be more interesting and informative than I would have ever believed."

Lady Amberley nodded thoughtfully. "Then you would not object if we invite him and his mama to accompany us to Vauxhall Gardens on the twentieth? There's to be a fete in honor of the victory at Vitoria, and your grandpapa has already bought tickets for it."

"It won't be anything like those dreadful illuminations when I first arrived, will it?" Lucy asked, for she had read in *The Times* that there had been a great deal of mischief on that occasion, unauthorized fireworks let off in the streets, and some fifty persons arrested.

"You need not worry. It will not be at all like that, though there will, of course, be fireworks displays there." Lady Amberley looked pleased, for they were one of her favorite entertainments. "Tickets are much in demand, and as it gets closer, I understand they are being sold at anything from three guineas to ten guineas each. Lord Amberley feels strongly that as you were there at Vitoria, you should also be at the celebrations."

When they paid a call the next day on Lady Mortimer, they stayed on after the other callers had left, to talk about the fete. It was agreed that they should all go, but stay very close together, for it was bound to be a dreadful crush.

"Do you really want to attend?" Anthony asked Lucy when they were both standing near the window.

"No, but I must," she said softly so that Lady Amberley wouldn't hear, "for Grandpapa seems to feel it will be a treat for me, and I'd hate to disappoint him."

"Do you see much of Lord Amberley, or is he at his club most of the time?" Anthony asked, for he knew that many older men preferred to escape much of the evening activity of their families, attending only the occasional event.

"We talk every morning over an early breakfast while Grandmama is still abed," Lucy informed him quietly, "and he tells me all the latest news about the war and other things that are going on."

Anthony grinned. "Does he, indeed? He must have taken a real liking to you to allow you to disturb him with his newspaper."

"Oh, we each read a piece of it while we're eating, and talk afterward," she said glibly. "He's a wonderful gentleman and he really cares about what happens both in England and abroad."

Anthony was strangely pleased that Lucinde and Lord Amberley had become so close, but at the same time he felt an odd pang of jealousy. It sounded to be a most pleasant way to start the day.

Then he remembered that he had meant to speak to her about her horse, Beauty, which she had left with him in Spain, in exchange for the money he had given her and the passages he had paid for when he sent her home.

"That reminds me," he said. "I've been meaning to ask you if you'd like to go for an early-morning ride in the park occasionally. I still have Beauty and I'm sure she would be overjoyed to see you again."

"Oh, yes, I can't think of anything I'd like better," she said enthusiastically. "What day are you free?"

He could not help but compare her eager response with the languid acceptances many young ladies carefully cultivated so as not to appear too eager. It was most refreshing, and he sincerely hoped she would never lose her natural exuberance.

"How about tomorrow morning?" he suggested. "Just tell me what time and I'll bring the horses around."

"Would eight o'clock be all right, and I'll forgo my visit with Grandpapa?" she asked, glad that they had not returned the black riding habit with the matching shako. How good it would be to see Beauty again!

"Of course. I'll see you at eight sharp, then," he agreed, and they went over to where Lady Amberley was standing near the door, ready to leave.

"We were just arranging to go riding tomorrow morning," Lucy explained as they stepped into the carriage.

"Can he mount you?" Lady Amberley asked. "I'm sure your grandpapa means to get a horse for you from Tattersall's, but he has so many things to think about that it's probably slipped his mind."

"Lord Mortimer still has my horse, Beauty. I gave it to him in exchange for our passages on the ship and some cash to pay any other expenses of the journey," Lucinde said casually. "But it will be so good to see her again."

"I'll speak to your grandpapa," Lady Amberley said firmly. "I'm sure he'll wish to buy your horse back from Anthony, if he's willing to part with her."

"Did you make all the arrangements for the fete?" Lucy asked. "Lady Mortimer must enjoy fireworks as much as you, for she seemed quite excited at the prospect of attending."

"I don't know if you realize it, but it's quite an event, my dear," Lady Amberley told her. "All of the royal dukes will be there for a private banquet first, and I'm sure that they'll do a reenactment of the actual battle in fireworks that will be more fearsome than the battle itself was."

"Are they going to have big guns firing and actors playing soldiers and throwing themselves on the ground to portray the hundreds of dead and wounded? Is that what everyone is paying so much to see?" Lucy asked bitterly, recalling not the victory but the horror of those great guns that had relentlessly poured round shot and canister into the British infantry.

As Lady Amberley turned to make a sharp retort, she saw a tear roll down her granddaughter's cheek, quickly followed by another.

"My dear, I am so sorry," she said as she slipped a kerchief into Lucy's hand. "I heard there were heavy losses, and it must have been dreadful to be so close to the fighting. I suppose you could hear the guns from some distance away."

"But I was not some distance away, Grandmama. We were waiting close by for a lull in the fighting so that we could get the wounded off the battlefield and give them what help we could," Lucinde said, her voice husky with the tears she hated herself for shedding now, when she had certainly not done so at the time.

"You and Gussy?" Lady Amberley asked.

Lucy nodded. "And the wives of the enlisted men. They all helped one another out there."

Lady Amberley was completely shocked, for she realized now, for the first time, just what her granddaughter had been doing and just why it was so difficult for her to accept the way of life here in London. She would be more patient with her in the future. And when next she saw Anthony alone, she meant to thank him with all her heart for sending Lucy back to them while she was still in one piece.

"If it will upset you, you really don't have to go to the fete, my love," Lady Amberley said gently. "I'll explain to Lord Amberley and I know he will understand."

Lucy shook her head firmly. "Of course I want to go, Grandmama, and I promise not to be a watering pot when the fireworks begin. Please don't say anything to Grandpapa."

Lady Amberley did not promise, for she had every intention of telling her husband what Lucy had been doing over there in Spain; then he, too, would understand and make allowances.

Then something else occurred to her. "What on earth are you going to wear tomorrow morning? It's too late now for the modiste to have that green habit we ordered ready."

"I have a confession to make," Lucy said roguishly. "I tried to stop you ordering that green one, but there was no gainsaying you. You see, I didn't put the black one into the box to take back to the modiste. The military style looked better in black than it would have in any other color, so I hid it in the back of the wardrobe."

Lady Amberley laughed out loud. "One would have to have the eyes of an eagle to watch you, young lady," she declared. "But as long as your horse is not black, the outfit will look exceptionally well."

"Now, Grandmama, with my hair do you think I would ride any horse other than a chestnut?" Lucy asked, teasing. "She lives up to her name, too, for she is a real beauty and I just can't wait until morning to see her again."

As they stepped out of the carriage and entered the house, Lady Amberley tried to recall what it had been like before Lucinde came to stay, and simply could not remember. Though it was almost the end of summer, the chit had brought a breath of spring into their lives, and while she wanted only the best for her, she almost dreaded the day when she would wed again and leave them.

Lucy was awake the next morning long before she need get up and dressed, for, after riding for days on end in Spain each time the army either advanced or retreated, it now seemed an age since she had been on horseback. She was looking forward to this morning's ride more than she would have thought possible.

She rang for Gussy, who brought hot chocolate with her, and the two of them sat talking for some time, Lucy telling her all she had heard of the fete she would be attending.

"I've been 'earin about it," Gussy told her, "and if you're

not needing me once you're dressed for it, maybe I'll be there, too."

Lucy looked surprised and pleased. "Are you seeing somebody, Gussy?" she asked.

"Not the way y'mean, milady," Gussy said with a laugh. "But Morgan, one o' the fellers that took us to the ship, looked me up yesterday. 'E's still working for the colonel, and 'e asked me if I'd like to go. I'd be sure an' get back in time to get y' to bed."

"But of course you're going, Gussy," Lucy said at once. "And you don't have to come back early. I've been getting myself into bed all my life until now."

Gussy shook her head firmly. "I'll be 'ere, for it just wouldn't be right not to."

Lucy was delighted that her friend was finally going to enjoy herself, for she knew her life had been a hard one until now. She said as much to Anthony when they set out for the park a little later.

"You didn't waste any time with your matchmaking, did you?" she asked him.

"Before I spoke to you, I already knew he was much impressed with her and intended to look her up if he could find her. I just made it easier for him by telling him where she was," he said with a grin.

"And by giving him tickets to the fete?" She was going on a hunch only, but where else would Morgan have got them?

His sheepish grin was much like that of a small boy who had been caught in an act of mischief. "I bought tickets for it myself, but when your grandpapa invited us, I thought it only right that Morgan and Mrs. Bradbury should join in that celebration also. You have given her the night off, haven't you?"

"Of course, but I feel strange doing so, for I cannot think of her as a servant. She feels that working at Amberley House is wonderful," Lucy said, "so I suppose it's a matter of comparisons. You know, despite her rough speech, I've never met anyone who didn't have a healthy respect for her once they got to know her. Grandmama thinks her a treasure, for when she had a megrim the other night she called for Gussy, then later told me she'd never before recovered from one so quickly."

Lucinde leaned forward and let her fingers slide through Beauty's chestnut mane, and seeing the gesture, Anthony smiled. He had tried to look the other way when, a short time ago, she had hurled herself down the steps of Amberley House and flung her arms around the mare's neck, whispering her name over and over again.

Before she mounted, he had handed Lucy his kerchief and told her to take a good blow, and even now her eyes were still a little pink. But he had to admit he liked her all the more for it, and now he wondered how he was going to be able to give Beauty back to her without having her tell him she could not accept the gift.

His problem was solved a moment later when Lucy told him, "Grandpapa had intended to buy me a horse at Tattersall's, but I told Grandmama that you had my horse, so I'm sure he'll be approaching you to buy her back for me. You will agree to do so, won't you?"

"If it's what you want, my dear, I'm sure Lord Amberley and I can come to terms," he said with a smile of satisfaction, "but you'll not be able to take her out on your own, you know."

She looked at him sharply. "Is that another of those stupid London rules?" she asked. "I always rode alone in the country."

"I've no doubt you did, though even there it was not quite the thing for a lady to do," he said. "But aside from propriety, it's just not safe for you to ride alone in London. Hasn't Lady Amberley ever explained to you the dangers of going out alone here?"

When she shook her head, he sighed, for he thought her

grandmama more astute than that. Lucy was the kind of person who always needed to be given a reason. "It would be a simple matter for someone to kidnap a lady who was out on her own, and then hold her for ransom. There are a great many people in this city who live on their wits, and even if they had no idea who you were, your looks alone would bring them a good price if they sold you to a brothel."

Lucy reined in Beauty, then turned to look at Anthony. "If you're trying to frighten me, then you have succeeded very well. But why didn't Grandmama explain that?"

"I think she has probably forgotten that you were brought up in the country, where there are lots of people who would watch out for you," he said thoughtfully. "And you are quite possibly a little more headstrong than her other grandchildren. When she says 'no,' I doubt that they would ever think of disobeying her."

"You're forgetting that I'm also an old married lady," she told him, "no longer accustomed to having to do what parents and grandparents tell me."

"But now that I have explained, you will be careful not to go out alone, won't you?" he asked, his eyes twinkling with amusement.

She grinned a little ruefully. "I most certainly will, for you quite decidedly have a way with words, sir. And now, do you think we might break another of Grandmama's rules? There is no one at all around to tell her, so do let's have a race. The last one to that old oak tree is a duffer!"

As she urged Beauty into a gallop, he pretended to look around and make sure they were alone, but he was really letting her get a good start. His gelding was much more powerful than the chestnut mare, and he wanted her to beat him by at least a head.

Lucy knew what he had done, and she felt warmed by his kindness. He was the same man who had made her return to England against her will, but she now knew deep down that it had been in her own best interests.

She was starting to realize, also, that Henry had never

really given a thought to what was best for her. He had always done what he wanted to do, and she had been the one who must adapt to his every whim. She was very young and had not minded then, but she would probably have started to do so had their marriage lasted much longer. She was a very different person now that she had been at barely eighteen years of age.

They walked the horses back to the park gate and along the streets that led to Berkeley Square. Anthony raised his crop to return the greetings of other riders, but they did not stop until they reached Amberley House.

"Did I tell you how lovely you look this morning?" Anthony asked, knowing full well that he had not, and thinking that it was about time he did.

Lucy gave him a cheeky grin and shook her head. "I don't think anyone has ever said that to me, and I'd not have believed them if they had."

"Not even Henry?"

"Good gracious, no," she said. "You should know that wasn't his way. He'd tell me quickly enough if I looked a mess, but he wouldn't flatter, for he didn't want my head to get too big."

"I think that was hardly likely to happen, for I don't believe you're at all vain. Once the Little Season starts, though, you'll hear it from all the young bucks who are bound to hang around you."

"I don't think I'd like that very much," Lucinde said, frowning. "I'd far rather people say what they really mean."

"Just take a careful look in the mirror when you go inside, and you'll see exactly what I mean," he told her. "Your skin is still a little too dark from the Spanish sun to be fashionable, but I happen to like it that way, though it will soon fade in the damp English climate. There is a vitality and a glow there, however, that make you stand out."

There was definitely a glow now, for her cheeks went a rosy red with embarrassment, and she looked away from him. "I wish you wouldn't say things like that," she muttered, "but I wouldn't mind if you told me how well I ride."

He lightly touched her flushed cheek with his finger. "I didn't need to tell you that, for you already know it," he said quietly, but there was laughter in his voice. "I'm willing to bet that in a couple of months there won't be a blush left in you."

He watched her as she turned and ran up the steps and into the house, then he remounted and set out for his own residence not far away, in Grosvenor Square, leaving the groom to bring Beauty with him. His last words to Lucy still echoed in his ears, and though he had meant them, deep down he hoped he was wrong.

The fete at Vauxhall Gardens was only a few days away, and unlike Lucy, he was quite looking forward to it, for it had been years since he had been there. He knew the gardens quite well, for in his youth he and his friends had gone there often and had enjoyed the pleasures that some of the ladies who frequented the darker pathways had to offer.

An evening there with Lucy would, he was sure, be equally enjoyable, but in a different way.

5

Vauxhall Gardens had never been more festive than on the evening of the public fete to celebrate Wellington's victory at Vitoria a month before.

Prior to their arrival there, the Mortimers and the Amberleys, traveling in Lord Amberley's coach, had taken a short drive past Carlton House and Wellington's own house, so that Lucy might see the illuminations. The words WELLINGTON and VICTORY were prominent everywhere, and many of the theaters and shops they passed were festooned with garlands of colored lanterns and blazing flambeaux.

To Lucinde, these displays gave a dreamlike quality to the evening, and the lengthy coach ride before they reached the gardens served only to emphasize the illusion, for her grand-mama was sitting between the two gentlemen and Lucy was seated across from Anthony. Though she was sure he was completely unaware of it, the sway of the coach forced his leg to brush against hers on occasion, causing her to feel the most extraordinary, quite embarrassing sensations.

As they alighted from the coach, Lady Amberley said, "I believe we should first find the supper box Lord Amberley reserved, so that we all know where to return to. Lucinde, I think you should stay close to Lord Mortimer and keep a tight hold of his arm at all times. It wouldn't do at all to get lost in a place of this sort."

Lucy looked considerably amused, for she was fully aware that Anthony had not yet invited her to do so.

"Do you mind if I follow my grandmama's instruction, my lord?" she asked, mischief glinting in her eyes, "or did you, perhaps, have some other, more interesting—"

"Assignation?" he suggested, grinning. "As a matter of fact, I had, but as the lady does not seem to have arrived as yet, I don't at all mind making do with the nearest red-haired minx." He held out his arm. "Allow me, my dear. Shall we lead the way?"

They began to stroll along the Grand Walk, Lucinde looking with interest at the variations in attire, for this was a place both the rich and the poor enjoyed to the full. Now she understood why Anthony had given his tickets to Morgan.

"That lady is wearing a mask," she whispered in surprise as he bent his head to catch what she was saying. "Why would she do that here?"

"She is probably meeting a lover and does not want any of her friends to know who she is," he told her. "And she may be a lady, but I would very much doubt it."

Then a group of young men in evening dress brushed past them, causing her to grasp his arm more firmly, and he placed his other hand on hers to hold her even tighter.

"Those are the ones to watch out for," he said. "They have probably been imbibing Vauxhall punch and are eager to have some fun with any female they can find."

"Just what is Vauxhall punch?" Lucy asked, eyeing the young men with some apprehension.

"It's a very potent drink that is popular here, but I'm sure you wouldn't like it. Your grandpapa has probably ordered wines with dinner, for the gardens usually have a good selection." He smiled down at her. "I'm pleased to see that you do not seem as concerned about celebrating Vitoria as you did the other day."

"I've got used to the idea, I suppose, and I really enjoyed seeing all the illuminations as we drove past. What a pity that Wellington is too busy to see his name lit up everywhere."

"Do I hear a note of sarcasm, Lucinde?" he asked.

He was surprised when she quickly snapped, "Don't call me that," then added, "please."

"Why not? It is your name and your grandmama uses it all the time." He was more curious than annoyed.

"Because it's such a silly name. My mama chose it from one of Molière's works that she happened to be reading just before I was born. Lucinde was a girl who pretended to be dumb or something, and I suppose Mama hoped I would not be quite the chatterbox I turned out to be. She was only eighteen at the time, and Papa was in his fifties, so I suppose she had little to do but read romantic poetry and dream a lot."

"I imagine so," Anthony said dryly, wondering what on earth the Amberleys could have been thinking of to permit their daughter to wed someone so old. Then he recalled something his mother had told him to the effect that Lucy's mother had eloped.

They were close to the Grove now, and they soon found the right box, then waited for the older people to catch up with them.

"Why don't you take Lucinde over to the South Walk, Anthony, so that she can see the archways?" Lady Mortimer suggested. "By the time you return we should have supper all ready to eat."

Anthony looked at Lucy and raised his eyebrows. She smiled and nodded, and soon they were strolling across the gardens to a walkway of similar proportions to the one they had just come along. Set at regular intervals were huge archways featuring realistic paintings of the ruins of Palmyra.

It seemed that the gardens were becoming more crowded by the minute, but it was, on the whole, an exhilarating scene. Lucy found it most refreshing to be among so many of her own age, rather than that of her grandparents.

The dress was varied, but the purpose was the same, as the people strolled carelessly along. They came from all walks of life, laughing and calling out to their friends, hugging old ones and greeting new ones, all of them out to have a good time and show how pleased they were that the

Frenchie was on the run at last and the war all but over.

Lucy's eyes shone and her cheeks glowed, and when Anthony looked down at her and asked if she was enjoying herself, she told him, "Tremendously. I had no idea it would be like this."

They soon rejoined the older people and sat down to nibble on small quantities of turtle soup, chicken, pigeon pie, and ham, washed down with a good vintage wine.

Then the bell sounded to signal the beginning of the fireworks, and they stepped out of the supper box and over to what they felt would be the best spot from which to view them.

At first Lucy stood with her hand upon Anthony's arm, but then, as the first crashing roar of a fireworks cannon sounded and she jumped in surprise, he placed his arm around her shoulders, and there it stayed while the battle was reenacted.

As they started back to the supper box and he removed that comforting arm from her shoulders, she felt the loss and wished for its return. Then she silently scolded herself for even thinking of such a thing.

Anthony was pouring more wine for them when Lord Amberley said, obviously a little disappointed, "I, personally, thought it terribly noisy. But you were both there. Did it bear any resemblance at all to the real thing? I could be mistaken, of course, but it seemed to me that we were losing."

"Your granddaughter was closer to that actual portion of the battle than I was," Anthony said gravely, and turned to Lucy. "What do you think, my dear?"

"The fireworks were terribly noisy, as you say, Grandpapa, but they were not a quarter as loud as the real thing. However, it was far more entertaining than I expected it to be, and at that point we were losing," she said diplomatically. "What are they doing for an encore, capturing the guns or depicting King Joseph trying to flee?"

"Oh, capturing the guns, I'm sure, for I believe the latter

is too sore a subject, because of the terrible looting that took place. Neither Wellington nor Prinny approved, of course," Anthony said grimly.

Lord Amberley raised his eyebrows. "Were our boys the only ones who did the looting?" he asked. "What really happened?"

"When Joseph left the carriages he'd loaded with money and treasures, to flee for his life, it seems they were then fair game for any who came along. The first to go through them were the French soldiers themselves, but they left most of it because they were in rather a hurry, as you might imagine."

"Naturally," Lord Amberley murmured dryly. "Who came after that?"

"Spanish soldiers, British soldiers, camp followers. And then the gypsies, of course. I heard tell of soldiers becoming wealthy overnight and deserting, for there was considerable gold and silver coin among the stuff left behind." Anthony sounded quite disgusted.

Lucinde was glad of the low lighting in the box, for her cheeks felt so hot that they must surely be crimson at the thought of the locket that the woman had thrust into her hand as she boarded the ship. She often took it out and looked at it before she got into bed of a night, for she had never before owned anything half so lovely. What would Anthony think of her if he knew that she possessed a small but obviously valuable piece of that loot?

A bell had sounded again and the others were discussing whether or not to go and see the waterfall, which was about to commence, but the final decision was to remain where they were until the next fireworks display.

They stayed in the box and watched people from all walks of life hurrying to see the elaborate display. At one point Lucy was sure that she saw Gussy and Morgan at the far left of a footpath, but before she could ask Anthony if he thought it was them, they had disappeared in the crowd.

By the time the second fireworks display was at an end,

all five of them were tired of the noise and the pushing to and fro of the crowd, which seemed to have increased even more during the last hour. While Anthony went back to the box to pick up his mother's wrap and make sure nothing else had been left behind, the others made their way to the entrance where the second coachman was waiting to fetch the coach. Anthony joined them then, and not ten minutes later they were on their way home. All were agreed that, though they were tired, it had been a grand fete and well worthwhile.

"I'm sure you'll be too tired to ride in the morning," Anthony murmured in Lucy's ear, "but would you, perhaps, enjoy a drive to Kew Gardens in the afternoon? I hear that the roses are at their best now, but will not last long. The gardens are not open to the public, of course, but private visits can be arranged at short notice."

Lucy's smile was hard to see in the dimly lit carriage, but the enthusiasm could clearly be heard in her voice.

"I would love to go, for I've heard so much about them and have not been there as yet," she said eagerly. "What time do you want me to be ready?"

"I will call for you at whatever time is most suitable to you," he said, quietly marveling at her artlessness, for she was never afraid to express her delight in the smallest things. He hoped that she would not lose that special quality when she mingled with some of the more jaded members of the *ton*. "Two o'clock, perhaps? And I suggest you wear something suitable for walking, for I am sure that you will wish to get close enough to smell each individual variety."

"Doesn't everyone?" Lucy asked in surprise.

"No, everyone does not, my dear, as you'll see for yourself tomorrow."

Lucy looked puzzled, but did not question him further. It was enough that she would be able to ride again in that handsome curricle instead of having to pay more of those wretched calls with Grandmama.

When Lady Mortimer and her son had alighted at their

home and the others were on their way to Berkeley Square, Lady Amberley remarked to Lucy, "Anthony seemed to be paying you a good deal of attention tonight, Lucinde. Did he say anything about when he might see you again?"

"Yes, he's going to call for me at two tomorrow and take me to see Kew Gardens," Lucy said happily.

Lady Amberley looked eminently pleased. "I do hope the weather holds up for you, for Kew is dreary in the rain," she told her. "And I suppose he'll be taking you in that curricle of his?"

Lucy nodded. "Won't it be lovely? I am so looking forward to it."

The old lady nodded as the carriage drew to a halt outside the house. "You'll like Kew at this time of year, my dear. Just get a good night's sleep to be sure you're looking your best tomorrow. And tell Gussy to put some of that lemon cream on your face again tonight. It has lightened it considerably, but there's still some way to go."

Lucy followed her grandmama inside, but did not bother to tell her that she had finally insisted that Gussy take the whole night off. If she could not get herself into bed for once, there was something sadly wrong with her, and there would be time enough in the morning to get ready for her drive.

"Do you know much about Kew Gardens?" Anthony asked. "Did your governess, perhaps, tell you its purpose?"

"My governess was more interested in arranging assignations with the curate in the village than with teaching me anything other than reading, writing, and fine needlework," Lucy retorted.

He smiled. "What an interesting childhood you must have had," he remarked with some amusement. "I don't recall everything I learned about the place, but I do know that it started with Sir Henry Capel who had an orangery and my retetum at his home in Kew, which was later leased to one of the royal princes. After that, first one and another of the interested parties have made additions to it, including

Lancelot 'Capability' Brown. In recent years, Sir Joseph Banks, as honorary director, has organized several scientific expeditions abroad for the purpose of collecting plant specimens and increasing the stock at the gardens."

Lucy's expressive face suddenly sprang to life. "Do you mean you're taking me to a true botanical garden?" she asked, quite obviously excited at the prospect.

Anthony looked slightly amused at her sudden enthusiasm. "Yes, that is where I'm taking you, but I thought you knew. I am inclined to forget occasionally that you have spent almost no time at all in the South of England. Kew has been known as an official botanical garden for more than sixty years, and so its gardens are arranged according to botanical classification rather than just to create a beautiful effect."

"How I wish Gussy was here, for she would be beside herself with excitement," Lucy exclaimed. "Do you think we will be able to pick a leaf or two to take back for her?"

The last person Anthony wished to have with them at this moment was Lucy's abigail. And, in any case, he could not imagine the rather dour woman showing even a fraction of Lucy's undoubted enthusiasm.

"Decidedly not, young lady," Anthony growled. "There are strict rules against anyone doing such a thing."

"Oh, Anthony, what an old marplot you are at times," Lucy exclaimed angrily. "As though anyone would notice if a few small leaves were missing from one little plant!"

"May I remind you," Anthony said quietly, keeping his face averted so that she could not see the smile he was trying to conceal, "that we have not reached the gardens yet, and if you persist in calling me names—"

"You couldn't be so mean as to bring me this far and then not take me inside?" Lucy asked, now close to tears, for she had wanted so much to see the gardens and she still recalled how adamant he had been in Spain.

"As I was saying," he went on, ignoring her outburst, "if you persist in calling me names, I may not try to use my influence to get you into the Herbarium to see the collection of dried and pressed plants. It is not, in the usual way, open for viewing."

He reined in the horses to allow a coach to pass, and as he turned his head to look at her she saw the hint of laughter in his eyes and was immediately contrite.

"You're not a marplot," she told him, reaching out a hand to touch his arm, "not even an old one, and I know you will make sure I see everything you can possibly arrange. Are we almost there?"

"In about fifteen minutes we'll be at the gates, then we'll drive to the Orangery and the Great Pagoda, and my tiger can walk the horses while we wander through the rose gardens." He glanced down at her feet. "I see that you wore something sensible for walking, as I suggested."

"Of course I did. I'd not have dared do anything else, though I noticed Grandmama eyeing my feet with disapproval when I came down. The very next time I go shopping with Gussy I'm going to have a pair of more sensible shoes made for just such an occasion. It's a pity I'm so small or I could borrow Gussy's."

The very idea of Lucy trying to walk around in a pair of her maid's shoes caused Anthony to burst out laughing. He had never known a young lady who made him quite so light-hearted and he knew it was one of the reasons why he enjoyed her company so much.

When he had first arrived in London, he had told himself that he would take her about to help her adjust to the ways of society before most of the *ton* arrived in town for the Little Season. But he had soon found how much he enjoyed her company, for she was genuinely interested in his views but not afraid to voice her own, whether in agreement or not. He had never known any lady behave in such a forthright manner, not even one of his sisters, and it made her very comfortable to be with.

She was also tireless when she was enjoying herself, he soon found, for he had already seen more of Kew in one visit than in the half-dozen or so previous visits put together.

And they still had to see the Herbarium, which he had succeeded in arranging.

An hour later, with a happy expression on her face and a package of unusual herbs clutched in her hand, Lucy allowed him to help her into the curricle, and they started back to London.

"Your grandmama will wonder where on earth we have got to," Anthony said as they moved along at a steady clip. "I hope she does not start to worry."

"She'll not do that," Lucy said airily, "for Gussy and I always return from expeditions much later than we mean to unless, of course, there is a reason for coming back early. It's been such a wonderful afternoon and I do thank you very much for arranging it, and for being so patient with me."

He chuckled softly. "Wild horses couldn't have dragged you out of that place until you had seen absolutely everything there was to see. And I still don't know how you managed to persuade that grumpy old custodian to give you those specimens. It just isn't done, you know."

"He wasn't grumpy with me," Lucy protested. "Perhaps because Papa was one, I've always got along better with older men than with young ones."

He let his glance rest on her for a moment until she realized what she had said, and her cheeks went a deep pink.

"I'm not sure whether I should be pleased that we usually get along because you think me old, or pleased that you think me young even though we don't get along," he told her, amused at her shocked expression.

Once more she placed a hand on his arm. "I was speaking only of comparative strangers, Anthony. You and I can hardly be classed as such, can we?"

"Very deftly handled, young lady, I must say," he told her, grinning. "And there I have been worrying as to how you will go on in society with your habit of saying exactly what you think."

The smile left Lucy's face. "I don't at all wish to go around in society, Anthony. Isn't there some way I can get out of it without upsetting Grandmama?''

''Now, Lucy, after she's bought all those gowns—two sets of them—I can see no way out for you. But it's nowhere near as difficult as you seem to think. All you have to do is listen and incline your head as though you're agreeing with whatever nonsense the ladies of the *ton* spout. You don't have to actually disagree with them, you know.''

''But that implies that I agree with them when I don't, so it's just as bad as saying something,'' Lucy protested, frowning.

''No, it's not,'' Anthony countered, ''for if you watch some of the other ladies, you will see them doing exactly the same thing. It's really just being discreet, by saying nothing, but keeping your own opinions intact.''

''I'll try to do what you say,'' Lucinde said softly, ''but please don't think too harshly of me if I find myself unable to do so at times.''

''Just as long as you try,'' he murmured, feeling unaccountably pleased that she was going to at least make the attempt for his sake.

When they reached Amberley House and she had thanked him prettily for the outing, she once more forgot all decorum and ran into the house clutching her dried specimens, eager to show Gussy at the first possible moment.

Lord Mortimer shook his head as he watched her unseemly flight, but there was a smile on his face and a light in his eyes that had not been there when he had left his own residence earlier in the day.

6

"Has Grandpapa not bought Beauty from you as yet?" Lucinde asked Anthony. It was a few days after their visit to Kew and they were on their way to the park for an early-morning gallop.

"He did broach the subject one afternoon in the club," Anthony said, "but we have not had an opportunity to discuss it further. Is there some reason why it should be done quickly?"

"No, not really," Lucy admitted, "for there would be no one else but you to ride with anyway."

At his loud "Humph," she looked startled, then realized that she had committed a social solecism once more.

"You know very well that I did not mean it that way," she said impatiently. "There is no one else I wish to ride with, but I would like to know that I have a horse of my own on which to do so, should a suitable occasion arise."

"I'll speak to Lord Amberley about it when next we meet," he said stiffly, "but I'll see that the mare is in the Amberley stables before nightfall."

Lucy could see no reason for him to take umbrage at her request, though it was more than obvious that he had done so. They rode along in an uncomfortable silence for some time until they reached the spot where they usually galloped, but as luck would have it, a carriage came into sight and they had to wait until it had passed. The delay made her even more irritated with him, for his insistence that they gallop only in private had always annoyed her.

To add to her discomfort, another early-morning rider came into view, and when he saw them, came over to have a word with his old friend.

"Algernon," Anthony said a little grimly, "what a surprise to see you in town so early. Lucinde, I'd like to present Sir Algernon Winters. Algie, this is Lady Lucinde Coldwell."

"Pleased to meet you, Sir Algernon," Lucy murmured, inclining her head slightly and noting with distaste how the high points of his collar poked into his chin and forced him to hold his head ridiculously high. In the center of his elegantly tied cravat a large diamond glittered in the morning sun.

"Delighted, my lady," the gentleman gushed, reaching over to grasp her hand and almost causing an accident as Beauty tried to dance away.

When Lucy had her mare under control once more, Sir Algernon begged, "Please call me Algie, dear lady. Everyone does, don't they, Tony?"

Her glance encompassed the man's pale-green riding jacket, cream breeches, and black boots topped with the same shade of cream. This must be one of the dandies she had heard Henry refer to with scorn. She did not miss Anthony's frown at the abbreviation of his name.

Without waiting for a response, Algernon went on, "Where did you find such a beauty before the Little Season has yet begun, my boy? I don't recall having heard of any Coldwells except in the wilds of Yorkshire."

"Lady Lucinde is the widow of Sir Henry Coldwell, Algie. He was killed in action on the Peninsula, and he was one of my very good friends, despite the fact that he came from a spot just a little south of those wilds."

Anthony's voice held a hint of sarcasm but it was wasted on Sir Algernon, who was looking more closely at Lucinde, noting that though her well-cut riding habit was black, she wore a bright-green scarf at the neck and a matching feather in her black shako.

"Sorry to hear of your loss, my lady," he murmured, "but that's what happens when grown men want to play at being soldiers. They should stick to the toy ones and there'd be no wars, would there, now?" He gave a high-pitched laugh as though he had made a huge joke.

Lucy eyed him with distaste, but said nothing, leaving it to Anthony to break the uncomfortable silence.

"And what are you doing in town so early, Algie?" he asked.

"Oh, you know what it's like, Tony. My mama wanted my youngest sister, Mary, to get a little town bronze before she comes out next year. What with all the gowns and things she absolutely has to have, they needs must be here at least two weeks ahead of time, and someone had to escort them to town." He gave a helpless shrug of his thickly padded shoulders.

"Only thing is, though, London's getting worse all the time. The government should do something about all those frightful-looking men with half their limbs missing who sit at street corners, asking their betters for handouts. And they smell so dreadful that I could be ill on the spot."

He took a lace-edged kerchief out and fluttered it under his nose as if just talking about it had brought it all back to him.

Lucy had been quite proud of the way she had controlled herself and said nothing before, but Sir Algernon's last statement was just too much for her.

"Those men lost those limbs fighting for their country, trying to keep England safe for women and children and even for fops like you," she said angrily, her blue-green eyes flashing. "You're not fit to lick their—" She stopped as she felt Anthony's hard grip upon her arm.

A decidedly red-faced Sir Algernon swung his horse around and started back in the direction from which he had come.

"I hate to think what you were about to say," Anthony said icily, "but I'm glad I stopped you in time. Do you realize that you've made your first enemy?"

"I made my first enemies in Lord and Lady Coldwell almost three years ago," Lucy retorted, "and I'd far rather count that effeminate dandy my enemy than my friend, as apparently you do."

"You need to keep a tighter rein on your tongue, young lady, or you'll damage not only your own reputation but that of your grandparents as well," Anthony said severely. "You can't just go about in this town saying whatever comes into your head, and the sooner you realize it, the better."

"You forgot to mention your own reputation, for you'll most certainly be tarred with the same brush as my grandparents if you continue to associate with someone like me. But wasn't that what you really meant?" she asked him bitterly. "Perhaps you should go after such a dear friend and offer him sympathy at having encountered the sharp edge of my tongue. Then you can make sure that when he tells everybody what a terrible person I am, he does not link his dear Tony's name with mine," Lucy almost shouted, so angry that she scarcely knew what she was saying.

"Perhaps you have the right of it, for once," Anthony growled, signaling the groom to come over.

Lucy swung her mare around so that he would not see the tears she could no longer hold in check, and as she heard him tell the groom to follow her home, she started back toward Park Lane.

She was grateful that it was still early enough for her to meet no one else, and glad, also, that the groom stayed well behind until they reached Amberley House. When he stepped over to assist her dismount, the man said quietly, "His lordship said I was to take Beauty to the Amberley stables, milady, if that's all right with you."

"Perfectly all right," Lucy said. "Tell them to take good care of her and I'll be around later to make sure that they have done so."

He half-smiled and nodded, then Lucy ran quickly up the steps and into the house, not even pausing to speak to Duffield as she made a hurried escape to the privacy of her own bedchamber.

For the next two days Lucy avoided both Lord and Lady Amberley as much as she could. She feigned tiredness and had Gussy bring her breakfast to bed each morning, then hurried around to the stables to talk to Beauty for an hour or so. Once Lord Amberley left for his club, she crept into the library, leaving the door open just a crack so that she could hear the comings and goings in the hall. Then she buried her head in one of the huge leather volumes, learning little as she read the same words over and over again without even knowing or caring what they meant.

She was forced to tell Gussy of her quarrel with Anthony, for she was the one person with whom she could not pretend, but though Morgan had told the maid that his master was in a strange, unhappy mood also, Gussy did not pass the information along. She had learned that it was usually best to let these things take their natural course.

Then, on the afternoon of the third day, as Lucy sat in the study looking out over the back garden and pretending to be reading a book on landscaping, she heard a voice in the hall that was only too familiar, and she scolded herself for being such a fool. She should have written and told her mama that she was here, then that lady would not have ventured near. But she had put it off, as she had put off a great many other things since her arrival in London, and now it was too late.

She tiptoed to the library door and opened it just a little further so that she could hear as much as possible. In addition to her mama's voice there was another, presumably that of the new husband, and all Lucy now hoped was that they might be staying somewhere other than at Amberley House.

They were in the drawing room now and Duffield was

offering them a glass of sherry. Then Lucy heard his slow step as he walked up the stairs, and his light knock on the door of the master-bedroom suite. Grandmama must have been taking a rest.

What Lucy did not expect, however, when she peeked around the massive wing chair in which she had hidden herself, was to see Duffield standing in the doorway of the study, then very carefully closing the door behind him before walking across the room in her direction.

He cleared his throat. "Lady Amberley requests that you join her in five minutes in the drawing room, milady," he said, then added, "If you would like to change your gown first, it might be best to use the back stairs."

Lucy grinned, bowing to the inevitable. "Thank you, Duffield. How does my mama look?" she asked him.

She saw the flicker of amusement in his eyes, then he said, "Not much like you, milady. You're the image of the countess when she was young, if you don't mind my saying so."

"I don't mind you saying so at all, Duffield," Lucy said cheerfully. "I'd like nothing better than to look like Grandmama. Please tell her that I'll be down in about ten minutes."

"I'll send Gussy up to you, milady," he murmured, then went to the drawing room to tell the guests that Lady Amberley would join them shortly.

Lucy hurried out of the study and up the back stairs, which she seemed to use as often as she used the grand front staircase these days, for it was so much more convenient, especially as a shortcut to the stables. Once in her room, she started to unfasten her gown and, a moment later, Gussy entered.

"Now don't you go rippin' off some of them buttons, milady. I'll do that," she said as she hurried across the room. "Which gown do you want to wear?"

"Oh, any old thing, Gussy, so long as it's clean and not creased," Lucy told her, caring little as to how she looked.

Gussy unfastened the rest of the buttons, then went over to the armoire and picked out an afternoon gown in a soft-green sarcenet that seemed to echo, but not copy, the green in Lucy's eyes.

Her mistress's delicate brows rose. "Do you think they're worth that, Gussy?" she asked.

"They're not, but you are. You show 'em 'ow lovely you really are, Miss Lucy, and put 'em to shame," Gussy told her, using the name she had used most of the time they were on the Peninsula.

Lucy smiled. "Why not? I'm sure Grandmama would completely agree with you."

Five minutes later, looking extremely elegant, Lucy stepped carefully down the grand staircase and, for once, allowed the footmen to open the drawing-room doors before she went slowly through them.

"Mama," she said softly. "How lovely to see you looking so well. Have you been in town long?"

There was no question but that it was a lie, for Lady Summers did not look at all well at the moment, but had visibly paled, and she looked completely shocked. Her own mama had not once mentioned in the five minutes since she entered the room, that she had her granddaughter staying with her.

"Lucinde, I thought you were . . . you were in Spain or somewhere," Lady Summers said quickly, quite agitated. "Are you staying here?"

"Of course," Lucy said quietly as her mother clasped her in an embrace carefully calculated not to disturb her own coiffure. "Where else was there for me to stay?"

There was a sound of someone clearing his throat, and Lady Summers suddenly seemed to realize that she could not escape the inevitable. She would have to introduce her daughter to her husband.

"Edward, dear, I'd like you to meet my little daughter, Lucinde," she said, taking Lucy's hand and turning toward a tall, fair-haired gentleman who appeared to be in his early thirties. "This is Lord Edward Summers, my dear, your new stepfather. It was such a pity that you were sick and could not be at our wedding, but I know that you two will get along famously."

He took Lucy's hand in his and bowed low over it; then, before releasing it, he gave it a meaningful squeeze. "I'm sure we'll have a chance this week to make up for lost time," he said, looking warmly into Lucinde's eyes.

Lucy frowned slightly, wondering what he was about, then said to her mama, "I was not sick when you got married, I was in Spain, Mama. I received your letter not long after my husband died, as I recall."

"You are a widow, my dear?" Lord Summers sounded more pleased than sympathetic. "You should have come to stay with us while you were in mourning. In fact, I insist that you come back with us when we leave, for a young widow needs the care of her mother."

"You are very kind, my lord, but Lady Amberley and I have made plans for the next several months, haven't we, Grandmama?" Lucy said, turning to face that lady and slowly closing one eye.

"We most certainly have, my dear," Lady Amberley responded at once, "and I forgot to tell you that I invited your cousins, Jennifer and Richard, to stay for a month or two and keep you company. They should be here in a week or so."

Lord Summers did not mean to be put off so easily. "But that would fit in very well with our plans, for we're not staying here more than a few days, and Lucinde could come back with us for a short visit, couldn't she, Penelope?" He turned to his wife, who was looking decidedly put out by the whole conversation.

"I had thought to stay longer in London than just a few days, Edward," she pouted. "Perhaps Lucinde could come some other time."

Lady Amberley had hoped to have an entertaining few hours listening to her pleasure-loving daughter converse with the outspoken Lucinde. But on meeting her new son-in-law, she realized the mistake she had made. There was no doubt about it, the man was far too young for her daughter. What could Penelope have been thinking of marrying first one too old for her and then one too young? And there was no possible doubt about it, he was a womanizer: Penelope would have her hands full with him.

When tea was brought in, Lady Amberley offered her new son-in-law a second glass of sherry instead, and he accepted with alacrity and was about to move a chair closer to where Lucy was sitting when Lady Amberley spoke up.

"Come and join me on this sofa, young man, for I'd like to get to know my daughter's new husband a little better." He had no option but to do so, and when he was settled, she continued, "Penelope has told me almost nothing about you. Are you, perhaps, related to the Summers family whose seat is in Bristol?"

"Only very distantly, I'm afraid," he told her. "My father was from the Norfolk branch of the family and my mother was a Chatham before her marriage."

"Not Clara Chatham, by any chance?" she asked eagerly, recalling someone by that name who she had once known well.

"I'm afraid not, but I do have an Aunt Clara on my mother's side of the family," he offered. "She never married, for I understand she was the oldest daughter and she had to stay home and help bring up a quite large family."

"That must be the one, but what a shame. She was so very popular at her come-out that everyone was sure she'd be wed in no time at all." Lady Amberley shook her head sadly. "It's unfortunate, but these things do happen."

Lucy was grateful to her grandmama for monopolizing Lord Summers. Moving closer to her mama, she asked softly, "Where are you staying?"

"The Summers family have a house not far away, on Grafton Street." Lady Summers' quiet voice held a note of regret, for it was easily within walking distance. "We were actually going for a ride in the park when I stupidly pointed out Amberley House. Of course, it was Edward who insisted on calling and paying our respects."

Lucy could not help but smile at her mama's frankness, but then she had never been one to dissemble in her dealings with her daughter.

"You needn't worry, Mama," she murmured. "I have no intention of joining you in the country, either now or at any other time. I've always understood, you know."

"He's very persistent. When he has an idea in his head, he's like a dog with a bone," Lady Summers said petulantly. "There doesn't seem any way to stop him, once he gets going."

They had pulled their chairs close together, and now Lucy placed a comforting hand on her mother's arm. "Grandmama seems to be keeping him occupied, anyway," she said. "I'm sure she'll understand if you don't wish to pay a second visit."

"There'll be a second visit," Lady Summers said sadly, "and also a third and fourth if you give him any encouragement."

Lucy smiled gently. "But I won't, so you need not worry about that. You are glad you married him, aren't you?" She felt for a moment that their relationship had been reversed, but then it had always been a little that way.

"He's good to me, my dear, if that's what you mean. It's far better than being an unwanted widow," Lady Summers said firmly. "You'd do well to get yourself a husband as soon as you can. But Mama will see that you do, I'm sure."

In her inimitable way, Lady Amberley must have discreetly brought the visit to an end, for Lord Summers rose. "If we're going to take that drive, we'd best be leaving, Penelope," he said, then he turned to Lucy.

"You may be sure, my dear, that we'll be seeing quite a lot of each other from now on," he said, smiling and taking her hand in his once again and brushing her palm with the tips of his fingers in a most disgustingly familiar way. "Until then, I will bid you a good day."

Lady Summers slipped her arm possessively through his and steered him toward the door. Lady Amberley walked with them into the hall, but Lucy remained where she was, feeling a terrible sadness for her mama, who seemed to have an extraordinary knack for attracting the wrong men.

She heard the sound of the front door closing and Lady Amberley joined her a few minutes later. They looked at each other for a moment, then Lady Amberley said, "My daughter only did one sensible thing in her whole life, and that was having you, my dear. But this is her problem, not yours. Do you realize that he thought you were a very young girl?"

"Yes, but I forgot to ask Mama where I was supposed to have been all this time," Lucy said with a short laugh.

"Staying with your cousins. But Penelope's done it now and been caught in an outright lie. I can just imagine what's going on in that carriage at the moment," Lady Amberley said with a grunt. "And she deserves every bit of it."

"Not really, Grandmama, for she can't help it. She really doesn't look old enough to be my mother, you know, so I don't blame her for pretending."

Lady Amberley looked disgusted. "She must be at least six years, maybe ten years older than he is. And though I agree that it doesn't show now, wait yet another ten years and then see them together."

Lucy had her doubts that the marriage would last so long, but she did not wish to put them into words, so she said nothing.

"And as for you, young lady," Lady Amberley went on, "it's high time you and that young man of yours mended your quarrel, for I'm tired of seeing you moping about the house."

"I don't know what you mean," Lucy said, resenting the interference, "or whom you can be talking about. I don't have a young man. If you're referring to Lord Mortimer, he is just an old friend of Henry's who has been trying to look after me for his friend's sake. And I don't need anyone looking after me."

Without another word, she swept out of the room, leaving her grandmama with an expression of amusement on her face. She reached for the bellpull.

"Was there something, milady?" Duffield asked a second later.

"Yes, there was. You may pour me a glass of sherry—a large glass. Sometimes I wonder about procreation, Duffield—and you don't need to answer that," she snapped.

The old servant smiled fondly at the old lady as he bent down to place the sherry on the table beside her, then he straightened up and walked sedately out of the room. If anyone was making bets, his money would be on her every time.

7

Lord and Lady Summers called again the next day, just after Lady Amberley had gone to leave her card at the homes of some of her friends who had just arrived in town.

"You did say that they are both here, Duffield?" Lucy asked, and the old servant disdainfully inclined his head, for he did not make mistakes of that sort.

"Now, come along, Duffield, there's no need to get on your high horse. The only reason I questioned you was because it would not be proper for me to see Lord Summers alone," Lucy said impatiently.

A trace of a smile showed on his face for just a moment. "They are together, milady," he said firmly, "and should Lady Penelope leave for any reason before you go down to see them, I'll most certainly let you know."

Five minutes later, dressed in a rather severe morning gown, Lucy entered the drawing room and went immediately over to her mama to kiss her cheek. After dropping a brief curtsy to Lord Summers, she took the wing chair opposite her mama and assumed that her stepfather would sit on the sofa.

It seemed, however, that he had no plans to sit down for the moment, for he remained standing just behind her chair.

"I suppose you came to see Grandmama, but I'm afraid you just missed her, and she won't be back now until just before luncheon," Lucy said apologetically. "Is there anything I can do for you?"

Her mother glanced toward Lord Summers and nodded, a little hesitantly.

Lucy turned around to hear what her stepfather had to say.

"Actually, we saw Lady Amberley leave the house, but did not think to detain her, for our purpose in calling was to see you," he said a little ponderously.

Lucy raised her eyebrows but remained silent, waiting.

"Your mother has told me how very unhappy she was when you married at such a young age and immediately left for the Peninsula. She feels that, at the very least, you should come home with us and stay for several weeks, so that she may have a chance to get to know you again," he said, trying to appear most earnest.

Lucy did not even pretend to believe that her mother felt anything of the sort. "Lord Summers—" she began, trying to be as patient with him as she knew how, but he interrupted her at once.

"Please, my dear, you are like a daughter to me. I will understand if you cannot call me papa, but you must at least call me Edward," he begged.

Lucy looked for a moment as though she could not believe her ears. Then she said quietly, "You are quite right that I cannot call you papa, and neither can I call you Edward, for I do not know you well enough as yet, sir."

"But you will, my dear. You may be sure of that," he told her softly, with the utmost self-confidence.

"However, as I was about to say," she went on, "you cannot possibly know the existing circumstances when I married, for you were not acquainted with either my mother or me at that time—"

He interrupted her once more. "But your mother has—"

Lucy was, however, fast losing her patience. "Lord Summers," she said sharply, "would you please take a seat, on that sofa. I find it both disconcerting to me, and rude to Mama, to have to turn my head around in order to converse with you."

Though he looked extremely put out, he took his place on

the sofa, and Lucy continued in as calm a voice as she could muster. "At the moment I am under a decided obligation to Lady Amberley. I arrived here with scarcely a penny in my purse and little to wear except the gown on my back. She has spent a great deal of time and money completely outfitting me with appropriate clothes so that I may mingle with her friends without putting her or myself to shame. It is not my intent to let her down now."

It was only too obvious that Lucinde meant what she said, and her mama looked appealingly at her husband. "Edward, my dear, don't—" she began.

He put up a hand to stop her saying more, then got to his feet. "You are quite right, my love. There is no point in saying anything further at this time. But it is by no means the end of it. I will try again later, however, to persuade your daughter to make us both happy by sharing our humble abode in the country."

They left quickly then and Lucy sank back into the large chair feeling quite exhausted. She had met a lot of men overseas, but never one as persistent as Lord Summers. Her mama had been right when she said that he was like a dog with a bone. She would make sure, in future, not to have them admitted unless her grandmama was home.

The next morning he came alone, but went away after being informed that neither lady was at home. From her hiding place in the study, Lucy heard him question Duffield further, making sure that both ladies were out and not just Lady Amberley. She smiled at the icy tone in which the very proper butler replied.

That evening, however, she decided it had gone far enough. She would not allow him to continue calling and being turned away indefinitely. She had a plan she meant to put into effect.

Lady Amberley was home when Lord Summers came the next morning, and when he was shown into the drawing room, the expression on his face was one of almost triumph.

Once more, he fumbled with Lucy's hand as he greeted her, and her grandmama, to whom she had mentioned this little trick, looked extremely annoyed.

Just before coffee was served, Lucy announced that she was going through to the conservatory to procure a specimen of a flower they had just been talking about. As she had expected, he had claimed an interest in botany as soon as she had spoken of her own research into the subject.

Before she had scarcely got out of the room, Lord Summers professed a need to wash his hands and excused himself to Lady Amberley.

Though Lady Amberley knew that one of the large footmen was hiding behind some bushes in the conservatory, she still sat on the very edge of her chair waiting for one of them to return. She sincerely hoped that it would be Lord Summers and that she and Lucinde had been imagining things, but after witnessing his behavior toward her granddaughter today, she doubted it would be the case.

When she heard him in the hall, she breathed a sigh of relief and waited for him to return to his seat, then realized that his voice sounded strained and that he was asking for his hat, gloves, and cane.

Going over to the window, she watched him through the curtains as he walked stiffly down the steps and out into his carriage. He drove away without a backward glance.

A moment later, Lucy came in looking more than a little satisfied, and at the same time, a maid brought in a tray of coffee.

When they were finally alone, Lady Amberley raised a questioning eyebrow in Lucy's direction.

"I don't think he'll be back, Grandmama," she said quietly. "Shall I pour?"

"Are you all right? Did that man try to attack you?" Lady Amberley asked, now more curious than concerned, for Lucinde did not appear to be at all upset.

"I'm quite all right," Lucy murmured, "but what

happened in the conservatory is strictly between my stepfather and me. He now understands that I will not permit him to make advances toward me, and I'm sure that he will not trouble me again.'' She smiled and held out a cup of coffee. ''Cream and sugar?'' she asked.

The old lady glared at her granddaughter for a moment, then said, ''Very well, we'll not discuss it further. You may add one spoonful of sugar and just a little cream, please.''

They sipped the fragrant coffee in silence for a while, then Lady Amberley asked, ''Is your quarrel with Lord Mortimer irreconcilable?''

''I sincerely hope not,'' Lucy said unhappily, ''but I don't think it would be seemly for me to make the first move.''

Her grandmama frowned. She had been hoping, at first, that Lord Mortimer was just out of town for a while, but the girl's obvious unhappiness as the days went by had seemed to indicate a quarrel. ''Is it something else you don't want to talk about?'' she asked.

Lucy shook her head. ''I insulted one of his friends in the park one morning. At my suggestion, Anthony went after him and had the groom bring me home.''

''You could always send him a note of apology,'' Lady Amberley suggested. ''There's nothing unladylike about that.''

Lucinde smiled faintly. ''I don't think he would accept an apology for upsetting him unless it also included his friend,'' she said, a little bleakly.

Lady Amberley could not disagree with her granddaughter's reasoning, but she was nevertheless pleased to find that the girl's feelings for Anthony were so strong. It would work itself out, she was sure, and before very long two of her other grandchildren would be here to help liven the place up. She had heard just this morning that they were coming a little earlier than expected so that she could get Jennifer a few new gowns and things.

But it was a pity, just the same, that Anthony had not been around when her new son-in-law was here, for he would have sent him off very quickly with a flea in his ear and Lucy would not have needed to do anything about it herself.

She must remember to tell Lord Amberley about the events of the last few days when they retired to bed this evening, for he would get a good chuckle out of the whole thing, she was sure. He would be sorry, of course, that he had missed seeing Penelope, but he had long since given up trying to understand the girl, just as she had been forced to do.

The very next afternoon, as Lucy entered through the back door after a visit with Beauty, she heard an unusual amount of noise and laughter emanating from the drawing room. She knew that it was not her grandmama's day for receiving friends, or she would have been pouring tea for her, so she hurried into the main hall to find out what was going on. She was wearing one of her old black gowns, now used only for visits to the stables, so whoever it was, she could not let them see her.

She was so intent on making no sound as she moved toward the drawing room, from which the noise seemed to emanate, that she failed to see the young man who had just entered the house until she collided with him.

"I'm sorry, miss," he said, grabbing her to stop her from falling. "You must be new here. I'll see if I can find your cap."

To Lucy's amazement he started groveling on the floor, obviously searching for something. Then she realized what he had said, and she began to laugh helplessly. The young man with the coppery-colored hair could only be her cousin Richard, whom she had not seen since she was a little girl.

"What on earth is going on out here?" Her grandmama was standing in the drawing room doorway, watching Richard crawling around on the black-and-white tile floor.

"He's l-looking for m-my cap," Lucy said between gales of laughter. "He th-thinks I'm a new s-servant."

"Richard, get up this minute," Lady Amberley ordered, smiling broadly, "and meet your cousin Lucinde."

Before he was back on his feet, however, Lucy grabbed a napkin from the sideboard and placed it on the top of her head.

"Will this do, milord?" she asked, dropping him a quick curtsy.

It was an uproarious start to what would prove to be a most happy visit. Lucy, of course, had to go upstairs at once and let Gussy make her look more presentable, but it was not long before she was back, enjoying reminiscences of the visits she and her mama had made to her cousins' home.

Richard was almost the same age as Lucy, and Jennifer, who had black hair and silver-gray eyes and the sweetest disposition, was just two years younger.

"It's a very good thing that only family saw you in that dreadful gown, Lucinde," Lady Amberley said sharply when her grandchildren had tidied themselves and come down for afternoon tea. "I can't think why you've held on to it, unless it's because not even a servant in this house would want it."

"I was just returning from the stables, Grandmama," Lucy protested. "Would you prefer me to wear something like this for such visits?" She lightly fingered the skirt of the lace-trimmed cream sarcenet gown she had changed into.

Lady Amberley frowned. "I was wondering why you sometimes come in through the back of the house, and meant to ask about it. What is so interesting about the Amberley stables?"

"My horse, Beauty, of course. Didn't I tell you that she was delivered here for my use?" Lucy realized that it must have completely slipped her mind. "Grandpapa was going to buy her back for me from Lord Mortimer, but I don't know if he has yet had the time to do so."

"I'll remind him tonight," her grandmama said, "for now that Jennifer and Richard are here you'll be able to ride every morning if you wish. Not tomorrow morning, however, for we have to go with Jennifer to the modiste. Did your mama make a list of what additional gowns she wishes you to have, my dear?''

Jennifer smiled. ''It's upstairs, in my reticule. I think there are only a couple of gowns needed, but the ones Mama had made for me at home need gloves, slippers, and such to match. She said that the selection and quality would be far superior in London.''

Lady Amberley nodded in agreement, then said to Lucy, ''And what are you frowning at, young lady? Is it too much to ask that you accompany your cousin on a shopping expedition?''

''I'd much rather go riding with her or with Richard,'' Lucy said frankly, ''for you know how I detest standing to be fitted for gowns, or going from shop to shop to find just the right shade of green or blue or whatever—as if anyone is going to notice.''

Jennifer was staring at her in complete disbelief. ''But, Lucinde, all ladies enjoy shopping. It's one of the things I was so looking forward to. And once the Season starts, you meet all your friends and stop for a cup of tea or one of those delicious ices at Gunter's. Do say you'll come with us'' she begged.

She was so very earnest that Lucinde had not the heart to refuse, which was what her Grandmama had been counting on.

''Very well. I'll come just this once,'' Lucy agreed. ''It was the thought of the ices that did it, for Grandmama has never suggested stopping for some.''

This was just what Lady Amberley had been hoping for when she invited her two other grandchildren to town. They were well-mannered and accepted their place in society with complete equanimity. Surely, after several months of close association, some of this would eventually transfer itself to Lucinde and make her more content with her role in life?

''Is there any reason why our cousin cannot enjoy both shopping and a ride in the park?'' Richard asked. ''It would be my pleasure to escort her at, say, about eight o'clock in the morning, leaving ample time for her to join you on your shopping expedition. I'm sure you'll not leave before ten."

Lucy positively beamed. "I thought that perhaps you were tired of riding after your long journey, but if you're not, then that would be wonderful. And at eight o'clock there's not usually anyone else about and we could gallop."

He grinned. "Make the most of it while you can, Cousin Lucinde, for in a couple of weeks there'll be many more people in town and even at eight o'clock the park will have quite a number of riders."

They both ignored Lady Amberley's frown of disapproval, but the old lady was wise enough to let it go for now.

"There's one other matter I'd like to bring up. I realize, Grandmama, that you prefer not to use abbreviated names, and that if you wish to call me Lucinde, you will do so. And you do, at least, pronounce it properly." Lucy grinned. "However, I think my cousins might be persuaded to call me Lucy, the name I've been using ever since I left home."

"Lucy does seem to suit you much better," Jennifer agreed, "and if you prefer it then, of course, we will do so—except when we're cross with you. Mama always calls me Jennifer Margaret when I've been misbehaving."

"I'm willing," Richard agreed, "as long as you don't call me Dick. That is one name I abhor."

"How about Ritchie, then?" Lucy teased.

"Not if you wish to live a long life," he threatened, then he added on a serious note. "I'm awfully sorry about Henry, and sorry, too, that we never met him. It must have been very difficult for you, all alone over there."

"Thank you, Richard," she said quietly, "but actually it's been more difficult here in London, having to learn so many new things. You see, in Spain there were no choices, you just did the very best you could, whereas here I'm constantly doing the wrong thing, or saying the wrong thing, and getting into trouble."

She looked unhappy for a moment, remembering the last time she had got into trouble. She missed Anthony more than she would have believed possible. Then her face brightened, for she was extremely pleased to be with her cousins once more and to have the chance to ride again.

The next few days passed happily enough. She rode in the park each morning with Richard, and though she found herself looking for a glimpse of Anthony much of the time, she was quite relieved when he did not come into sight.

And although she still found no pleasure in the seemingly endless visits to first one shop and then another, it was obvious that Jennifer was having a wonderful time.

To procure a pair of gloves in exactly the right shade to suit Lady Amberley meant going down a narrow side street off Bond Street to the warehouse that supplied most of the modistes in London.

The carriage set them down on the corner and the ladies walked the short distance. Lady Amberley and Jennifer proceeded into the warehouse, but Lucinde paused, for she had seen something that was an all too common sight in certain parts of London these days, and one that she could not pass by.

A man sat propped against a wall, wearing the torn and tattered red uniform of the 14th Light Infantry. One leg of the dirty white breeches had been cut off above the knee and the ends roughly tacked together.

Lucy reached for the change purse she always carried and emptied it into the private's hand. The watery blue eyes brightened and he mumbled his thanks.

"Where did you lose your leg?" she asked softly.

"At Salamanca, miss," the gruff voice answered, "just abaht a year since."

"I know," Lucy murmured, "that was where my husband was killed—Colonel Henry Coldwell."

"I was in 'is regiment," the private said in surprise, "but I'd no idea 'e was 'it there. Now I see yer 'air I remember you, for you were with 'im, weren't you? 'Ere, I can't take this from you," he began, trying to give the money back to her, but Lucy stopped him.

"He'd want you to have it," she told him. "Put it in your pocket. Has your leg healed all right?"

"Aye. I was one of the lucky ones, if y'can call it lucky," he said. "There's lots o' things I could do instead o' sittin' 'ere beggin', but nobody wants to 'ire a man wi' only one leg."

She gave him one of the cards her grandmama had ordered for her. "If things ever get really bad, come to the back door and tell them I said you should ask for me. What's your name?"

"Jim Baker, miss," he told her, "an' God bless you."

Lucy saw through the glass panes in the door that her grandmama was about to leave the warehouse. "I must go now, but don't forget, will you?"

The warmth in his eyes made up for all the scolding Lucy received from her grandmama on the way back to Berkeley Square.

"I'm surprised at you, Lucinde, after what I've said to you about this before," Lady Amberley began as the carriage got under way. "I know that you feel sorry for these men, but they're rough and ready and could kill you for the change in your purse. Though, come to think of it, you probably gave him every penny you had."

Lucy said nothing but inclined her head to indicate that she had.

"What are you going to do now if you need a piece of ribbon or a reel of thread?" her grandmama asked angrily.

"I have at least a dozen reels of thread and I can always take a ribbon off of something else," Lucy said gently, knowing that she would never be able to make her grandmama understand.

"I'm not saying you should be hard-hearted, Lucinde, for it's just not in you. And you've seen me throw them a coin sometimes. But it's dangerous to stop and talk to them as you do," Lady Amberley went on. "Why didn't you just give him something and then follow us into the warehouse?"

"I'm sorry to upset you like this, Grandmama," Lucy said,

placing a hand over that of the older lady. "I had to stop and talk to him, for he was wearing the uniform of Henry's regiment. He lost his leg in the same battle as Henry was killed."

Lady Amberley squeezed the hand holding hers. "I know you can't help it, my dear," she said, "but please try to be a little more careful. You've come to mean a great deal to me in these last few weeks."

"I promise," Lucy said with a smile.

Reaching into her reticule, Lady Amberley took out her own purse. "Here, take this and let me have yours, for I don't like you going around with an empty purse," she said gruffly, and Lucy did as she asked.

Jennifer, who had been listening to the exchange of words with interest, decided that she had just learned a great deal about both her cousin and her grandmama that she had not known before.

8

Lady Amberley was going to pay a call on her good friend Lady Mortimer, and as she did not wish Lucy to hear her questioning that good lady about her son, she suggested that her two granddaughters might like to stroll over to Gunter's for ices.

"You must take a maid with you, of course, even for that short distance," she reminded them, for she knew that Lucy would never think of doing so, and it had seemed to her these last few days that Jennifer might have started to emulate Lucy just a little.

"We'll take Gussy with us," Lucy said when they were ready to set out, "for I'm willing to wager that she's never had an ice in her life."

Jennifer's eyebrows rose, but she decided to wait and see what her cousin had in mind.

The three of them started to walk down the street, Gussy staying a few paces behind the other two despite the number of times Lucy turned around and frowned at her.

"Let's eat it over there," Jennifer suggested, pointing to where a bench was placed beneath some trees.

"That's a good idea. You stay here and I'll just go and get them," Lucy began, but was interrupted by her maid.

"No, milady." Gussy looked for a moment as if she would like to hit her mistress over the head and knock some sense into her. "Y'can't leave Lady Jennifer alone over 'ere. If ye'll give me the money and tell me what you want, I'll go and get 'em for you while ye get settled."

Lucy had not given a thought to leaving Jennifer alone, and when she did, she had to agree. "Very well, then. Now, be sure to get three of them, for I'm determined you're going to have one, Gussy."

"It's not proper, milady," the maid protested. "What will people think?"

"You know very well that I have never cared what is proper," Lucy told her angrily, "and if you don't bring three back with you, I will walk over myself and get another."

Jennifer started to laugh, and said, "You may as well get three, Gussy, for when she says she's determined, she means it."

Muttering to herself, the maid went over to the pastry shop and came back a few minutes later with the three dishes of their special ice. Try as Lucy might, however, she could not persuade Gussy to sit beside them while she ate hers.

"You just don't understand your place, milady," Gussy snapped at her. "I'll eat mine over there by that old oak. And when you've done, I'll take 'em their dishes back."

"You're very fond of her, aren't you?" Jennifer remarked when they had started to spoon the delicious concoction into their mouths.

"We've been through a lot together," Lucy said. "Foraged for food when we had to, worked side by side, and shared anything either one of us was given. She is my equal, whether society cares to think so or not."

"That's fine when you're alone," Jennifer said gently, "but you embarrassed her just now, Lucy. She's happy just to be with you, I can tell. But she has her own sense of place, and as long as she knows how you feel about her, that's all that matters to her."

Lucy bit her lip. "I suppose you're right," she admitted reluctantly, "and I'm sure she'll give me a scold when she's helping me dress tonight."

"What are you going to wear for your first London ball?" Jennifer asked. "Aren't you even a little excited?"

Lucy had just taken a spoonful of the ice, and she let it dissolve slowly in her mouth to give herself time to think of an answer that would not disappoint her cousin. The truth was, of course, that had she and Anthony still been friends, she would have been more than a little excited, but she could think of no one else she would like to dance with.

"We had dances quite frequently when Henry and I first went to Portugal, for there was little to do but wait for the French to retreat, and Massena was terribly stubborn about it. I and the other officers' wives would plan parties where we frequently danced if we could find a fiddler to play for us." Lucy's eyes looked dreamy as she remembered those early days of her marriage.

"It must have been very exciting," Jennifer said, a little enviously, "for there were probably four men to every woman."

"More like forty men to every woman," Lucy told her. "The enlisted men who wished to take their wives with them had to draw lots, for only a small number were allowed to get on the ship in England. It was sad to see the ones who had been unlucky standing there, often with their children in their arms, watching as the ship carried their husbands farther and farther away."

She saw no reason to tell such a young girl as Jennifer about the camp followers who took the place of many of the wives once the men landed on foreign soil.

"But you still have not told me what you are going to wear tonight. I must know, for it would not do for us to arrive in the same color," Jennifer explained.

"That makes the decision an easy one," Lucy said cheerfully. "Tell me what color you're planning to wear and I'll be sure not to choose the same color."

"The gown I would like to wear is a pale-peach lace over white satin," Jennifer said, "with broad white satin ribbons falling from under the bodice almost to the floor."

"That will be so lovely with your creamy complexion and dark hair that you're bound to be the belle of the ball, my dear," Lucy assured her as she made a mental note to always check with Jennifer as to what she was wearing in the future. For the younger girl's sake, she would not like to wear anything that clashed or put her cousin's outfit in the shade.

The gown she finally chose that evening was a simple sleeveless column in a soft apple-green satin. It had a deep neckline and absolutely no trimming whatever, which was completely to her liking. When Lady Amberley saw her, however, she insisted on lending her a pearl necklace and matching pearl earrings, and she had to agree that they put an excellent finishing touch to the outfit.

"It seems just like old times," Lord Amberley said as he and Richard escorted Lady Amberley and their two granddaughters to the Stockbridges' ball. Lady Amberley would stay with her charges, but her husband meant to retire to the card room immediately they arrived.

"Now, my dears," the countess admonished her granddaughters, "do be sure to get up to dance no more than twice with any gentleman. And though you're allowed considerably more freedom, Lucinde, you still may not dance with or speak to any gentleman to whom you have not been properly introduced. This will not be at all like the dances you attended in Spain, and I would not care to see Jennifer's chances impaired by any thoughtlessness on your part."

"You need not worry, Grandmama, for I will be the epitome of discretion this evening," Lucy said quietly, feeling quite hurt at Lady Amberley's words, "but I believe this will be the last ball I shall attend, for I have no wish to damage either yours or Jennifer's reputation with my gauche behavior."

"What nonsense," Lady Amberley said sharply. "I was merely reminding you of the damage that can be done by a thoughtless remark or action."

Lord Amberley loudly cleared his throat and glanced pointedly at his lady, who had the grace to look embarrassed, and they were all quite relieved when, a moment later, the coach came to a halt outside the Stockbridges' door.

They alighted and went up the steps and into the house, where, to Lady Amberley's delight, they found Lord Mortimer and his mama just ahead of them, waiting to go through the receiving line.

The difficult moment quickly passed for all except Lucy, who had suffered so many rejections as a child that she thought she had built up an immunity, only to discover it had been but surface-deep. While her grandmama performed the introductions, she kept her eyes averted, and it was not until Anthony's deep voice addressed her directly that she looked up.

She was startled to see the gentle expression in his eyes as he smiled at her and said softly, "I'm delighted to see you looking so very lovely, my dear. Will you grant me the first waltz and the supper dance with you?"

Though her grandmama's remark still rankled, Lucy's spirits rose as she greeted him and then allowed him to put his name on the appropriate lines of her program. She knew it was quite silly to be so easily pleased, but it seemed she had little control over her feelings insofar as Anthony was concerned. She had missed him quite dreadfully—much more than she cared to admit even to herself.

He requested the dance after supper with Jennifer and then stepped to one side with Richard as the latter started to ask him questions about the wars.

"What a handsome gentleman," Jennifer said quietly to Lucy, not taking her eyes off of him as he conversed with her brother. "Have you known him for very long?"

Lucy could not help but smile, for her young cousin seemed quite mesmerized. It would pass, she was sure, once the dancing started and she met many more young men.

"Let me see," she said with a grin that Jennifer, still looking at Lord Mortimer, missed altogether, "I believe I first met him in Portugal in the year 1811. It must have been about February, for the weather was quite cold, as I recall, and he insisted that I wear his cape about my shoulders."

"He was a friend of your husband's," Jennifer inquired, turning back to Lucy, "that's how you know him so well? I thought for a moment that he was someone you had but recently met."

Lucy still looked amused. "You're correct on both counts actually, for I had not seen him for ages until just before I left Spain. He arranged for mine and Gussy's passage on the ship, and for us to be safely escorted to it," she said, omitting the fact that their departure had been at his instigation and command.

"I see." Jennifer sounded somewhat disappointed and added wistfully, "But he has the kindest eyes and the warmest smile. Does he, by chance, have a younger brother?"

Lucy laughed softly. "I believe he has, but you must ask him that when he claims his dance. That is, if you're not too tongue-tied to do so."

They both watched him as he gave his full attention to the younger man, obviously explaining something most carefully and using his hands to help illustrate a point.

Lady Amberley and her bosom bow, Lady Mortimer, though they had seen each other only the day before, were so engrossed in their own conversation that it took a small nudge from Lord Amberley to make them realize that they were next in line to greet their host and hostess. Lord Mortimer was watching, however, and was at his mother's side in a moment, taking her arm and escorting her forward.

Then it was the Amberleys' turn, and as the older granddaughter, Lucy was to be presented first. She frowned for a moment, for she should have been watching what the other young ladies did, and had been too busy watching Anthony. A curtsy had to be the right thing, she quickly decided, and was grateful to see her grandmama's smile of approval as she sank low.

"That was very prettily done, Lucinde," Lady Amberley told her. "You must not take my rough tongue to heart, my love, for it was not my intent to hurt you. But you're so much like me when I was a gel that I know how easy it is to do the wrong thing."

Lucy gave a shaky laugh. "I'll not mind if you give me a little nudge sometimes," she said softly, "for I've no wish to make an exhibition of myself. Perhaps we could devise signals of some sort. You know, one pinch means curtsy, two pinches means smile and hold your tongue, three pinches . . ." She stopped at the sound of a deep chuckle just behind her and noticed the twinkle in her grandmama's eyes.

"It sounds very much as though someone is going to be black and blue before the evening is out," Anthony remarked, smiling at Lucy as she swung around to face him, "but I suppose it is important to make a good impression at your first ball. Don't worry, for in a couple of weeks you'll do everything so automatically that you'll not give it a second thought."

"That is what I'm afraid of, my lord," she told him, a little ruefully. "I don't want to become one of those empty-headed ladies I meet at afternoon teas, who can talk of nothing but which gown they will wear that evening and how many times they have dined at Carlton House."

Fortunately, her grandmama had turned away to speak to one of her friends and did not hear her remark.

"You have to give it time, Lucy," Anthony said quietly. "You'll learn quickly enough which of the ladies you meet are worth cultivating. They don't go around actually wearing blue stockings, you know, but many of them have a great deal of influence in what goes on in this country. And now, I believe this is our waltz."

She slipped easily into his arms and a moment later felt as if she were floating on air as they swirled around the room.

"Do you recall, when Henry and I first arrived in Portugal, how you refused to dance with me?" she asked, looking up at him with a deceptively innocent expression.

"Now, young lady, that is a slight distortion of the truth, and I'll not let you get away with it," he warned. "As I recall, almost as soon as you arrived at what was supposed to be a ballroom, Henry decided to go into the card room for the evening and leave you in my charge."

A smile teased the corners of her mouth as she waited for him to continue.

"He told me, I believe, that he had the utmost faith in my honor as a gentleman," Anthony said a little scornfully, "and I told him in no uncertain terms that the only way I could trust myself was if I did not dance with you."

Lucy's eyes resembled saucers and she mouthed the word, "Oh," then added, "That was not at all what Henry told me."

"If you recall, he did not try to leave you alone in that ballroom again, did he?" Anthony was fascinated as he watched the changing expressions on her face as she tried to recall those times of comparative peace when it had been imperative that they do something to relieve the interminable boredom.

"No, he didn't," she said thoughtfully as the dance drew to a close, "and now I think on it, he was a little more attentive for a while. But then, after you transferred, he started to volunteer once more for all the most dangerous assignments. He was kind and gentle with me, but he must have found an eighteen-year-old chit a most boring companion."

Anthony chuckled. "You kept him on his toes," he said, placing her hand on his arm and starting across the room toward her grandmama. "Speaking of which, I must thank you for not seeking revenge for imagined past sins and treading on mine this evening. I cannot recall when I enjoyed a waltz so much, my dear, nor how I will survive until I can claim you once more for the supper dance."

Lucy frowned, for that was just the kind of meaningless remark she most disliked, and she had not expected it of Anthony.

He raised questioning eyebrows, but when she simply murmured her thanks, he bowed, then turned on his heel and joined Richard, who was standing talking to some of his contemporaries.

As he walked away, Lucy suddenly realized that she would probably not see him again for quite some time, for there were many dances before supper would be served, and she wished that it might pass quickly. Was that what he meant? she wondered. Did he really feel the same way?

Jennifer had been watching them dancing the waltz with an expression of longing on her face, for envy was not a part of the girl's nature. "You dance so well together that anyone would think you had been doing it for a long time," she remarked to Lucy, "but then, I suppose you did dance with him sometimes when you were overseas."

"As a matter of fact, I did not, for he was transferred shortly after I arrived there," Lucy explained. "It's strange that you should mention it, for we were just saying that this was the first time we have ever danced together."

A young man, the son of one of Lady Amberley's friends, came over to claim the next dance from Jennifer. When they had left to take their places in the set, Lady Amberley asked slyly, "Did that waltz serve to change your mind about forgoing balls in the future, Lucinde? I must say you appeared to be enjoying it to the utmost."

"The evening has only just begun, Grandmama," Lucy murmured. "I'm promised to a number of other gentlemen for contredanses, cotillions, and the minuet, and though I know I learned them once, it was a very long time ago. I see that my next partner, the young man with the collar points that gouge his neck, is coming for me now, so you will soon see for yourself how I behave."

"That young man is Lord Thane, the new Earl of Coventry, Lucinde, and one of the richest men in England, so you'd best mind your manners," Lady Amberley murmured. Then she said quite loudly, "Lord Thane, how nice to see you enjoying yourself once more. How is your dear mama?"

After a few polite responses, Lord Thane led Lucinde out onto the floor to join a set that was waiting for them, and the music commenced once more.

It was some two hours later, and with feet a little the worse for being trampled upon, that Lucy got up for her second dance with Anthony.

"Immediately after supper a few of us, including Richard, are planning to leave and go on to White's," he told her. "I believe my mama is arranging at this moment for Lady Amberley to take her home, but I didn't want you to wonder where I had gone, my dear."

"I have heard that it is customary for people to attend as many as three and four functions per night, so I suppose you have really spent a long time here already," Lucy said, unable to hide her disappointment that he was leaving her behind.

"As I will be unable to dance with you again, there is little point in my staying," Anthony murmured, his blue eyes showing his regret. "May I take you for a ride early tomorrow morning, or has your cousin already promised to do so?"

She shook her head. "You may take me," she said with a happy sigh. "Eight o'clock?"

He nodded. "And if Richard or Jennifer should ask, please don't tell them they may come along, for I would prefer it if there were just the two of us," he said, adding, "I've missed you."

Although Lucy did not admit to it, she felt sure he could read in her eyes how much she had missed him, but all she said was "You'll bring a groom, of course."

"Definitely," he agreed, "and now tell me how to do this wretched dance, for I've completely forgotten the figures."

Lucy's peal of laughter could be heard even by her grandmama, sitting watching on the side. "Oh, no, not you, also," she said. "We'd best keep a sharp eye on the others and do what they do."

Fortunately, the movements were not too complicated and they soon had the hang of it enough to be able to converse between movements.

"Is Grandpapa leaving also?" she asked him.

"He left some half-hour ago," he told her, "for the card play was too tame for him here. I'm sure Lady Amberley did not expect him to stay very long but just to put in an appearance."

"He's a very dear person, and I'm so glad he is willing to talk to me and tell me what is going on in the world," Lucy said earnestly. "If it were not for him, I would not know anything."

Anthony said nothing, but his eyebrows rose, for he had not realized that Lord Amberley was capable of being on such terms with his granddaughter. He had always held him in high respect, but now felt even kindlier toward him.

As soon as the dance came to an end, he led her over to the supper room, where her grandmama was sitting at a large table with his mother and young Jennifer. Waiters were already coming around with platters of the most delicious food and drinks of all kinds.

"It's a far cry from what is served at Almack's," Anthony murmured in Lucy's ear. "Stale cakes and lemonade is all you get there, so be warned when you grace their portals."

"From what I've heard about the place, I don't think I'm going there," Lucy said firmly. "I would be sure to cause a scandal the minute I entered the room."

"I'd like to see you wriggle out of it," Anthony challenged. "Your grandmama will most certainly have procured vouchers for you and will be horrified if you refuse."

He had seated himself between Jennifer and Lucy and now turned to have a word with her young cousin. Though she could not hear all the words, Lucy was aware of the excited tremor in Jennifer's voice. She leaned forward, supposedly to reach for a slice of bread, and saw that her cousin was giving him a look of almost adoration and hanging on his every word. Jennifer had most decidedly developed a girlish *tendre* for Anthony, and this might prove awkward in the weeks ahead. She had to admit, though, that he was handling her very well.

Though she danced every single dance until Lady Amberley decided they should leave, it was somehow not quite as enjoyable once Anthony departed. She did, however, meet quite a number of young men who asked if they might call on her at Amberley House. Though she smiled and inclined her head in agreement, as her grandmama had told her to do, she secretly hoped they might find something better to do with their time.

9

It was a rather tired young lady who awoke somewhat later than usual the morning after the ball, but quickly arose ready to have Gussy help her into her riding habit then hurry downstairs to meet Anthony. Much to her surprise, Gussy had not yet brought up the jug of hot water for her to wash in.

She had bathed in far too many basins of cold water to make a fuss about that, however, so she quickly poured some of the water remaining from last night into the flowered china bowl and began to open her eyes as the water refreshed her face.

Then she realized why Gussy had not put in an appearance, for now she could not only see but also hear the steady rain that was falling outside. There would be no ride in the park with Anthony this morning.

Feeling unreasonably disappointed, she sat down again on the bed and tugged sharply on the bellpull.

A few minutes later, Gussy knocked and entered, a tray with a pot of hot chocolate in her hands.

"After such a late night, I'd 'oped ye might sleep late this morning, milady," she said, "for ye'll not be riding in this weather."

"Oh, Gussy, I was so looking forward to it. You probably noticed that I've not seen him for more than a week, and then last night everything was as though we'd never quarreled." She smiled ruefully. "I believe he wanted to talk about it this morning, for he emphasized that he did not wish either of my cousins to accompany us."

She jumped up and went across to the small room off hers where a maid could sleep, make repairs to or press garments, and she came back with a cup in her hand. Picking up the chocolate pot, she poured a cup for Gussy.

"Now it's like old times, when we'd sit and sip that awful stuff they called tea in Spain, and talk over the happenings of the previous day," she said with a sigh.

Gussy sipped the delicious chocolate and watched as Lucinde piled the pillows behind her and stretched out on the bed. She had not needed to be told who "he" was. "Aye, and listen to it rainin' like this, often enough, but we never 'ad owt as good as this to warm us in them days," she remarked. "So you quarreled, did you? I thought as much, for you've been moping about 'ere for a week or more."

"It was because of a fop we met one morning. He made some unpleasant remarks about the wounded soldiers on the streets. I started to tell him what I thought about him, but the man rode off," Lucy told her.

Gussy was a good listener, and she sat and waited for Lucy to continue.

"Anthony was furious, and then when I angrily suggested he go after his friend and try to make amends, he agreed and told the groom to take me home," she said, a little lamely.

"Most likely 'e did it to stop 'im telling the story all over London an' givin' you a bad reputation," Gussy said dryly. "You'll not be popular 'ere for long if ye go around callin' people names. I remember 'ow you even called 'im a few when 'e said 'e was shipping you 'ome."

Lucy looked at the maid for a moment, then started to giggle. "I did, didn't I, Gussy? But he deserved them."

"I'm not sure that 'e did at that," Gussy said. "You'd no business bein' out there takin' such chances. Sir 'Enry should never 'ave let you start 'elping, but 'e didn't seem to care what you did as long as you let 'im do what 'e wanted to."

"Gussy, you know that I couldn't have sat around in Lisbon with the other officers' wives, drinking that wretched tea and talking about the latest fashions in London. I'd never been one of them, just as I'm not one of them here now. At least I was happy doing what I could to be useful."

"Now don't you take on so, milady." Gussy looked quite upset. "I never said as you didn't 'elp as much if not more than I did. But it wasn't what you shoulda been doin'."

"I know what you mean, Gussy, but I can't turn back the clock and pretend that those years didn't happen. They're as much a part of me as the ones when Mama took me to stay with first one aunt and then another, as if we were a couple of gypsies. She hated living alone in my papa's old house in the country."

"You're not the least bit like 'er, milady, from what I can see. You're more like Lady Amberley, and she's right proud of it, I can tell." She got to her feet. "I'd bet any money that Lord Anthony'll be at that front door in 'is carriage the minute the rain stops, so we'd better get you ready for breakfast."

A half-hour later, Lucy went down to join Lord Amberley in the breakfast room. He had just finished eating, and was sitting back reading his morning paper.

"Did the rain put a damper on your riding, my dear?" he asked. "In case none of those scamps told you, you looked very lovely last night, and I was proud to escort you there."

He started to rise, but she shook her head, bending over him and kissing his cheek. "Is there anything interesting in there?" she asked, nodding toward the paper.

"Crime is widespread and people are feeling insecure, if you call that news," he told her. "And there's been more trouble on board the *Samson*, the ship that houses the French prisoners. Three of them escaped and engaged the wherry to take them to Ryde, but once they set out, they tried to persuade the boatman to take them to France instead. The fool refused so they stabbed him to death and threw him overboard."

"How dreadful, Grandpapa," Lucy exclaimed. "But they must have been caught or no one would have known what happened."

"They were pursued by several other wherries, captured, and taken on board the *Centaur*. I suppose that they hear little news while in captivity, otherwise they'd realize that the war will be over now before very long and they'll be freed without going to the trouble to escape." He turned over another page and announced, "Sir Walter Scott is among those being considered for the new poet laureate."

Lucy grinned. "I'm afraid I really don't recall who the last one was," she told him. "I suppose that once they get the position, they have it for the rest of their lives."

"Seems like it," Lord Amberley grunted. "The last one died in August and was a fellow by the name of Pye, but I don't recall ever having read anything he wrote."

He looked up and chuckled as he saw his granddaughter's obvious amusement. "Well," he said, "you took lessons much more recently than I did. Do you know any of his poems?"

She bit her lower lip to try to stop laughing, but it was hopeless. She shook her head. "No, Grandpapa, I don't, but then I never was very good at poetry."

"What were you good at, then? We missed knowing those kind of things about you, for your mother never brought you here except just that once. She didn't like the blunt way your grandmama criticized her, so she stayed away." He watched her with a faint smile on his face as he spoke.

"I know. And it's funny but that's one of the things I like best about Grandmama. You always know where you stand with her, for she says exactly what she means," Lucinde said emphatically. "But one of the things I was good at was riding. Henry often said that there were few men who could keep up with him the way I could. And he prided himself on being a neck-or-nothing rider."

"Oh, yes, that reminds me. That young man of yours wants so little for your horse that I feel as though I'm cheating him. But he says it's what he advanced to you for your trip back to England, and he'll not take a penny more." He waited, eyebrows raised, to hear what she thought about it.

"It's true, I'm sure, for Anthony doesn't lie. I'm sorry I can't pay you back for her," she said softly.

He glared at her. "What kind of nonsense is this, young lady? Buying things for the young 'uns is part of the pleasure of being a grandparent. You wouldn't want to take away our fun, would you? Your grandmama has not been so happy in years." He got slowly to his feet. "Now, I'd best be getting along, for my man of business is coming this morning and I want to be ready for him." He glanced outside, watching the rain as it bounced off the roof of the tool shed. "It'll clear up soon and you'll get your ride, mark my words."

Lucy had eaten as much as she wanted to already, so she jumped up and slipped a hand through her grandpapa's arm. "If you don't mind, I'll find myself a book from the study before your man comes, for it's a good day to curl up in a big chair in front of a fire and read."

She did not get much reading done, however, for no sooner had she made herself comfortable in the small sitting room on the second floor than Jennifer came hurrying in.

"What a gloomy day," she said, looking not at all gloomy herself but much like a breath of spring in her morning dress of deep pink. "I just wanted to tell you how much I enjoyed the ball last evening, Lucy, and I know you did also, for you looked happier than I've ever seen you look since we arrived."

She was such a thoroughly nice young lady that, though Lucy much preferred to be alone this morning if she could not be with Anthony, she put aside her book and smiled warmly at her cousin.

"I must admit that I did enjoy it," she told Jennifer. "It was a lovely evening."

"It was also the first of many such evenings now that the Little Season has started." Jennifer was clearly delighted at the thought, but Lucy groaned inwardly, for though she had enjoyed the early part of last night, she knew it was something she would rather take in small doses.

"And did you hear Grandmama tell Lord Mortimer that he might call at any time? I heard her saying to one of her friends that he would be such a very good influence upon Richard," Jennifer's cheeks went a deep pink as she added, "And I must say that I liked him very much. I think he must be the most handsome man I have ever seen."

Lucy sighed inwardly, for she had been afraid that this would happen. Her cousin had quite obviously developed a girlish *tendre* for Anthony, and it would only get worse as she saw more of him. She wondered if he had any idea of the effect he had on the girl.

When Duffield appeared in the doorway a moment later, she knew at once who was calling. Like one of the jinni in the *Arabian Nights*, Jennifer must have called him up.

"Lord Mortimer is here, milady," he said to Lucy.

"Send him up right away," Jennifer told him eagerly.

Some other time Lucy would have found his shocked expression amusing, but this morning she just said quietly, "You may show Lord Mortimer into the drawing room, Duffield, and please tell him that we will be down shortly."

Jennifer's cheeks had turned a deep pink and she looked decidedly shamefaced for a moment, then pouted a little, saying, "I know it was you that Duffield told, but don't you think, perhaps, that was because you are the elder? I've forgotten something and must run back to my bedchamber. Will you wait here for me?"

It was so very unusual for the girl to be even the slightest bit rude that Lucy chose to ignore it. She saw no reason to tell Jennifer that she and Anthony had quarreled just before she and her brother came to stay, so she merely said, "No, I'll not keep Lord Mortimer waiting any longer. You may join us when you're ready."

Once she swept out of the room and down the stairs, she forgot all about her cousin in her own eagerness to see Anthony once more. A footman quickly opened the door and she stepped inside as Anthony, who had been facing the fireplace and gazing at a painting of Lady Amberley as a young woman, swung around.

"I believe you're a little taller than she was then," he told her, smiling broadly, "for I noticed that the chair against which she stood is over there. Stand against it and let me see if I'm right."

She moved swiftly across the room and took up the same pose, her eyes dancing with fun as she looked at him.

His gaze went from her to the painting and back a couple of times. "Two or three inches, I would say, but there's no mistaking the relationship," he assured her. "I wanted to bring my curricle, for I was hoping that the rain might have stopped by now and we could have gone for a drive, but I'm afraid there's little sign of it letting up. Shall we plan on riding in the morning if the weather is fair? Eight o'clock again?"

She nodded, then through the open door she heard the sound of light footsteps hurrying down the stairs.

Anthony had heard it also and murmured, "We can talk privately then."

Her cousin did not look any different to Lucy, and she could not help but wonder why the girl had gone to her bedchamber again, for she had quite obviously not wanted Lucy to go ahead and see Anthony without her. She was now smiling up into his eyes, having dropped him a low curtsy, and there was a look of adoration on her face.

"Won't you ladies sit down so that I may do so also?" Anthony asked. "I cannot stay long for I have an appointment at White's at eleven."

"You wouldn't care to drop me off on Old Bond Street, would you, Anthony?" Richard came hurrying in, having recognized the voice of the visitor as he came down the stairs. "I'm due at Weston's in about fifteen minutes, and I had intended to stroll across there until I saw the rain."

As Anthony indicated his willingness, Lucy could not help wondering how such a young man could afford the finest tailor in London. But perhaps Grandmama was footing the bill for both of her cousins' clothes as well as for hers.

"I've ordered a jacket in his light *bleu céleste*. Only hope that the color suits me," he said, looking a little worried.

"You have the same coloring as I have," Lucy remarked, "and I've always found light blue most becoming. Just don't go and order anything in pink, or I'll not allow myself to be seen near you."

He laughed good-naturedly. "There's little fear of that, for I believe Weston would send me packing if I even dared suggest such a thing. He's an arbiter of good taste and disdains the latest fads."

The two men left shortly after that, for though they had only a short distance to travel, wet weather always seemed to slow down traffic in the London streets.

"What on earth are we going to do with ourselves on a day such as this?" Jennifer was staring through the window-panes at the slippery wet leaves on the ground that made walking dangerous, and watching Lord Mortimer's carriage as it proceeded slowly around the square. "London is such a dreary place in the rain."

"I, for one, am going back upstairs for the book I had started to read before Lord Mortimer arrived," Lucy declared. "But I believe Grandmama will still wish to make calls this afternoon, for since I have been here I have not seen a few drops of water deter her."

In this she was quite correct, and as she seemed eager for their company, the two young ladies went with her in the large closed carriage, for Lord Amberley had taken the smaller one.

At her friend, Lady Highsmith's, they saw Sally Jersey, a lady Lucy had heard much about but had not yet met. She was one of those who could grant or withhold vouchers for Almack's, which did not perturb Lucy in the least, for she had no desire to go there, but in order not to upset Grandmama she did her best to copy Jennifer's good manners.

"How fortunate you are to have two such lovely but quite different granddaughters," Lady Jersey said to Lady Amberley. "All you need is a blond-haired one and you can satisfy the taste of any gentleman in London. And what pretty manners they have, though the redhead looks as if she could live up to that hair if she wished."

"You're too young to recall, Sally, but I had the same coloring when I was a gel, and sometimes it was a trial, I'll admit," Lady Amberley told her.

"I'd never have believed it," Lady Jersey said with a knowing smile, "for you've always seemed the very epitome of decorum. I'll have vouchers sent to you within a couple of days, in plenty of time for the first assembly."

After saying all that was proper, the three of them left, but just as Lady Amberley was about to step up into the carriage, her foot slipped on a patch of wet leaves and she slid partway underneath.

A lady who was coming down the steps behind them saw her fall and let out a scream so loud that it frightened the horses. Though the coachman held them as best he could, the carriage jerked forward slightly, and the left rear wheel went partly onto Lady Amberley's right leg.

Lucy saw at once what had happened and threw her whole weight against the wheel to push it away from her grandmama, and while the first coachman held the horses as still as he could, the second coachman lent his weight to Lucy's and her grandmama was freed, but she was moaning pitifully.

"Quickly. Tear your petticoat into strips," Lucy told Jennifer, then she looked around.

As usually happened in such a case, a crowd started to gather, and Lucy looked quickly over them to see who could be of help. She saw that two of the gentlemen carried canes and asked at once if she might have the loan of them. Then, crouching on the road beside her grandmama, she put one on either side of the injured leg and bound them in place with the torn-up petticoat.

The rain was still pouring down, and though someone was holding an umbrella over them, she knew that she must get Lady Amberley under cover as quickly as possible, but small though the old lady was, she was still too heavy for two young ladies to lift.

Then a familiar voice called out, "Make way there. Let me through," and Anthony was by her side.

"We've got to lift her into the coach without hurting her leg, Anthony. Can . . . ?" Before Lucy had finished the sentence he had Lady Amberley in his arms. Lucy slipped past him and into the coach so that she could help him place her on the seat.

"Now let's get her home as quickly as we can," she said as she knelt on the floor by her grandmama's side, cradling the old lady's head in her arms. Lady Amberley's eyes were closed and she moaned softly.

"I'll follow you and help get her out at the other end," Anthony called as Jennifer stepped into the coach, and then they started for Berkeley Square.

"When we reach the house, you go first, Jennifer, and get Gussy right away," Lucy said. "It'll take the three of us to get her out without hurting her."

"Is she going to be all right?" Jennifer's voice quavered, and her cheeks were wet with tears.

"Of course, she is," Lucy snapped. "My grandmama's a tough lady, and I'm sure she's been through worse than this." She put a finger to her lips to warn Jennifer to say no more in front of Lady Amberley.

It seemed to take hours to reach Berkeley Square, but it was actually no more than ten minutes; then, once they were there, Jennifer did as she had been instructed, so that Gussy and Anthony arrived at the carriage door at almost the same time.

The doctor was sent for, against Gussy's better judgment,

and while they waited for him to arrive, she and Lucy took off the old lady's clothes, cutting most of the garments rather than trying to lift her. Then they slipped her into one of her own warm flannel nightgowns.

A fire had been lit in her bedchamber, but she was still shivering, so they piled blankets upon her to try to prevent a chill setting in.

All Gussy's worst fears were realized, however, when the doctor arrived and said that the first thing he must do was bleed the old lady to let out all the bad blood that would have formed around the broken bone in the leg.

If Lucy had not been watching her grandmama closely when the man spoke, she might not have been quite so angry with him. But she saw the blue-green eyes open and the look of horror in them before she heard the first word the old lady had said since the accident. It was a firm "No."

Dr. Debenham's head turned, for he had obviously thought his patient was unconscious. Then he gave a little shrug of his shoulders and started to get out the equipment with which to start bleeding her.

"Just a moment, Doctor," Lucy said. "You heard my grandmama say 'no' quite distinctly."

"She doesn't know what she's saying," he told her. "I'll need—"

"What other treatment do you propose?" she asked, looking across at Gussy, whose face was set in grim lines.

"Now, look here, young lady," Dr. Debenham snapped. "You must be in shock yourself and need to go lie down for a while. Go and get a couple of the servants in here to help hold her, and then do as I advise."

"I asked you what you are going to do about the broken leg?" she persisted, a stubborn look coming into her eyes.

"There's nothing to do about the leg. She'll never be able to use it again, even if by some remote chance it does not become infected." He was starting to get annoyed. "Just be a good girl and get me those servants I asked for."

Lucy went over to her grandmama and put an ear close

to Lady Amberley's mouth. "Get him out of here," came quite distinctly, and even the doctor heard her.

"You may pack up your bag, Dr. Debenham, and leave," Lucy said firmly. "My grandmama does not want you to treat her."

When he continued with his preparations, completely ignoring her, Lucy walked over to the door and called, "Lord Mortimer, are you still here?"

He took the stairs two at a time and was at her side in a moment, looking into her strained face.

"Please escort Dr. Debenham out of the house," she requested. "Lady Amberley does not wish him to treat her."

"Are you sure?" Anthony looked worried, for he knew that Dr. Debenham was used by some of the best families in town. "Do you want to send for someone else?"

"That's up to Grandmama," Lucy said quietly. "If she prefers it, then Gussy and I will take care of her. We've both dealt with much worse breaks on many occasions."

"But not on someone of her age, I'm sure," Anthony warned. He looked at her face for a moment and then said, "If you'll come with me, Dr. Debenham, I'll see you out."

With a snort of disgust the doctor followed him out of the chamber and down the stairs. "That young lady will be very sorry when her grandmama dies of blood poisoning," he said, "but you may tell her that she need not send for me, for I wash my hands of the case."

10

A tall thin woman, gray-haired and sad-eyed, stood with shoulders erect gazing from her living-room window at the oak and elm trees lining the long drive up to the house. Here in the North of England the leaves had fallen a month ago, leaving bare branches that reached like graceful silvery brown arms up to the clear blue sky. But the sight of them brought no pleasure to Lady Coldwell, for they seemed only to mark the beginning of another cold, long, lonely winter.

Her husband would be on his way back now, after meeting with his estate agent and discussing with him what should be done before the winter really set in. They went through the motions, as they had for half of their lives, but nothing seemed to really matter since their only son, Henry, was gone—this time for good.

As though he had heard her thoughts and come to commiserate with her, Lord Coldwell came into sight. He trotted up the drive, dismounted, then gave his horse to the waiting groom. A moment later he entered the drawing room, smoothing down his thinning hair, then reaching out both arms to draw her close in a comforting hug.

"I'm but cold comfort to you today, my love," he said gently, "for there's a nip in the air and my nose and cheeks must be red as cherries."

"Becket will be here in a moment with some hot tea to warm you through," she told him, stroking his icy cheek with gentle fingers, "and then I believe we should talk, for I've been thinking about what that friend of Henry's, Lord Mortimer, said to us."

Lord Coldwell raised an eyebrow, for it was the first time she had brought up the subject of the young man's visit since the day he had left.

The elderly servant came in with the tea tray, placing it in front of Lady Coldwell, who poured a cup and handed it to her husband. She took a sip of her own tea to make sure it was to her liking, then placed it carefully on a table by the side of her chair and looked into his watery blue eyes.

"He said that the gel was good to Henry, didn't he, and that though she stayed out there after he'd gone, she kept herself to herself?" She was obviously hurting still, but finally trying to be fair.

Lord Coldwell nodded, then got up and poked at the fire until it started to blaze and burn brightly. He stood with his back to it for a moment, looking at the uncertainty in his wife's face that had not been there before.

"It wasn't her fault he went and got himself killed, my love. She wouldn't have been able to control his wildness any more than we could. I'm glad you're starting to realize it, for I believe we've both done her a great disservice."

She nodded. "I'd like to write a note to her. We don't have her direction, but if I send it to Lord Mortimer, I'm sure he'll have found her by now and will see that she gets it," Lady Coldwell said quietly. "I want to thank her for making our son's last year and a half happy."

"And for sending his body here, too. Young Mortimer said she spent all the money she had on seeing it was done properly," he added. "I'd have liked to have seen her bring it, but we didn't exactly make her welcome, did we?"

She shook her head sadly, then said, "I asked Vanessa and her brother, Nigel, to join us for supper tonight. She's still young and she's mourned Henry for too long. It's high time she went out and about and met someone else."

Lord Coldwell was glad to see his wife's change of heart, for he had worried that she would go into a complete decline if her bitterness continued.

He reached over and patted her hand. "That's the way, my love," he said gruffly. "Encourage the girl to make a new life for herself instead of behaving like a widow woman. The Langdons should not have let her go on about it this long, but she's a trifle headstrong to my way of thinking, and they probably can do little with her. She'll listen to you, though, for she always has."

"That's why I invited them this evening, for I suddenly realized that she behaves more like my daughter than theirs, and it's my fault for permitting her to do so. She'll listen to me, I know, when she won't heed a word either her mama or papa say to her." She looked thoughtful for a moment, then added, "You know, when I think about it, she would not at all have made a suitable wife for Henry, for he was not the sort to have put up with that willfulness for a moment."

Lord Coldwell nodded and his eyes twinkled. "I've thought of that many a time this last year. He showed more sense than we did by marrying someone who'd make him happy. But when Vanessa told us she meant to stop him going back to the Peninsula, all we could see was that he'd be home and safe. I suppose he thought it was the Langdons' land we wanted, and it was, in a way, but we wanted it for him, not ourselves."

She finished her tea and carefully placed the cup back on the tray. "I must go and tell Cook that we're having guests tonight, and then I think I'll lie down for a while so that I'll be well-rested. Vanessa will not at all like what I have to say to her, but she's not a widow and it's time she stopped behaving like one."

He rose and helped her to her feet, then gave her his arm. "I'd best go up and change early, I suppose, for I'd not want to be shown up by that young man. Whenever I've met him lately he's been dressed up to the nines. If he should ever get to London, he'd make the dandies pale by comparison."

They separated in the hall and he stood for a moment at the foot of the stairs, watching her slow upward progress and realizing that he'd not even noticed when the spring had left her step, but she still held herself ramrod-straight.

Two hours later, they greeted their guests in the drawing room. They were a contrast in styles. Lady Vanessa wore a high-necked gown of black bombazine, with black gloves and shoes, and her black hair was ornamented with a pair of ebony and pearl combs.

Her brother, Nigel, would scarcely have looked under-dressed had he been attending a fashionable dinner party in Mayfair. He wore an indigo velvet evening coat with pale-gray knee breeches, a silver brocade waistcoat, and a faultless white cravat fastened with a black onyx tiepin.

"How kind of you to invite us, Mama Coldwell," Vanessa said, going over to her hostess with outstretched arms that she flung around that lady's shoulders in an exaggerated hug. She stepped back and gave her a questioning look. "Are you sure you feel quite up to entertaining guests so soon after . . . ?"

Lady Coldwell waited for her to finish the question, but the young woman left it unsaid, as though it was just too difficult for her to put into words.

"I have decided that it is high time we all went about our affairs once more, my dear," Lady Coldwell said quietly. "Our son is dead, and no amount of sorrowing will bring him back. We can never replace him, but you, Vanessa, can most certainly find yourself another young man on whom to lavish your affections."

Lady Vanessa looked as if she could not believe that she had heard correctly. "How can you say such a thing?" she asked hoarsely. "Henry was everything to me, and I will never be able to replace him in my heart."

"Henry was a married man," Lady Coldwell said sternly.

"Lord Coldwell and I were at fault, for we should not have continued to regard you as our future daughter-in-law after our son was wed to someone else. But it's time now, Vanessa, that you cast off those drab black gowns. I intend to speak to your mama and suggest that you have your somewhat belated come-out next Season."

There was a momentary flash of anger in Lady Vanessa's cold blue eyes, quickly hidden, then she said softly, "Sir Henry was the only man I ever wanted for a husband. The thought of spending a Season in London in order to find someone to replace him goes against everything I have ever believed in. I don't know how you can even think of such a thing, Mama Coldwell."

Sir Nigel Langdon had been listening to the interchange with considerable interest. He had originally been of the opinion that his sister was putting on an elaborate act, but had gradually come to realize that where Henry Coldwell was concerned, she had become slightly deranged. Now he wondered what effect Lady Coldwell's plain speaking might have on Vanessa.

It was fortunate that Becket entered at that moment to announce that dinner was served. Lord Coldwell held out an arm to escort Lady Vanessa inside, while Sir Nigel took in Lady Coldwell.

By mutual consent the subject was dropped during dinner, but as soon as the two ladies went into the drawing room for their tea, Lady Coldwell brought up the matter once more.

"A few weeks ago, Lord Mortimer came looking for Henry's wife. I didn't mention it to you at the time, my dear Vanessa, for I thought that it would only make you more unhappy, but I now realize that I should have had no such qualms," she began. "He was a friend of Henry's, and he had found her, a few weeks before, helping the wounded on the battlefield, and had quite rightly sent her back to England, for it was most certainly no place for a lady.

"When, not more than a week later, he obtained his release from service with Wellington to attend to urgent affairs here, he first tried to make sure that his friend's widow had reached home safely, so he called upon us." Lady Coldwell looked pained. "I'm afraid that I made it quite plain to him that I neither knew nor cared where she might be, and he seemed quite shocked at my attitude, but I made it clear that I meant it."

"I should think you did, Mama Coldwell," Vanessa said heatedly. "The very last thing you need is for that hussy to try to make herself at home here."

Lady Coldwell shook her head, and a faint trace of a smile showed in her eyes. "I have thought about it a great deal since his visit, and I know now that I was completely at fault. I refused to even meet her after they were wed. Henry brought her here, you know, and I sent word that unless she waited outside in the carriage, I would not see him." She paused. "By doing so, I missed the last chance I had to see my son alive—and it was not her fault, it was entirely my own."

Vanessa sighed. "You're upset, Mama Coldwell, and I can fully understand it," she said, then a crafty look came into her eyes. "Do you have no idea where she is now? Did she, perhaps, stay in London?"

"I really don't know, but I soon will, for I am going to write a note to her tomorrow and send it in care of Lord Mortimer. I shall ask her to reply to me, and if she's the gel the young man described, she will do so," Lady Coldwell said, then she looked up as her husband and Sir Nigel Langdon came into the drawing room.

"I'm afraid I have completely tired you out, Mama Coldwell, with my chatter," Vanessa said, giving a prearranged nod to her brother. "I think that perhaps we should take our leave now, but I will come back in the morning to make sure you are all right, my lady."

Lady Coldwell smiled. "I shall look forward to that, Vanessa," she said politely, and rose to see her guests to the door.

Once Lady Vanessa was settled comfortably in the

Langdon coach, she turned to her brother. "How would you like to come with me to London?" she asked.

A slow smile spread over his face. "I thought you would never suggest it, dear Vanessa," he drawled. "You mean right away, of course, for the Little Season has just begun."

"Of course," she replied. "Why not? I've no intention of waiting until next year. We can stay with Aunt Hermione, in Golden Square, and though it is not the best address, I understand it is still in the Mayfair area and, of course, will not cause us unnecessary expense. I'm sure that Papa will be only too happy to pay for however many gowns I need, for I've bought so few these last two years."

"And Mama will, of course, pay for my attire, as she has been doing now for some time. When Papa positively refused to pay more for my clothes than he did for his own, Mama came through, as I knew she would." He grinned. "Just what do you mean to do once you get to town, my dear?"

"Find Lady Lucinde Coldwell, of course." There was no point in prevaricating, for she would need considerable help from Nigel. "I intend to make her suffer the way she made me when she stole Henry Coldwell right from under my nose."

"And if, at the same time, you should come across some wealthy young man who wants to marry you, I'm sure you won't turn him down, my dear, for you're getting a little on in years to be too particular, aren't you?"

"Now, don't you go around telling people how old I am, or you'll be sorry you were born," Vanessa snapped. "Our aunt has such a poor memory she'll have no idea what our ages are, so I'm sure I could take off a couple of years without anyone being the wiser."

"I'll keep quiet about anything you wish, my dear sister, for the right sum of money," he told her. "Or, perhaps, the right piece of jewelry."

"I'll have to see about that when I get to London," Vanessa said thoughtfully. "I might need your help with a small matter, and would, in that case, be most generous."

Sir Nigel raised his eyebrows. "I'll do anything, short of kidnapping the lady in question, for the right consideration," he said, "payment in advance, of course. Have you any idea what she looks like?"

The hard blue eyes glittered. "I got a glimpse of her once, when she was waiting outside Coldwell House in the carriage. She would be difficult to miss, for she has a head of the most atrocious fiery red hair."

He laughed. "Were you hiding in the bushes, my dear, trying to see what your rival for dear Henry's charms looked like? How very droll—and most unbecoming. What would you have done if they had seen you?"

Furious with him for realizing what she had done so long ago, Vanessa swung around with the intent of slapping his laughing face, but her wrist was caught in an iron grip that made her gasp with pain.

"You should know better than to try something so foolish, my dear sister," he said, his voice soft but menacing. "Aside from the fact that I can hit harder than you can, you are forgetting that you need me. Unless I agree to accompany you, there will be no trip to London, as you well know. And then what would happen to your little plan?"

He released her wrist and she began to rub it to get the circulation back into it. Her action had been foolish, for he was right: she did need him—far more than he needed her.

"There's no point in our quarreling, Nigel," she said quietly, "for together we can achieve what we both desire. Can you be ready to leave in a week?"

"Of course, sooner than that, if you can," he told her. "Talk to Mama and send a note to Aunt Hermione tomorrow, and I'll take care of the travel arrangements."

The next morning, when Vanessa went back to visit Lady Coldwell as she had promised, she told her that she and her brother would be leaving for London within the week. She had discussed the matter with her parents and they had agreed that it was the very best thing for her to do, provided Nigel went with her.

"My dear," Lady Coldwell said, "I know that you are doing the right thing, and will never regret it. You have to start a new life for yourself, make new friends, and forget the past."

"I'm sure you're right, Mama Coldwell," Vanessa said sweetly. "Is there anything I can do for you while I am in London?"

Lady Coldwell was about to say that there was not, when it suddenly occurred to her that her letter to Lord Mortimer would be much safer if it was delivered in person.

"There is one little matter, my dear," she said. "As I told you last night, I am writing a letter to my daughter-in-law, and as I do not know her direction, I proposed to post it to Lord Mortimer, who, I am sure, will have found her by now, for he seemed a most determined gentleman. I would much prefer it if you would take my letter with you and deliver it to him in person at his Grosvenor Square address. You could introduce yourself to him and his mama, and perhaps, if they were so inclined, you might make more friends through them as well as through your aunt."

Vanessa tried hard not to let Lady Coldwell see how pleased she was at being given this commission. She would not, of course, take the letter to this lord at all, but would burn it before she reached London. Then the Coldwells would believe that their daughter-in-law had no wish to have anything more to do with them.

She forced a smile. "It will be my pleasure, Mama Coldwell. I'll come by the day after tomorrow to get it from you, and will see it safely into the hands of your Lord Mortimer without delay."

When she had gone, Lord Coldwell, who had been reading his newspaper in the breakfast room and had heard everything, gave an unusual snort. "If you don't hear anything from our daughter-in-law, in, say, three months, I believe you should follow with a second letter. That young miss seemed just a little bit too eager to take it with her, to my way of thinking."

"How can you say such a thing, my dear? Vanessa has always been the most affectionate daughter-in-law a mother could have," Lady Coldwell protested.

Her husband sounded as though he was about to explode. "Now you're doing it," he almost roared. "She's almost made me a candidate for Bedlam with her Mama Coldwell this and Mama Coldwell that. You're neither her mama nor her mother-in-law. You never were and you never will be."

"Now, my dear, don't take on so. I know what you mean, for, to be honest, I believe it was her still calling me Mama that made me realize it was time she got herself a husband of her own." She smiled faintly. "Isn't it interesting how it's the little things that eventually bother us the most? And I had every intention of writing to Lord Mortimer again if I received no acknowledgment from him, for he seemed to me to be the kind of gentleman who would let me know that my letter had been received."

Lord Coldwell came over and patted her hand. It had taken a long time, but finally she had come to terms with the loss of her son. She would never forget, but she had finally decided that she could, and would, go on with her life.

A couple of days later, Lord Coldwell was in the village when he saw the Langdon carriage pass through on its way to London. A lace kerchief fluttered at the window, and as he gave an answering salute, he felt an overwhelming feeling of relief.

The kerchief was withdrawn and slipped into Vanessa's reticule as the coachman whipped up the horses to a faster speed once they were through the village.

"Do you have any idea of what you will do when we get to Aunt Hermione's?" Nigel asked.

"Find Lady Lucinde Coldwell, of course," Vanessa said. "It can't be very difficult, for the members of the *ton* love to gossip, and there cannot be more than one person among them with such an unusual first name. All I have to do is wait and listen."

"And when you have found her?" He raised one eyebrow. "What, then?"

"I'll just mingle with her friends and await an opportunity, any opportunity, to cause her as much hurt as she has caused me."

There was so much venom in her voice that, for a moment, Nigel felt sorry for the unknown widow, but it did not last for long when he remembered that he would be generously repaid by his sister for his own services on her behalf.

11

"What do you think, Gussy?" Lucy asked when the door closed behind the doctor. "The leg is badly bruised and is swelling, so I believe we must keep it immobile and as comfortable as possible until the swelling goes down."

"It's all we can do for now. I 'ave some 'erbs for a poultice that'll bring the swelling down a bit faster. Did ye try to put the break together afore ye tied it wi' these fancy canes?" Gussy asked.

Lucy nodded. "It was badly bruised and was already starting to swell, though," she said. She turned to the old lady, touching her cheek and saying softly, "It hurts, I know, Grandmama dear, but in a while Gussy will make a potion to put you to sleep."

She put her cool hand on her grandmama's forehead and felt the heat starting up. The fever would probably be the worst thing of all. If they could just pull her through it, Lucinde somehow felt sure that everything else would be all right.

There was a tap on the door and Lord Mortimer opened it and put his head around.

"Is there anything I can do to help?" he asked. "I'm more than willing to play errand boy if you'll tell me what you need."

It was Gussy who spoke up first. "We're goin' to need lots of wood, milord, for the fire mustn't go out. An' three or four extra blankets."

"And we need a better splint than these two canes, which, by the way, must be returned to their owners. I have their directions in my reticule," Lucy told him. "Ask Mrs. Waterhouse to tear up a couple of old sheets into six-inch strips, if you please, Anthony. And ask her also to be sure to have plenty of warm water ready at all times." She went over to her grandmama and bent down so that she could hear without straining. "Is there any other doctor you would like us to send for, Grandmama?"

Her shake of the head was not strong, but nonetheless emphatic. "You and Gussy," she said in a whisper.

Lucy looked at Anthony and shrugged helplessly. "Did anyone go to get Grandpapa?" Lucy asked softly.

He nodded. "He should be here at any moment. I'll take care of some of the things you need now, and be right back."

Lord Amberley made his presence known in no uncertain terms. He came storming into the bedchamber without even removing his topcoat.

"What's this nonsense about sending the doctor away?" he demanded. "Lady Amberley is to have the finest possible care and—"

Lucy almost launched herself at him to make him lower his voice. "Hush, Grandpapa. You know better than to come in here shouting like that."

He had not yet seen the small figure in the big four-poster bed, and Lucy took his hand and led him over to where his wife lay, a worried frown on her brow and her cheeks already looking flushed.

"No doctor, George," she whispered. "The girls know best."

He patted her hand gently and said, "Don't you worry, my love, we're going to have you up and about again in no time at all. Try to get some sleep now." He kissed her forehead, then rose and walked toward the door. "Come outside for a moment, Lucinde," he said quietly. "I want to talk to you."

He walked her far enough away from his wife's chamber so that she could not hear even if he raised his voice, then he said, "I've been told you sent the doctor away. Debenham's a good man, and she's going to need him."

"Grandmama sent him away. He was ignoring her leg because he said she would never use it again. All he wanted to do was to bleed her," she told him, and for the first time since the accident her eyes filled with tears.

"He told her she'd never use the leg again?" Lord Amberley could not quite believe it.

"He said it to me, but he did not even try to lower his voice," Lucy said bitterly.

"I'll kill him when I see him," he growled. "No wonder she sent him packing. But there are others, you know. We can call the king's physicians in if we want to."

"You felt her face, Grandpapa. She got soaked to the skin out there, and she's already starting to run a fever. That's going to be the worst thing for the next day or so, and there's little anyone can do but keep her as cool as possible until it breaks." She stared bleakly at him. "I don't know what to say. Should she die, you'll never forgive me and I'll not forgive myself. If you know a really good doctor, tried and true, then by all means send for him, but don't bring someone like that stupid Dr. Debenham."

Lady Amberley's fever started to rage that night, and for two days and two nights Gussy and Lucy took turns at looking after her, bathing her with cool rose water when she was at her hottest and getting her to drink healing herb potions when she was more lucid.

Lord Mortimer found a doctor with a deservedly good reputation, but when he stopped by, he told them frankly that there was nothing he could do that they were not already trying. It was just a case of waiting for the fever to run its course. He looked at the leg, saw that the swelling was going down, and agreed that here, too, they would just have to wait.

Lucy was sitting by the window for a moment, watching

the sun start to peek through the trees, when she heard a croaky voice call, "Lucinde." She was at the bedside in a moment, placing a hand on her grandmama's forehead and looking into the tired blue-green eyes.

Suddenly she felt exhilarated, for the fever was down. She wanted to shout it to the rooftops, but instead she poured a little cool water into a cup, placed an arm around her grandmama's shoulders to raise her a little, then held the cup until she had drunk enough.

A few minutes later Lady Amberley slipped into the most peaceful sleep she'd had for three days.

When Gussy relieved her, Lucy went to her own bedchamber to wash her face and change her gown. It was strange, but now that her grandmama was passed the crisis, she no longer felt tired. She sat down on the bed for a moment to change her slippers and the next thing she knew it was late morning and she felt as if she had not eaten in a month. She hurried down the stairs to see if breakfast was still being served, then looked in frustration at the sideboard, which was quite bare.

"It's almost time for luncheon, my dear, but I'm sure Duffield can find something to stave off the hunger." Lord Amberley's face had grown surprisingly lined in just three days, but his smile showed her at once that he had heard the good news. He put an arm around her shoulders. "Jennifer and Richard are out riding in the park with Lord Mortimer, but they should be back very shortly. Come into the study and tell me when exactly the fever left her."

Lucy was surprised to feel a distinct pang of jealousy at the thought of Anthony out with Jennifer, but it left as quickly as it had come.

"It was just after dawn, Grandpapa," she said gently, "and she called my name. I gave her a little water and then she fell into the best sleep she has had in days."

"Thank God it's all over," Lord Amberley breathed, placing his hand on her small but obviously capable one.

"Now we can concentrate on getting her strength back up again."

"And on getting her on her feet again," Lucy reminded him. "We've been checking the leg frequently, and the swelling has just about gone down now, but the bones have still to knit together again. When is that doctor—"

She was interrupted by Jennifer, who burst into the study and flung her arms around her cousin's neck. "We heard the good news and went out for some fresh air, for we thought you would sleep half the day away," she said happily.

Richard and Lord Mortimer stood smiling in the doorway, and the butler stood behind them with a tray in his hand.

"I awoke because I was hungry, and here is Duffield with something to put me on until luncheon. Why don't we all adjourn to the drawing room and let my grandfather finish his work in peace?" She turned over her hand, to clasp his and squeeze it gently. "Will you excuse us, Grandpapa?"

"No, I'm coming with you, for I'm still not quite sure how your grandmama came to be injured, and I'd like to hear what you saw of it," he told her.

Once they were all settled in the drawing room and she had taken a sip of the glass of wine that Lord Amberley insisted was strictly medicinal, Lucinde looked sadly at the waiting faces.

"It was my fault entirely," she began, "for I should have taken a hold of her arm when she was getting into the coach, but it was raining quite heavily and I was trying to stay under the umbrella and not get any wetter than I could help."

"Don't you dare blame yourself, young lady," Lord Amberley scolded, "for I'll not have it. She was probably trying to hurry inside before she got too wet herself."

Lucy gave a helpless little shrug, then continued, "The road was covered with wet fallen leaves, making it difficult to walk. Her foot must have slipped on them as she tried to step into the carriage, and she fell backward. I was not expecting it, of course, and before I knew it, she had slid partly under the carriage. Then, just as I bent down to try to help her, something startled the horses."

"It was a woman who was waiting just inside the doorway for her own coach to come after ours. She apparently screamed when she saw Grandmama fall," Jennifer added.

"Anyway, the wheel came onto her leg, and though I threw all my weight against it to try to push it back, I could only stop it from going any farther over. I don't know who it was who came to help—one of our coachmen I think—and he managed to push it off her, but the damage had already been done." It was not until Jennifer passed her a kerchief that she realized that tears had rolled down her face.

"Is the bone crushed?" Lord Mortimer asked quietly.

"I don't think so. We couldn't tell at first when there was so much swelling, but now it seems as though it may just be a break, though the leg is, of course, black and blue. Is that second doctor coming back again today?" she asked hopefully, for both she and Gussy had felt that this one knew what he was doing.

"He'll be here in a little while. I sent word to him again this morning," Lord Mortimer said. "He's not like the other one. This one is a good man."

The doctor came as they were almost finished with luncheon, so Lucy excused herself and took him up the stairs and into her grandmama's bedchamber. He examined the leg, complimented Lucy on the way she had kept it stable, and told both her and Gussy that he could use them in the London hospitals.

"Lady Lucinde 'as done more than 'er share of looking after wounded men," Gussy told him bluntly.

His eyebrows rose and a smile of disbelief played at the corners of his mouth. "Not in the hospitals here, I'm sure, or I would have seen her," he said.

"In Spain and Portugal, young man." Lady Amberley's voice had lost much of its strength, but it still held a note of authority, and the doctor immediately turned to the head of the bed, where his patient lay glaring at him.

"My apologies, Lady Amberley," he said gently. "You were sleeping when we came in and I did not wish to disturb you."

"Well, I'm awake now, and I know you're not that stupid fellow we've used in the past. So, who are you?" she asked, her voice ending on a slightly querulous note.

"I'm Dr. Charles Waters, my lady, at your service," he said with a quiet smile.

"You are as long as you don't try to tell me I'll never use that leg again," she snapped, then lay back, tired.

"I would not be foolish enough to make any absolute promises, my lady, but I'm certainly not going to say you won't use it. It's far too early to make any pronouncements. I will tell you, however, that I'll do my very best to get you back on your feet," he promised. "But a lot will depend on you, also. You don't look like a quitter, though, to me."

Lady Amberley's smile was tired, but it was the first in several days. A moment later her eyes closed again and she fell into another restful, healing sleep.

Lucy escorted Dr. Charles Waters down the stairs and into the hall, where Lord Mortimer waited.

"I'm sure you would like a word with Lord Amberley," he said. "He is, of course, most anxious to have your opinion on her condition, Charles."

Lucy waited until Anthony took the doctor into the study, left him with her grandpapa, and came back into the hall.

"I didn't know that he was a friend of yours, Anthony," she said. "I like him, for he's nothing like that dreadful man they were using."

"He does only enough private practice to supplement his own income, for he prefers to work in the hospitals. I didn't tell him anything about you, for I'm not sure how much you want people to know," he said quietly. "When he was here last time, however, he seemed very impressed with what you and Gussy were doing."

"He knows now, for Gussy set him straight when he said he could use us both in the hospitals. I'm glad you were able to get him, however, for I'm too close to Grandmama to think as clearly as I should. I suppose it's always like that with someone you love."

He nodded understandingly. "Could I persuade you to go for a ride into the country in my curricle—alone except for my tiger?"

Lucy found his question amusing. "I can be persuaded quite easily, but I'm not sure that my grandpapa would give his approval," she said, her eyes sparkling with fun.

"You just go and get ready and leave your grandpapa to me," he told her. "And bring something warm with you, for the weather has turned cooler these last few days."

She went upstairs, but before going to change her gown, she stopped by her grandmama's chamber to have a word with Gussy.

"Will you be all right here on your own for a couple of hours?" she asked her friend. "Lord Mortimer wants to take me for a drive and I'd much appreciate a little fresh air."

"Of course she'll be all right, Lucinde." The voice that came from the bed was becoming decidedly stronger. "You've been cooped up in here with me for far too long. Did that doctor leave?"

"Not yet, Grandmama. He's in the study telling Grandpapa how well you're doing."

"He's the man I want to look after us in the future when aught ails us," Lady Amberley said. "I trust him and he listens to what you have to say."

"I'm sure Grandpapa feels the same, Grandmama." She bent over and laid her own smooth cheek against Lady Amberley's wrinkled one. "I'm so glad I came home and was here to look after you when you needed me."

The small, bony, beringed fingers wrapped around Lucy's and squeezed hard, then the old lady said gruffly, "Don't keep your young man waiting. We'll manage very well for a while here without you."

Smiling happily, Lucy hurried out of the room and into her own, changing her gown at about the same speed as she had been used to when she was on the Peninsula. Grabbing a warm shawl for her shoulders, she ran down the stairs to join Lord Mortimer.

They rode in a comfortable silence for a while as Lucy drank in the cooler, sweeter air, then Anthony said quietly, "Have you any idea how dangerous it was to go under a carriage and try to hold back the wheel while someone at the horses' heads tried to calm them? I've thought of nothing else since I heard about it, for you might so easily have been killed."

"Are you saying I was foolish to try to save my Grandmama?" she asked, a note of warning in her voice.

He shook his head. "No, not foolish—just remarkably brave, my dear. I'm sure you knew the danger you were in, didn't you?"

"I must admit that I felt much more comfortable when that coachman came and added his weight to mine," she said with a short laugh. "But let's not talk about it anymore. It's so good to be outside again, even if it is a little chilly."

"If that shawl is not warm enough for you, I'll put my coat around your shoulders," he said, "for we can't do with you catching a cold."

"I never catch colds," she bragged. "Gussy says it's amazing that a little thing like me can be healthy as a horse, but I am, thank goodness. I hope you kept Jennifer company a little while I was so busy upstairs."

It was a lie, for she did not hope that at all, but it was the only way she could find out how much he had seen of her cousin.

"Your cousin is a very sweet young lady. In fact, I might add, she has a far more compliant and agreeable disposition than you have. However, since I met you again in Vitoria, I've grown so accustomed to our arguments and even the occasional fight that Jennifer is too tame in comparison,'' he said, grinning wickedly. ''Does that answer your question?''

''You are being kind to her, though, aren't you? I would not like her to be hurt,'' Lucy said earnestly. ''It seems so strange. I'm quite sure that Grandmama invited her to stay so that I would see how easy it is to become accustomed to the ways of the *ton*, for Jennifer accepts them without question. But she is a complete innocent in worldly things.''

''And are you so wise in the ways of the world?'' he teased.

''Some of them,'' she offered. ''For example, she could never have lived, as I did, for more than a year without ever having so much as a penny in my pocket.''

''Did it not worry you, though, that if you should ever really need something, you had not the means to procure it?'' Lord Anthony was curious indeed, for he had no idea that she had lived such a hand-to-mouth existence.

''If we had food, clothes, and medicines, what else could we need?'' she asked innocently.

He shrugged helplessly, for it was true also that although she did not have the money for her passage home, anyone would have given her a good price for Beauty.

''There are many women—and men also—who need a sense of security. But then they are not usually as able or willing to work to achieve this as you were. You're quite remarkable, but I hope this independence of spirit has not set you against remarrying.'' He watched her carefully, wondering if she would give him a flippant or thoughtful answer. He did not have long to wait.

''Despite my grandmama's urging, there is only one reason why I would remarry,'' she told him, ''and that is if I felt my life was not worth living except with that one particular person.''

He was completely shocked, for he had not thought her a romantic by nature. When he could continue the discussion calmly, he asked, ''Was that how you felt about Henry?''

She smiled. ''Oh, no. Henry was like having the papa I

never really knew, a big brother I had never had, and my own little boy, all rolled up into one. He needed me to take care of him, and at the time we were married he was just right for me."

"Did you not want a child of your own?" he asked, more than a little anxious to know why she and Henry had not produced at least a couple of little ones.

"Oh, yes, I would have loved a child, but I would not even think of bringing one into the world of war and disease surrounding us out there," she declared.

She was quite emphatic, but as he could not imagine Henry having lived for long like a monk, his question had not really been answered.

"Are you implying that you had a choice in the matter?" he asked, attempting to sound as casual as possible.

Lucy looked closely at him, trying to see if he was simply curious, as he had sounded, or if her answer was of importance to him.

"That's a very personal question," she said quietly. "I don't believe that, at the moment, I want to answer it."

He gave a careless shrug. "Just as you like, my dear. I am only surprised that you did not tell me it was none of my business. You must be growing more tolerant than I thought."

They talked of other things until they arrived back in Berkeley Square, but the question still hung in the air between them, to be answered when the time was right.

12

Lady Amberley, who was becoming stronger every day, insisted that Lucy spend less time in the sick room.

"If you will use Peters, my abigail, for now, and leave me in Gussy's hands, I know I'll do well enough," she told Lucy. "Please tell Anthony that I would dearly love his mama to pay me a visit when she has the time."

Her good friend came the very next day, of course, and when she left, Lady Amberley had a satisfied smile on her face.

"It's all arranged. Lady Mortimer will chaperon you and Jennifer until I'm up and about again. She is only too happy to do so, for she's never been one to sit at home, and it gives her an excuse to go around even more than she would otherwise," she told Lucy. "And you must take notice of her just as though you were with me."

Secretly pleased at any arrangement that would keep her in close touch with Anthony, Lucy readily agreed. She could not help but wish, however, that a similar arrangement was usual for a young man, for she was becoming more than a little concerned about the behavior of her cousin, Richard. He rarely accompanied her and Jennifer anymore, and she had seen him in the park in the company of ladies of doubtful reputation, but he at least still had the good sense not to bring them over and introduce them.

She would not think of worrying her grandmama with this, of course, and hoped that her grandpapa might not need to be concerned on the young man's account either. She did mention it to Anthony, however, when they were out for an early-morning ride.

"He's young, just sowing a few wild oats, I'm sure," he told her, trying to stop her from worrying. "Most young men go through that kind of thing before they marry and settle down."

"Did you do the same thing when you were his age?" she asked, unable to imagine him behaving as foolishly as Richard was doing these days.

"Oh, I'm sure I must have, but it's so long ago that I really don't recall," he drawled in a tone that left no doubt as to his disinclination to discuss such a matter with her. "Are you and Jennifer planning to go to Almack's on Wednesday?"

"I'm sure my cousin will want to go, for she has been brought up to believe that only the *crème de la crème* may pass through its portals and feels it an honor to be allowed entrance. We received vouchers, of course, as Lady Jersey promised, but I have little desire to even see what it is like." Lucy had heard so much about the things one could and could not do there that she was sure she would make some absolutely dreadful mistake on her first visit and shame her grandmama forever.

"Aren't you even a little curious about the place?" Anthony asked. "I have to admit that I would not go there in the normal way, but I most certainly went when my sisters were being brought out. And I know I would enjoy just seeing the expressions on your face when you go there for the first time."

"I suppose I have little choice but to go, for your mama is being so generous with her time in taking us about, that it would be most ungracious to refuse." She sighed. "I've quite forgotten everything I learned, when I first arrived, about what I can and cannot do there."

"You'd best ask your grandmama to list them for you again, for I would not like to lead you wrong. How is her leg coming along these days?'' he asked, genuinely concerned.

''It will be at least another month before we can be sure the bones have knit together, and then she'll have to exercise it carefully before putting the slightest weight on it. I'd like to bring her downstairs in the afternoons now for an hour or so, but she feels it undignified to let servants carry her around, and I think it's too difficult for Richard to manage on his own,'' she told him. ''Just imagine how awful it would be if he dropped her as he carried her down the stairs.''

''Have her ready this afternoon and I'll come around at about two o'clock and carry her down myself,'' Anthony said firmly. ''She needs to see a little more than those four bedroom walls.''

''Do you think you can manage her on your own?''

''If you recall, it was I who carried her from the coach up to her bedchamber when she was in far worse straits,'' he said dryly. ''Did you consider, perhaps, turning a downstairs room into a chamber for her temporary use?'' he suggested.

''I did, and I thought it an excellent plan, but she has refused to even consider it thus far,'' she told him a little ruefully. ''That's why I want to get her into a more congenial atmosphere, for she's become quite grumpy of late and difficult for even Gussy to please.''

''I daresay, under similar circumstances, you would be considerably more than a little grumpy,'' he said, grinning as he thought of Lucy behaving much like a caged tiger. ''It's more than likely, once she's been downstairs again, she'll change her mind. If she does, you might possibly have someone mount a small armchair on wheels so that she could be moved easily from room to room,'' he suggested.

He left her at the front door with the promise to return at two o'clock.

After Lucy had partaken of a large breakfast, she went to see the housekeeper and the two of them found just the right chair for the purpose. Mrs. Waterhouse assured her that there would be two sets of wheels on it and a handle in the back long before luncheon, or heads would fly.

But when Lucy went upstairs to inform her grandmama that Anthony was coming over with the sole purpose of carrying her downstairs that afternoon, she voiced her objections at once.

"I'm too heavy and awkward for Anthony to be carrying up and down the stairs, and it's surely young Richard's place to help, but he's never around when anything needs to be done. I've not seen that young man for several days," she complained, "and I have an awful feeling he's up to no good. His father should have bought him a commission in the army and let him get some of his wildness out of him."

Lucy applied herself to the task of soothing Lady Amberley's wounded feelings, and when that lady made no further objections to her trip downstairs, she knew that the battle was won. She determined to find out, however, what her cousin was doing, for, when she thought about it, Richard had not been home for either luncheon or dinner for near on a week.

When Richard was not down for luncheon again today, she went in search of him.

There was no answer to her first knock on his bedchamber door, so she knocked once more and called his name. This time there was a mutter that sounded much like "Go away," but, instead, she knocked again, this time loud enough to waken the dead.

"What do you want, Lucy?" came a muffled voice.

"I want to speak to you, Richard," she called angrily. "And if you do not come to the door in one more minute, I'm coming in."

Of course, she had no intention of carrying out her threat, for it would not have been at all the thing, but she thought it might bring results, as it did right away.

She was shocked at how terrible he looked as he stuck his

head around the door, blinking as though he had only just awoken. His chin was covered in a fuzz of red bristles and his eyes were most decidedly bloodshot.

"I don't know what you're doing still asleep at this hour, Richard," she said crossly, "but Anthony will be here shortly to carry Grandmama downstairs for a little while. I had thought that you might be able to give him a hand, but the state you're in I wouldn't trust you not to drop her," she declared, showing quite clearly the disgust she felt at his appearance at this hour.

His angry reaction was completely to be expected. "What state are you talking about?" he snapped, glaring at her. "Just because you've taken over here from Grandmama doesn't give you the right to barge into a fellow's room at any time, Lucy. Ask him to wait and I'll be down in an hour or so and give him a hand."

"He can probably wait," she snapped, "but Grandmama cannot. She's ready now, and if she has to wait at all, she'll change her mind after we've spent the best part of the morning getting her ready."

"Women . . ." he muttered. "I'll be there. Just give me a chance to get dressed."

Lord Mortimer arrived a few mintues later, and he frowned when Lucy told him the state her cousin appeared to be in. "Young fool," was all he said, however, before going upstairs to Lady Amberley's bedroom.

"My lady," he said, entering the chamber and bowing low. "I am to have the privilege of being the first person to take you out of this room and into the great big world below. Your servant, madam."

"Are you sure you won't let me fall?" she asked, starting to become alarmed.

"I've lifted people twice as heavy as you," he lied glibly, reaching down and placing one arm under her shoulders and the other beneath her legs. "Just put your arm around my neck. Gussy's going to hold up your broken leg and Lucy will lead the way."

"You would be the envy of half the ladies of the *ton* if they knew the service you are getting, my lady," he teased. "I hope you remembered to warn Mrs. Waterhouse that your grandmama was coming down today, Lucy, for yesterday I measured the dust at a quarter-inch-thick."

"Just you watch your step, young man," Lady Amberley said, chuckling in spite of herself, "for that marble floor in the hall is very hard."

But almost before she had the words out, they were at the foot of the steps, and a moment later he had carefully placed her on a couch in the drawing room and was packing cushions around her.

As he tucked a lap robe over her legs, she reached for his hand and held it a moment. "Thank you, Anthony. You know I would never have come down if you had not insisted, and I feel better already. Of course, I may have to stay down here forever . . ." She started to say jokingly, then stopped as she looked at each of their faces. "You two haven't been plotting anything, have you?"

Their innocent expressions convinced her that something else was planned, but she was much too happy to worry about that for now. This was a delightful room, even if she did say it herself, and though it was immaculate as always, she still ran a hand over the tea table to make sure about the dust.

Lucy saw her covert action and glanced at Anthony, and they both started to laugh. Suddenly Lady Amberley's worries about never walking again left her. She now knew that, come what may, these two would have her on her feet again before very long.

There was a knock on the door and Duffield entered, clearing his throat. He glanced over at Lady Lucinde, who smiled and nodded while her grandmama waited to see what was in store for her.

She had not long to wait for, right behind Duffield, Gussy came in, pushing before her one of the small, comfortable old chairs that had been relegated to the attic because the cover was wearing. It was now set upon four wheels and there were even leg rests on hinges, which could be lifted and locked in place when needed.

"It looks as if someone has been very busy," Lady Amberley said quietly, still a little nervous that she might fall out of it. "I suppose you want me to try it?"

"Whenever you're ready, Grandmama dear," Lucy murmured. "There's no rush, but we thought you might like to see it."

"You try it first," the old lady said dryly, "and tell me if it's comfortable."

Lucy was in the chair in a minute, putting up the leg rests and stretching out her legs upon them. "Come along, Gussy, take me for a ride," she instructed, and the maid proceeded to wheel her around the room.

When Richard finally came down, it was to see his grandmama sitting comfortably in the new wheelchair, both legs stretched out in front of her and a wrap covering them.

Lady Amberley looked at him closely. "Are you only just getting up, young man?" she asked sternly.

"Of course not," he blustered. "I was out riding early this morning, then took a nap and overslept."

Despite the attentions he had received from Higgins, Lord Amberley's valet, for which he had paid a considerable gratuity, he still looked a trifle pulled, and no one in the room failed to notice.

"Where's Jennifer?" he asked, not so much concerned about his sister as attempting to draw attention away from himself.

"I believe she went to pay calls with Lady Mortimer," Lucy told him. "She should be back shortly."

"Would you like me to take you for a tour of inspection, milady?" Gussy asked, trying to dispel some of the tension in the room.

"I should like that very much, Gussy, and then we can come back in here and have tea," she agreed, a little more brightly than she felt.

When they had gone, Richard said to Anthony, "Sorry

I was not here in time to give you a hand, but I see that you did well enough without me."

"But I'm not family, Richard," Anthony said quietly.

Richard flushed, then muttered, "I suppose I have to hang around for tea, for that sounded as though there'll be all hell to pay if I'm not here when she returns."

"Excuse me," Lucy said quietly as she rose and walked toward the door. "I think Grandmama's tour will be far more edifying."

As soon as they were alone, Richard grumbled, "Don't know what's got into her. Banging on a fellow's door and wakening him up from a sound sleep."

"She probably wonders what has got into you, to use such language in front of her," Anthony said quietly. "I doubt that you know any word she hasn't heard before, but she should not have to listen to it in a drawing room."

"I'll tender her my apologies when she comes back," Richard muttered.

"I wish you would. She's a much more sensitive little thing than you think, though extremely practical in many ways." Anthony paused, not knowing quite how to say the next without giving offense. "You seem to have made quite a number of friends since you came to London. If I can ever be of service, something you don't want to talk to your grandparents about, please feel free to contact me," he murmured.

"Good of you, Anthony, very good. I'll think on it, you can be sure," Richard said brusquely, then turned to the door as he heard voices.

Lady Amberley was returning with her entourage and it sounded as if she had enjoyed herself more than she expected.

"The small sitting room was an excellent choice, Lucinde"—her voice held an eager note that had not been there when she left—"and Gussy can sleep in the anteroom with the door between us open in case I should need her."

Anthony had come to his feet at the first sound of voices, and he now moved over toward the door as she was wheeled back inside. "It sounds as though you've had a most successful tour, Lady Amberley,'' he remarked, smiling down at her happy face.

''You two had it all planned, didn't you?'' she asked gruffly. ''You were not about to permit me to stay upstairs feeling sorry for myself, and I do thank you most heartily for it. What a relief it will be to have luncheon and dinner downstairs again.'' She took his hand in hers and squeezed it hard, then said to her nephew, ''I hope you'll be home for dinner tonight, Richard, for I will regard it in the way of a celebration.''

''I'm afraid, I have . . .'' he began, then felt the heel of Lucy's slipper come down hard upon his foot. ''I'm afraid I have commitments later on, but will be happy to join you in a family dinner, Grandmama,'' he finished.

When Jennifer and Lady Mortimer returned, they were delighted to see Lady Amberley downstairs, and after partaking of a quite delicious tea, the two Mortimers left so that the old lady could take a rest after all the excitement. They promised to return in a few hours, to help her celebrate.

Dinner that night was a merry occasion, and even though Lady Amberley had to sit a little awkwardly at the foot of the table, she was too thankful to be dining with her family and friends again to care.

Lord Amberley did not go to his club for once, but sat proudly watching his wife as she ate a great deal more than she had been eating of late. Afterward, she was content to join Jennifer as an onlooker while her husband and her granddaughter took on the Mortimers in a lighthearted game of whist. Richard had excused himself immediately after the meal.

It had been the most pleasant evening Lucy had spent since her grandmama's unfortunate accident, and as she climbed the stairs that night and entered her bedchamber, she wished that Gussy had been there waiting, for she needed her sound, sensible advice in the matter of Richard. Something was wrong, she was sure, and she had thought of talking to

Anthony about it if the opportunity arose, but hesitated to involve him in family matters.

She was in such deep thought that she did not at first take notice of a noise downstairs, but when it came a second time, she jumped up and went to the bedroom door, opening it a crack and listening. The sound of heavy breathing was clear now, but she could not quite see who it was, for the lights in the hall were usually left burning all night, but turned down to a mere glimmer.

Going back into her room for a moment, she went to her desk and lit a second candlestick from the one there, then returned to the door and stepped out into the hall. Someone was coming slowly up the stairs, and the glint of red hair in the dim light confirmed her suspicions that it was Richard. Moving soundlessly over the thick carpet, she went carefully down to where her cousin had paused to rest against the handrail.

He was hunched over as if in considerable pain, and when he caught sight of her, he whispered, "Go back to bed, Lucy. I'll manage somehow."

It was, of course, the worst thing he could have said to one of her temperament. She was at his side in a moment, placing an arm around him and whispering, "Try not to make a sound, but lean on me. I'm much stronger than you think."

He winced at her touch and she looked up at his face as she moved her hand a little higher. His eyes were closed, but it was obvious from his expression that he was hurting.

He made no further protest, but allowed her to lead him slowly toward his bedchamber. Once inside, however, he urged her to leave. "I'll be all right now, Lucy, once I get myself into bed," he told her, but his speech was labored and his breathing shallow.

She took not the least notice of him, but went around lighting candles until she could see him clearly enough to realize that though his face was unmarked, he was badly injured elsewhere.

"You'd best tell me what happened," she ordered, starting

to unbutton his jacket, "for I'll not leave until you do."

Slowly it all started to come out. He had got in with the wrong people, started to gamble for high stakes, and when he couldn't pay, he had been given a severe beating as a warning of what would happen if he did not find the money soon.

"But until a fortnight ago you escorted me and Jennifer everywhere. How could you lose so much money so quickly?" she asked, completely ignorant of the high stakes in the various clubs and gambling hells.

"Some lose much more than I did in one evening, but they let me win at first, to encourage me to make higher bids. I can see that now, and I swear I'll never gamble again—that is, if I ever get out of this mess," he declared.

She had eased off his coat and started to unfasten his waistcoat when she saw the bloodstains on his shirt.

"You shouldn't even be in here, Lucy," he muttered. "It's not at all the thing. Go back to bed and I'll stretch out for a while."

"I'm going to get Gussy," Lucy said. "She's a light sleeper, so I'm sure I can waken her without disturbing Grandmama."

He shook his head. "No. I'll be all right until morning, and then I'll get Grandpapa's man to give me a hand once the coast is clear. I mean it, Lucy. I'll lock the door after you and not let you back in. I may have recently done a lot of things I shouldn't, but I'll not let you compromise yourself by tending to me."

She saw that there was no gainsaying him, so she quietly left the room, but she meant to talk to Anthony in the morning when they went out riding, telling him no more, of course, than that Richard had taken a beating.

13

"What happened?" Anthony asked when Lucy told him that she was worried about Richard's condition. "Was he set upon by rogues?"

"I really couldn't say," she told him, "but he was hurting last night and will, I am sure, be feeling much worse this morning. He would not, however, permit me to take off more than his waistcoat, but I saw blood on his shirt."

Anthony frowned. "He was quite right, and by now you should know that, Lucy. You're not treating the wounded in Spain anymore, and it was not at all the thing for you to have been in his bedchamber. Do you want me to go up and see how he is when we get back?"

This was exactly what she had been aiming at, but felt that she could not ask him directly. She suddenly realized that she was learning to dissemble, like the rest of the *ton*, and did not like it one wit.

"Would you mind very much?" she asked. "He said he would ask Higgins for aid once Grandpapa had left the house, but that will be several hours yet. I would come with you, of course, and—"

Anthony looked exasperated. "No, you would not. You'll simply have to learn, my dear, that a lady does not visit a gentleman's bedchamber unless it is her husband's, her son's, or in some instances, her brother's. You would not wish to be compelled to marry Richard because of such an indiscretion, would you?"

"I am afraid you are speaking to the wrong lady, Lord Mortimer," she said coldly. "I would not under any circumstances marry my cousin or any other man to whom I did not wish to be wed. And if at any time my behavior embarrassed Grandmama to such an extent, then I would simply remove myself from a society that I never wished to be a part of in the first place."

He reached over and placed a hand on hers. "I did not make the rules, my dear, nor did I say that I endorsed them. All I'm trying to do is to explain why Richard would not permit you to remain in his bedchamber."

"But he needed help so badly last night, and he wouldn't even let me go for Gussy," she protested impatiently, then realized that he was being far more understanding than any other man she had known. Even Henry had raised objections at first when she had started to tend the wounded soldiers. She smiled ruefully. "I don't think that I will ever be able to live according to the dictates of the *ton*, for their rigid ideas go against everything I have come to believe in," she said quietly. "When I cannot render aid to someone who needs help, I feel that I want no part of them and their rules and regulations. I have already made as many compromises as I mean to."

He suddenly felt gravely concerned that she might remove herself to some place so remote that he would never be able to find her. "Will you make me a promise?" he asked gently.

"It depends on what it commits me to," she prevaricated.

"Will you promise not to suddenly go away without telling me of your intention?"

She thought of it for a long time, for she did not like to make commitments of this sort, then said, "Only if you will promise not to try to physically stop me from doing so."

Though he did not like it, he realized it was as far as she would go. "No physical restraint," he agreed somewhat grimly, and she gave him her hand on it.

"Now I think it's time we returned to Berkeley Square

and I found out what condition your cousin is in. Do you think you might be able to borrow Gussy, for I believe she would be much more capable than I in assessing his injuries?''

Lucy opened her mouth to protest Gussy's presence when her own was not allowed, then decided that in the interests of her cousin it would be best if she went along with the request.

''I don't believe Grandmama will be awake as yet, for she sleeps but poorly through the night, then catches up after day breaks. I'll send her maid in to take Gussy's place in case she should wake and need something,'' she agreed quietly.

They reached the house and left the horses for the groom to take care of, then went inside.

''Is Sir Richard down to breakfast yet?'' she asked Duffield, quite sure that he would not be.

''No, milady, he's not usually abroad for two more hours yet,'' he told her stiffly.

''Have one of the footmen show Lord Mortimer to his bedchamber, then,'' she instructed, and turned to Anthony. ''I most certainly hope that you are successful in teaching him how to tie a waterfall, my lord,'' she said with a faint smile.

He chuckled. ''Don't become alarmed if it takes me the rest of the morning to teach him,'' he told her, ''for I'm sure he'll waste a lot of neckties practicing.''

They parted company then, Lucy going along to the room next to her grandmama's temporary bedchamber, where she found Gussy pressing some of her gowns.

It took only a moment to explain the situation and then Gussy said, ''Of course you can't look after your cousin, milady. What were you thinking of? I'll put this away an' be up there in a couple o' minutes''—she reached for the bellpull—''just as soon as 'er ladyship's fancy maid condescends to answer.''

''You may as well go at once, Gussy. I'll wait for the maid and instruct her to remain with my grandmama until you return. I'll tell her that I am in need of your services for an hour or two, and she'll not try to argue the point with me," Lucy averred. "And don't forget that I'll want to know the fullest extent of my cousin's injuries."

After making sure that Lady Amberley was fast asleep, Gussy hurried upstairs, pausing only to pick up the bag of medicinal herbs and potions that she still kept at the back of her mistress's armoire.

Her knock on Sir Richard's door was light, but was answered at once by Lord Mortimer.

"Come in, Mrs. Bradbury," he told her. "He appears to have had a poor night's sleep and I was endeavoring to remove his shirt when I heard your knock."

Gussy took out a pair of scissors from her bag. "I think it'd be best to use these, milord," she advised, "in case there're bones broken."

Richard made no protest when he saw her coming toward the bed, and a moment later she had him sitting up with his shirt off and was shaking her head at the mass of bruises already forming. Then she examined him as gently as she could, pausing to listen to his breathing from time to time and nodding to herself. Finally she straightened up and said quietly, " 'Is lungs seem to be all right, milord, but 'e may 'ave a cracked rib or two. Wot we need t'do is to bind 'im up tight like. 'E'll be a mite uncomfortable while we do it, but 'is ribs'll 'eal faster that way."

They worked well together and soon Richard was feeling much more comfortable; then, while Gussy prepared a potion for him to take to ease the pain and allow him to sleep, he and Lord Mortimer had a long, quiet talk. As a result, word was put out that he had suffered a fall and would be abed for the best part of a week. Lord Mortimer paid calls on some of the younger man's so-called friends. After a most careful reckoning, money changed hands and it was agreed, on paper, that all scores had been settled.

Gussy took the young man's shirt back to Lucy's bedchamber and cleverly altered it so that he could button it completely down the front, and as she worked, Lucy questioned her.

"You're not being fair, Gussy," she complained after a while. "I obeyed the dictates of convention and let you look after my cousin instead of me, and in return you were supposed to let me know what happened."

"I never said I'd tell you anything," Gussy said. "But I will say you were right. 'E'd been beaten by them as knew wot they were doin'. 'E'll be sore for a week, but after that 'e should be out an' about again. It seemed to me that Lord Mortimer 'ad a long talk wi' your cousin while I made 'im a sleeping potion, an' I'm sure 'is lordship's goin' to take care of everything."

With this Lucy had to be content for the time being, but she meant to pester Anthony the very next time she saw him until he told her more of what her cousin had been doing. She assumed it was gambling, of course, but could not decide whether he had cheated and been punished, or if he had incurred debts he could not repay.

There was also the problem of repaying Anthony, for if he had extended monies on her cousin's behalf, he must be repaid as soon as possible.

All her worries went for nothing, however, for Lord Amberley's man, after seeing Sir Richard, told his master of his suspicions. An interview with his grandson followed and a note was sent to Lord Mortimer asking him to call at his earliest convenience.

"What did he say to you?" Lucy asked Anthony when he came out of her grandpapa's study early that afternoon. "I hope that my bringing you into family problems did not put you at odds with Grandpapa."

"Not at all," Anthony assured her. "He thanked me for taking care of the matter for him and gave me a note for the amount of monies I expended. You may not get off so lightly, however, for he asked me to send you in to see him next."

"Oh, dear," Lucy said with a heavy sigh. "You will wait

to commiserate with me when he's finished, won't you?"

He smiled. "I doubt that will be necessary, but I promise to remain to find out."

But it was still with some trepidation that Lucy entered the study and sat down opposite her grandpapa.

"The first thing I want to do is thank you for keeping this whole affair from Lady Amberley," he said. "She would have been quite beside herself, as I'm sure you realize. Though I believe that you made a sound choice in seeking Lord Mortimer's help, I could, however, wish that you had come to me instead, and kept the matter within the family."

"That would have been telling tales, Grandpapa," Lucy said firmly, "and I don't think you would have expected me to do that."

"And it wasn't telling tales to disclose everything to Lord Mortimer?" he asked sternly, not expecting her to answer back.

"I did not know what had happened, so I could not disclose anything more than that Richard had been injured," she said quietly. "My cousin needed medical attention and would not permit me to help him, so I had no alternative but to ask Lord Mortimer's aid."

"I should think he would not let you, his cousin, assist him," Lord Amberley said, quite obviously shocked. "That was absolutely out of the question. Had you persisted and been discovered, you might have found yourself compromised and forced to marry him."

Lucy's chin went up. "And I might not," she said coldly. "I would not think of marrying anyone for such a flimsy reason."

"Fortunately, such a thing did not become necessary," he grunted. "You used your head, though, I must admit. Can that woman of yours be trusted?"

Lucy had to smile. "With my life, if it came to it," she said. "Gussy's tried and true, Grandpapa."

He nodded his approval, then went on, "It seems to have taught that young scoundrel a lesson he'll not forget. He has made me a promise not to gamble for any but the most insignificant amounts, and I am sure he will keep his word."

"I believe he will also. Now that Jennifer and I are going out again, in Lady Mortimer's care, he will probably accompany us as he used to," she told him. "I think that he just went out looking for company and got in with the wrong people."

"Well, he came out of it a wiser young man, and we'll say no more about it in case word should reach my lady. Go and join young Mortimer and just remember to come to me next time. I had thought we were good-enough friends for you to tell me anything," he grumbled.

Lucy flung her arms around his neck. "Of course we are, Grandpapa," she murmured in his ear. "I just didn't want to worry you, that's all."

Anthony looked into her face as she came back into the drawing room, and made a suggestion. "I have my curricule outside. How would you like to go for a ride and blow away all that bad temper, for I can see from your eyes that all did not go well."

"It wasn't so bad," she admitted, "but a little fresh air sounds wonderful. I'll just run upstairs and get my bonnet."

There was more traffic than usual, for it was a little later in the day, and Lucy kept quiet at first so that Anthony could concentrate on steering his cattle around the other vehicles. It gave her time to think on what her grandpapa had said, however, and once they reached the park, she was eager to ask his advice.

"It was the manservant Grandpapa employs who gave Richard away," she said, "for my cousin has been using the fellow's assistance when he was available. I would like to approach Grandpapa about hiring a man for Richard's sole use and wondered what you might think of it. Surely it would not be unusual for a young man of his age to have a valet?"

Anthony grinned. "You're up to your tricks again, aren't you, trying to make your cousin feel a little less down-pin? However, in this case you do have the right of it. As I have the feeling that the Amberleys have no need to stint, Richard should most certainly have a man of his own, and you might be just the right person to broach the matter. That is, of course, assuming that you did not quarrel with Lord Amberley today."

"Not in the end, but we did have a few cross words," she admitted. "He's the dearest of grandpapas, but most conventional, I'm afraid."

This time Anthony chuckled, for he could well believe that Lucy had shocked the old man with some of the things she had said to him.

"Well, there's nothing unconventional about a young man about town needing a valet of his own, so you're safe enough on that count, and the sooner you approach him, the happier your cousin will be, for he needs help now more than ever," he told her.

He slowed the horses and took a good look at Lucy as she sat erect and waved to first one and then another of her acquaintances. Her appearance was delightful, though she had taken no more than two or three minutes to run up the stairs and put on a deep-green bonnet and pelisse. Her red hair was starting to grow a little and curled around her face in the most captivating way. He suddenly knew that he must have her for his wife, for he had never felt this way about any of the hundreds of young ladies he had met, but he felt sure she still thought of him only as a very good friend. He would have to approach it with the greatest of care or he was certain she would shy away.

"Will you be attending the Granvilles' rout this evening with my Mama and Jennifer?" he asked when they had once more entered a quieter section of the park.

"I had not thought to do so," she told him. Then she asked, "Are you going to be there?"

"Only if you are," he said softly, watching with interest as color instantly suffused her cheeks. "You have been confined too much to the house of late. Why don't you let Gussy handle your grandmama and come along?"

She sat for a moment carefully examining the tips of her gloved fingers, then said quietly, "I think I will, for it would please Grandmama, I know."

He wanted to tell her again that it would please him also, but decided that he had given her a little to think on and should leave it for now.

"Then I will look forward to seeing you there," he told her as he handed her down at her door.

He watched her as she ran quickly up the steps and into the house, then he leapt back onto his curricle, grasped the reins, and took off at such a pace that he almost left his tiger behind.

Sir Nigel Langdon eyed the elegant form of his sister from head to toe, then remarked, "My dear Vanessa, you had best achieve your objective as quickly as possible, for I do not at all like your attending parties while I must keep away from all but the lowest of gaming houses. I hope you understand that for every day I have to stay dressed no better than a country parson, you will have to pay most dearly."

"If you were to attend the affairs I do in the style to which you have become accustomed, I know that you could not fail to be noticed, and that, dear brother, would not fit in with my plans," Vanessa told him. "Just be patient, for the slut who stole Henry must attend the rout this evening. Aunt Hermione said that everyone who is anyone would be there."

"That may be, but you've been saying as much for the past fortnight, and you've still not seen your dear Henry's widow," he said nastily. "Even if she is there, what do you intend to do, walk up to her and tell her you mean to make her pay for your unhappiness? Come, now, did Henry really mean so much to you?"

"He was mine," she snapped. "It had been all arranged and would have gone through without a hitch had she not come into the picture. It was grossly unfair."

Knowing his sister so well, Sir Nigel had considerable

doubts about this, but he was not prepared to voice them at this time.

He shrugged. Why should he worry about someone he had never even set eyes upon? Vanessa was vicious, to be sure, had been ever since they were both quite small, so why should he be the only one to suffer at her hands?

"Very well, I'll go no further than the low places I've already attended. At least I'm getting practice for when I have the money to gamble for higher stakes," he said with a shrug.

A lackey came then to say that Aunt Hermione's carriage was waiting, and with a less-than-friendly smile, Lady Vanessa swept from the room.

When she and her aunt alighted at the home of the Granvilles, Vanessa glanced around her.

"You seem to have been looking for someone for the past two weeks," Aunt Hermione remarked. "I hope it's not some lover you have planned to meet."

"Merely someone I knew as a child," Vanessa replied. "I lost touch with her and would very much like to see her again."

She gave a little gasp and hoped that her aunt had not noticed, for Lady Lucinde Coldwell was in a group at the door now, waiting to greet their hosts. She looked so much more attractive and mature than had the young girl she had caught a covert glimpse of so long ago, that Vanessa had almost passed her over, but there was no doubt about it, for she could not forget that hair.

As the party moved around the room, she never let them out of her sight. What she must do now was to find an opportunity to become acquainted, and she saw her chance in the younger girl with the black hair who was at this moment excusing herself and going toward the ladies' retiring room.

Reaching down as though she had dropped something, she carefully placed the hem of her gown under her slippered foot, then stood up quickly. The sound of fabric rending drew

Aunt Hermione's attention from the old friend she was in conversation with.

"Was that your gown that ripped, Vanessa?" she asked sharply. "I suppose I'd best come with you and see what can be done."

"It's only the smallest of tears, I believe, and there's sure to be a maid or someone there to help. You need not trouble, Aunt, for I'll only be a moment," Vanessa said quickly, then hurried out of the room and up the stairs to the chamber reserved for the ladies.

To her relief, the maid in attendance was busy stitching a rip in her quarry's lace glove, so she sat down next to the young lady and lifted the hem of her gown, eyeing it with distaste.

"Oh dear, what a shame."

Lady Vanessa looked up at the owner of the sympathetic voice. "My aunt was right, for I should have been more careful, but I'm sure it can be stitched so that it does not show," she said with a bright smile. "I'm Lady Vanessa Langdon and I'm staying in town with my aunt, Lady Hermione Douglas."

"How nice to meet you," Jennifer said, immediately taking to the young lady with the warm, friendly smile. "I'm Jennifer Amberley. My brother and I are staying with our grandmama, but she was involved in an accident so her friend, Lady Mortimer, is acting in her stead."

This was just the kind of opening Lady Vanessa needed. "But how dreadful for your grandparent," she said in her most sympathetic voice. "What happened?"

"She slipped when entering her carriage and broke her leg, but she's going to be all right again," Lady Jennifer assured her. "Cousin Lucy made sure she got the best possible care."

This was going even better than Vanessa had dared to hope for. She smiled and raised her eyebrows, as if she did not know who Cousin Lucy might be.

Lady Jennifer smiled. "I'll introduce you when we go back

inside. She's Lady Lucinde Coldwell and she lost her husband in the Peninsular wars."

"How dreadful for her," Lady Vanessa said softly. "Does she have any children?"

The other girl shook her head. "No, I'm afraid not, for they could now have been such a consolation to her. Not that she's a sad person at all, as you'll see for yourself when you meet her."

"I'll look forward to that so very much," Lady Vanessa said, meaning every word of it.

14

Lucy did not feel quite as happy about Jennifer's newfound friend as did her cousin. There was something about that particular young lady that Lucy could not like, yet she was unable to quite put her finger upon what it might be. Her grandmama would have said that the girl was encroaching, and it was probably true, for she had not been presented, but had introduced herself to Jennifer. However, Lucy was certainly not one to pay heed to such minor infringements.

But Lady Vanessa Langdon was now invited everywhere they went. Lady Mortimer had some slight acquaintance with the girl's aunt, who claimed to be in poor health, and so the former had generously offered to take Lady Vanessa about also, in view of the close friendship that had sprung up between her and Jennifer.

This was the reason that Lord Mortimer now declined to escort them to most of the parties they attended, for he disliked being in the company of so many females. He was, however, keeping a sharp eye out for Richard and could often be seen with him at various functions, but not at gaming hells, for Richard was keeping his word and now regarded such places as if they were the plague itself.

Though Lucy missed seeing Anthony in the evening, their early-morning rides had resumed and were a source of constant pleasure to both of them.

"You look far too neat and tidy to be believed this morning," he said with a chuckle as they entered the park.

He pointed to a tree in the distance. "When we reach that lone oak, I'll race you to the clump of elms that lie beyond, and we'll then see how tidy you can remain."

"Grandmama's maid is driving me to distraction," she told him. "She won't let me out of my bedchamber until every hair is in place, and I can't be cross with her, for she's quite old and extremely sensitive. But I'll be so glad to get my dear Gussy back."

"I understand that Lady Amberley is coming along very well under her care, however, and that she's starting to put a little weight upon the leg each day," he remarked. "She'll be up and around again before you know it."

As he finished speaking, he started off at a gallop, for they had reached the oak, and he chuckled as he heard Lucy use a word that no lady should even know about. He had caught her off-guard, however, and she had not a hope of catching up with him.

"That was foul play, you scoundrel," she told him when she reached the elms, "and I'll get even with you next time, just you see."

He laughed. "You do and I'll tell Lady Amberley what I just heard you say," he threatened. "Unfortunately, though, I don't think she would even know the meaning of that particular oath."

"Oh, Anthony," she declared, "I do enjoy these morning rides, and I miss you quite dreadfully at most of the parties we go to. I don't know why your mama agreed to include Lady Vanessa in every single entertainment we attend. I'm probably being a wretch to say so, but I cannot like that young lady, and though she is always charming to me, I still feel it an act put on for someone else's benefit."

Lord Anthony frowned. "She's pleasant enough," he said, "and you of all people should feel sympathy, for I understand her come-out was delayed because of the death of her fiancé in the wars."

"So she says, but I have tried to question her as to his

name, regiment, and the battle he was killed in," Lucy said, frowning, "and she invariably prevaricates. Perhaps she has told you more than she has told me."

He shook his head. "On the occasion I asked her about him, she burst into tears and said it was still too raw a wound for her to talk about. It would have been quite heartless to pursue it further."

"She certainly does not give the appearance of having recovered from her loss. She is not at all a happy person, except, perhaps, when she's with Jennifer, who seems to enjoy her company very much indeed," Lucy remarked. "I believe I may soon stop attending so many functions and let your mama just take the two of them, for no one now brings me just the things I like at supper, as you did, and I miss standing up with you at balls."

She was not being flirtatious in the least, but spoke quite matter-of-factly. Nevertheless, a warmth came into his eyes and his voice was husky as he said, "Do you, by Jove? You almost tempt me to come with you this evening, but I made a commitment to Lord Melbourne that would be difficult to break."

"Oh, no," Lucy said at once, "you mustn't think of it. I believe I'll complain of a megrim and stay home for once. We were not attending a ball, anyway, but a musical evening, which would be certain to make my headache, if I had one, much worse."

He saw the mischief in her eyes and placed his hand upon hers. "Whatever function you are attending tomorrow night, I promise to be there," he said softly, "and I must tell you how delighted I am that you have missed me even a little."

She felt a warmth deep inside, something she had not felt since Henry was alive, and to Anthony's secret amusement, her cheeks took on a most becoming flush.

By the time they reached Berkeley Square she was most anxious to get upstairs and change out of the heavy riding habit, for she felt uncomfortably warm all over.

* * *

When Lucy told Jennifer that she would not be going with her to the musical evening, her cousin was quite alarmed, for she had never known Lucy to suffer from any ailment.

"Have you told Gussy that you do not feel well?" she asked with concern. "She might be able to mix up a potion that would have you feeling better in no time."

"Neither Gussy nor I have a cure for what ails me," Lucy told her cousin. "What I really need is to have a quiet evening and then a good night's sleep. I assure you that my usual robust health will be restored by tomorrow morning. Please give my regrets to Lady Mortimer and tell her to take very good care of you."

Jennifer promised to do so, then retired to her bedchamber to get ready for the evening, and a little while later Lucy went upstairs also to change into a simple dinner gown.

When a knock came on the door, she thought it must be her grandmama's maid wishing to assist her, and she was surprised to find that it was Jennifer who answered her instruction to come in.

"I was wondering if I might borrow the string of pearls that you sometimes wear," Jennifer asked. "The ones that Mama gave me are a little too long and I believe that yours would be just right."

Lucy looked a little embarrassed. "I'm afraid they belong to Grandmama," she told her cousin, "as does all the jewelry you've seen me wearing, for I have never owned any except my wedding ring. I borrow the pearls each time I need them."

Jennifer looked at her in surprise. "Didn't your Mama give you any of hers? What did Sir Henry give you on your birthdays if he didn't give you jewelry?" she asked, not meaning to be at all critical but simply not able to understand.

Lucy's laugh was a little forced. "Mama was a lively widow and wanted all the jewelry she owned for herself. And as for Henry, there was never enough money left for extravagances after buying all the things we simply had to have to survive. He had only a quite small allowance that an uncle made him, you know, for his parents strongly disapproved of his being in the army."

Her cousin was not quite contrite. "I'm so sorry I asked, Lucy, but I had no idea that you were wearing Grandmama's things. I certainly did not mean to embarrass you, or I would never have come in like this," she said, "and asked to borrow them."

Lucy had been disconcerted at first, but had now recovered and could not resist the temptation to brag a little. "I've steered you wrong, however, for there is one piece of jewelry that I own but would never think of wearing. It is most unusual and is, I believe, quite old."

She went to her desk and took out the jeweled locket the camp follower had given her. Carefully unfolding the scrap of fabric it had been wrapped in, she placed it on the coverlet of her bed.

The golden locket gleamed in the glow from the candles. It was oval, about two inches long and an inch and a half wide, and in the center was an emerald surrounded by diamonds. More diamonds ran like the spokes of a wheel from the center to a row of small pearls around the edge of the locket, and the gold between was richly engraved in a rose-and-leaf design. It hung on a very heavy gold chain some twenty-four inches long.

"Where on earth did you get this? It looks extremely valuable," Jennifer breathed as she picked it up to examine it closer. "Is there anything inside?"

Before Lucy could stop her, she had unfastened the catch and opened up the locket. Inside was a miniature of a beautiful young lady with long black hair and dark eyes that seemed to dance with joy.

"It was a gift to me," Lucy told her cousin, "and is obviously Spanish. I did not realize its value until it was too late."

"Sir Henry must have loved you very much to give you something like this," Jennifer said, becoming more and more curious about its origins.

"Oh, it was nothing like that . . ." Lucy started to explain, then realized it was better not to, and wished that she had not been so foolish as to show it to Jennifer. "You must not tell a soul that you've seen it, for I have a feeling you're right about it being valuable."

"She does look Spanish, doesn't she?" Jennifer said, looking more closely at the miniature. "And the painting is excellent, for you feel that you can almost touch her."

She sighed as she placed the locket in Lucy's outstretched hand. "How I wish I could wear it. Everyone would be looking at it, but I can understand how you feel. I'll not tell a soul about it, I promise."

Jennifer hurried out to finish her toilette and Lucy wrapped the locket once more and put it away, but she had an odd feeling about it now. It was one thing when only she and Gussy had known about it, but she had little faith in her cousin's vow to keep her secret. Jennifer had told her too many secrets of other people for her to have any faith in the girl's promises.

Gussy's knock on the door brought a message from Lady Amberley. She wanted her to come down to her ground-floor bedchamber at once so that she could see for herself that Lucinde was not about to succumb to some dreadful illness.

"There's nothing at all wrong with me," she said to her friend, "except that I miss you and wish you could teach Grandmama's own maid how to handle her."

"Then why did you say you'd the megrim?" Gussy asked. "The old lady's 'aving a fit in case you've caught your death ridin' out so early of a morning."

"I just couldn't listen to one more flat soprano or contralto screeching away in a roomful of people, Gussy. And can you believe that at these affairs they also expect the young ladies in the audience to give renderings of their favorite songs? Vanessa gets up every time."

Gussy had heard enough of her mistress's humming in the bathtub to appreciate what the others must sound like.

"Just come down and put 'er mind at rest, milady, then you can spend a nice quiet evenin' with a book," she said.

The two of them went out and down the stairs together, and once Lady Amberley had seen for herself that there was nothing wrong with her granddaughter that an early night would not cure, she allowed her to give her a kiss and promised not to tell her friend that it was all a hum and that Lucinde was simply suffering from an excess of society.

It was a relief to Lucy when Lady Mortimer collected Jennifer and she was able to partake of a simple supper and retire to her bedchamber with a copy of a current, quite scandalous novel.

With Lord Mortimer accompanying his mama once more in the evenings, and taking Lucy riding each morning, she no longer found her days at all tedious. He was a most congenial companion, and she completely forgot the stern side of him she had seen in Spain and just that once here in the park when she insulted an acquaintance of his.

Then one morning, as they left Berkeley Square and headed toward the park, they heard an altercation coming from the direction of the mews where the Amberley stables were.

"Off wi' you. M'lady don't 'ave nowt to do wit'e likes o' you. An' ye'd best gi' me that card."

They both glanced in the direction from which the voice came, then Lucy turned Beauty's head and started toward the mews.

"What do you think you're doing, Lucy? Stay with the groom and I'll see what's going on if you're so concerned," Anthony said, but Lucy was already across the street and approaching the place where a man in Lord Amberley's livery was so soundly berating someone.

Anthony grabbed a hold of her reins as she drew near to her grandpapa's groom, but before he could check her further, she slid down from the mare and walked over to where a man was leaning against the wall, a crutch under one arm. As she approached, he reached for his cap and took it off.

"I remember you," she said quietly, "and I'm very pleased you did as I suggested. What can I do to help?"

"The shelter where me an' a few others like me were livin' 'as been closed and we're out on the street now altogether. Yon feller's right, tho'. I shouldn't 'ave come, but I didn't know wot else to do. The nights are colder now and it'll get worse afore it gets better. An' there's no work to be found for the likes of us."

Lucy had not heard Anthony dismount, but she felt his hand on her arm before he spoke.

"Where did you lose your leg?" he asked, but before the ex-soldier could reply, Lucy said, "Salamanca."

"Then you do know him?" he asked, somewhat surprised.

"We met one day here in London, and I gave him my card and told him to come to see me if he should ever need help." There was a hint of defiance in her voice that Anthony did not not fail to note.

"I believe that I can be of more assistance at the moment than you can, Lucy," he said quietly, then turned to the ex-soldier. "Do you know the Three Kings' Yard behind Grosvenor Square?"

"Yes, sir, I know where it is," was the quick response.

"Then meet me there, with your friends, at three o'clock this afternoon," Anthony said grimly. "How many are you?"

"There're nine of us, sir," the ex-soldier said, some of the weariness disappearing from his face as he spoke.

"In case you don't know who you're meeting, this is Colonel Anthony Mortimer, a former aide of Wellington's," Lucy said, "and a friend of my late husband."

The man nodded as though he had guessed as much, and Anthony took Lucy's arm. "Are you ready?" he asked, quietly enough, but no one who knew him as well as she did could have missed the controlled anger in his tone.

Lucy nodded and preceded him to where his groom and horses waited.

He gave her a hand up, then mounted himself, and they continued toward the park in an increasingly uncomfortable silence. When they reached the old oak, he glanced over to her and she looked at him with eyebrows raised. It took only the merest inclination of his head to send her and Beauty racing for the elms, and this time he could not have caught up with her if he had tried.

She knew the reckoning was going to come, however, so she dismounted and walked through the trees toward a small pond. Then she waited for him to follow.

"Just how many more wounded ex-soldiers are there in London carrying your card with instructions to come for help if they need it?" he asked, his voice dangerously quiet.

She shrugged. "Maybe a half-dozen," she said in as casual a tone as she could muster.

"And what are you going to do if times get worse, as is inevitable, and all half-dozen of these ex-soldiers, and their friends, come looking for you at once?" he asked sarcastically.

"Whatever I can to help, of course," she told him. "I wouldn't have made the offer had I not meant it."

"Lucy, you're not safe to be let loose in London without a keeper," he exclaimed. "You have no sense whatsoever of what befits your position. What did you do, just walk up to these men on the street and introduce yourself?"

Lucy was about to deny it when she realized that was, to all intents and purposes, exactly what she had done. She bit her underlip thoughtfully, wondering just how she could make Anthony understand.

As she looked up at him, his face suddenly changed from exasperation to understanding. She could no more deliberately stop trying to help those soldiers than she could deliberately stop breathing, he realized. She had been doing it for so long overseas that it was completely natural for her to continue doing so here in London, and he would be willing to bet that she had given each of them the last penny in her purse. Wasn't that why he had grown to love her? he asked himself, and though he agreed, it did not stop him from delivering a severe scold that he knew went into one of her pretty little ears and right out the other.

She did, however, look appropriately chagrined when he was finished, and then asked, "What are you going to do with these men when they meet you this afternoon? Can I—"

"No, you cannot come with me to meet them," he snapped, guessing what she was about to ask, "and what I have in mind is sending them out to the country where I need work done on my estate before the land freezes over altogether. There's an empty cottage they can stay in and more food there than they've probably seen in months."

Lucy smiled. "I knew you'd be able to think of some way of helping them," she said happily.

"Just try not to make friends with any more of these fellows than you can help, please," he begged, "for there is a limit to my resourcefulness."

"I'll try, but I won't make any promises," she told him, "and perhaps Grandpapa needs work done in the country, too."

"If I were you, I would not count on it, or even put it to the test, for you might just be the next person who found herself packed off to the country," he warned. "And don't start asking me questions about them tonight at the ball, or someone is liable to get the wrong impression. I'll tell you tomorrow morning if everything went according to my plan."

"Men really do get all the fun, you know," she grumbled. "They're allowed to do so many things in the city that are completely forbidden to ladies, and they even get to decide what should or should not be done in Parliament, but they take far too long about it, as a rule. I'm sure that if the right women were allowed to take a part in it, things would be accomplished much more quickly."

He chuckled at the ridiculous ideas she got into her head at times. But one thing he had to admit: she was the most honest, straightforward young lady he had ever known, and time spent with her was never dull.

15

Although Lucy had known not to trust Jennifer, she was still surprised when Lady Amberley made mention of her locket when she went into her grandmama's bedchamber to check on the old lady's progress.

She was more than happy to see that the leg could bear quite a bit of weight with apparently very little discomfort.

"You're doing wonderfully well, Grandmama," she said, "and I guarantee you'll soon be walking alone with just a cane for support. I'm proud of you for the way you've worked to get back on your feet again."

Lady Amberley's shoulders noticeably straightened and her eyes brightened under such praise. "If it had not been for you and Gussy, I'd be lying on that bed still with not a hope of ever getting out of it again," she said gruffly. "The Lord knew what he was doing when he sent you both to me."

She allowed Gussy to make her comfortable in an armchair, then asked her granddaughter, "What is this I hear about your having a valuable gold locket? I thought you told me you owned no jewelry at all."

Lucy looked at Gussy and sighed heavily. "I knew I should never have shown it to Jennifer," she said crossly, "for she cannot keep a thing to herself. I told you I had no jewelry, Grandmama, because I don't think of it as such, for I would never dare to wear it."

"Could you, perhaps, be a little more explicit?" Lady Amberley asked, frowning.

"Whether the stones are genuine or not, it is the most costly gift I have ever received. I treasure it as something very beautiful that I can take out when the mood strikes, and recall some of the happier times in Spain and Portugal. If it were real, only a king or a queen would wear it, and then at only the most formal of occasions."

Lady Amberley looked thoughtful. "It wasn't Jennifer who told me, it was your grandpapa, and he had heard about it from Richard. He'll be visiting me in just a moment; perhaps you should have a word with him."

Lucy shook her head sadly. Jennifer's tongue had indeed been very busy. It was her own fault, of course, for she had known not to trust Jennifer but had been embarrassed and unable to resist claiming that she was not completely without jewelry.

Lord Amberley came in a moment later and went over to kiss his wife on the cheek.

"You're looking better every day, my love," he told her. "It won't be long now before you're completely your old self again." He turned and saw Lucy watching them. "Just the young lady I wanted to see," he said, putting an arm around her shoulder and steering her to a small couch. "What's this about your owning a priceless piece of jewelry?"

"I was just explaining to Grandmama that I don't really consider it so much a piece of jewelry as a memento. It was a gift that I enjoy mostly because of what it represents," she tried to explain.

"Is it very valuable, as Jennifer implied?" he asked. "For if it is, it might be wiser to keep it in my safe than in your bedchamber."

"Perhaps, but I treasure it for purely sentimental reasons. It might quite easily be valuable," Lucy agreed, "but how could I enjoy it if it was locked away all the time? It is hardly the kind of thing I could wear without causing considerable comment."

"I'll tell you what to do," Lord Amberley said. "Bring

it down for us all to see after dinner tonight. Richard has quite naturally become curious about it, and I'm sure Lady Amberley would enjoy seeing such an unusual piece."

"Very well, Grandpapa," Lucy agreed, though she had considerable qualms about doing so. But when she later remembered that this was the night Lady Vanessa Langdon and both the Mortimers would be dining with them, she felt an even stronger reluctance to bring out the locket, and hoped that it would be forgotten or put off to an evening when there was only family present.

An outing had been planned for the following day. An excursion to Hampton Court Palace and a private viewing of the royal residence. They would eat a picnic luncheon in the grounds before returning to London. As they must needs make an early start if they were to get back before dark, Lady Vanessa was to spend the night at Amberley House with Jennifer.

One glance in Jennifer's direction when Lucy had first entered the drawing room, where a before-dinner glass of sherry was being served, told her that her cousin was feeling exceedingly guilty and was most unlikely to be the one to broach the subject of the locket this evening.

The grave expression on Lord Mortimer's face, however, both before and throughout the meal, gave Lucy cause to wonder just how far word of the locket might have spread. If Richard had told her grandpapa of its existence, might he not have also told Anthony? And would Anthony not have guessed where it had come from? There was no point in upsetting herself because of a lot of suppositions, so Lucy decided to forget all about it until someone brought it up.

As soon as dinner was over, Lady Amberley signaled to Lucy, who rose and wheeled her grandmama into the drawing room. Lady Mortimer, Jennifer, and Vanessa followed, leaving the gentlemen to their port and cigars.

Jennifer and Vanessa, who became engaged at once in a quite heated discussion on the latest books they had read, sat together on the far side of the fireplace, while Lady

Mortimer went over to where Lucy had placed her grandmama's wheelchair.

"Will this be your first visit to Hampton Court Palace, Lucinde," Lady Mortimer asked, "or did your mama perhaps take you there as a little girl?"

"Mama rarely brought me to London," Lucy told her, "and when she did, she had much more important things to do than to entertain me."

"My daughter was too busy trying to catch a new husband, and the likely ones soon had her measure," Lady Amberley explained with a grunt of disapproval. "I took Lucinde to Astley's Amphitheater, as I recall, before it was burned down and rebuilt, and what a time she had watching the clowns and magicians and acrobats."

"I was very small, but I remember how exciting it was," Lucy said, her eyes shining with pleasure at the recollection, "much more interesting than Hampton Court would have been to me at that young age."

"Why don't you run upstairs and bring down the locket we were talking about this morning, Lucinde?" Lady Amberley suggested, apparently quite unaware of her granddaughter's reluctance to put it on display. "It sounds like such an unusual piece that I'm sure everyone would be interested in seeing it. Lord Amberley promised that the gentlemen would not stay long over port, so they'll probably be already here by the time you come back."

To protest would have seemed ungracious, so Lucy rose and went up the stairs to her bedchamber. She took out the locket from its place in her escritoire and looked at it for some time, wondering to whom it had originally belonged. It might, of course, have passed through a number of hands before reaching hers.

While she was gone, Lady Amberley explained to her friend that it must be something Sir Henry came across on the Peninsula and gave to Lucinde before he was killed, for it appeared to have great sentimental value to her granddaughter.

At the mention of Sir Henry's name, Lady Vanessa stopped listening to what Jennifer was saying, so that she missed some of her newfound friend's conversation and had to apologize, but she had finally learned of a way to hurt the girl who stole Henry. She awaited Lucy's return with eager anticipation.

The gentlemen came in to join the ladies, Lord Amberley going over and taking a seat beside his wife's wheelchair, while Richard sat near to his sister and Vanessa, and Lord Mortimer settled down on a couch in front of the fireplace.

All heads turned as Lucy came back into the room holding something in a large kerchief. She looked more than a little embarrassed by their attention.

"I hope no one will be disappointed," she said dryly, "for I had not thought to be the main attraction of the evening."

Anthony motioned for her to sit beside him, but she gave a little shake of her head and he resumed his seat as she went over to her grandparents, unwrapped the kerchief, and put the locket into Lord Amberley's outstretched hand. The two older ladies leaned over to get a closer look.

After a pause, Lady Amberley said, "Well, it's certainly a most unusual piece—very beautiful and with intricate markings—but I can see now, my dear, why you would not be comfortable wearing it."

Lady Mortimer asked, "Is it very heavy?" and the locket was slipped into her hand to let her judge for herself. "Quite heavy, I would say," she murmured as she handed it back to Lord Amberley. "Is there anything inside it?"

Unable to bear the suspense, Richard got up and went to peer over Lord Amberley's shoulder as he slipped the catch and revealed the miniature. Jennifer joined them a moment later to take another look at the painting.

"Isn't she lovely?" she said, stepping back to let Richard get a closer look.

"You know, Lucinde," Lord Amberley said as he rose at last and handed the locket to Lord Mortimer for his examination, "I'm sure that this is quite old, and if the stones are real, it must be quite valuable. It is not at all the sort of thing to leave lying around in a dresser drawer. It should be kept in my safe for now, I believe."

"Thank you, Grandpapa," Lucy said quietly, "but I have no wish to have it locked away. As I told you, I often take it out and look at it, for it brings back many fond memories."

"Just as you like, my dear," Lord Amberley said with a slight shrug. "But don't blame me if you lose it one of these days."

Lord Mortimer held it up by the chain, estimating its weight, and for the first time Lady Vanessa took a good look at it, noting how it sparkled and gleamed in the bright light from the candles. Then she looked away again as if not concerned with it in the least.

He opened it and looked closely at the lady in the painting, his mouth set in a quite grim line, then he snapped it closed and held it out to Lucy, and she took it and wrapped it in the kerchief once more.

This time when he indicated that she should join him, she felt unable to refuse and sat down gingerly at one side of the couch, waiting to hear what he was going to say. She did not have long to wait, but she did have to listen closely, for his voice was intended for her ears alone.

"I am extremely disappointed," he said softly, "for I had not thought you to be the kind of person who would deliberately take something that was not her own. I know where that must have come from, for after you left I saw quite a number of similar pieces that had been found among King Joseph's property and given to Wellington. Looting is stealing, no matter how the men and women who took part in it tried to justify their actions. You must know, I am sure, how strongly Lord Wellington felt about it."

"I heard that he was furious because, though there was much left for him to take, he did not get everything," she answered in the same quiet tones as his. She felt too hurt that he would condemn her out of hand to try to explain just how it had come into her possession.

"What he got was the spoils of war, and is now helping pay part of the costs of the final campaign," Anthony said with conviction. "And he was justified, in my opinion, when he called his soldiers who looted, 'the scum of the earth,' though I know he has been much criticized for the remark."

"They were not scum when they were facing those relentless French guns and still trying to advance, were they?" she asked sharply. "He was safe on the hillside, watching them. I could see him clearly from where I stood."

"If you could, then you must have seen also how upset he was at the delay in the planned counterattack. But that's neither here nor there. It does not make looting anything but a despicable form of thievery, in my estimation."

"I'll go and put this away," Lucy said, placing the offending item in the palm of her hand and rising. "If you will all excuse me, I'm a little tired tonight and we have an early start in the morning, so I'll retire now. Shall I send Gussy to you, Grandmama?"

"I'll send for her in a little while," Lord Amberley said. "Good night, my dear, and we'll see you bright and early in the morning."

She hurried up the stairs as fast as she could, for she was having difficulty holding back the tears that threatened to spill over. How could he assume that she had been involved in the looting that took place after Vitoria? It was stealing, no matter who took it, and she would never have played a part in anything of that sort. Had she known what the camp follower's gift consisted of, she would have returned it right away, but it had been only natural to assume that it was some small item of food and she'd not thought to look until it was too late.

He was a horrid, dominating man, and she had been a fool to think he might be anything else!

Once inside her chamber, she flung herself onto the bed to sob out her chagrin at the quiet but deadly lecture he had just given her. She wished with all her heart she did not have to see him tomorrow, but it would cause too much comment if she refused to go on the outing. And, besides, Gussy might need help with Grandmama.

She did not lie there for long, for she had always thought tears portrayed a lack of character. Her grandmama's maid had brought in fresh water earlier in the evening, so she bathed her eyes and prepared to retire for the night.

As she was about to put the locket back into the drawer where she had always kept it, she felt a distinct nervousness. All the fuss about its value had put her somewhat on edge, and she suddenly turned away from the escritoire and slipped the locket beneath her pillow. Tomorrow, she decided, before they set off on their outing, she would decide on a much safer place to keep it.

Although she was tired, sleep did not come easily for once, and she lay for some time remembering every single word that Anthony had said to her as she sat beside him on the couch. She would give him short shrift tomorrow, she decided, if he should attempt to make up for his surly behavior. But somehow she did not believe he would condescend to do so. She sighed, for she would miss their early-morning rides quite dreadfully, but he had made an incorrect assumption about her and she would not even try to make him see his mistake.

She must have slept for an hour or two, for it was still dark when she awoke with the strange feeling that she was not alone in the bedchamber. She lay still, listening, for some time, then must have fallen back to sleep, and the next morning did not recall having wakened until the maid had been with her chocolate and hot water. Then she noticed that several items on her dressing table were not where they had been the night before, and she remembered the strange feeling she had during the night.

Taking the locket from beneath her pillow, Lucy was looking around the chamber to find a suitable hiding place when Gussy knocked on the door and entered.

" 'Er ladyship is just drinking 'er chocolate, so I thought

I'd come up and see if you needed anything,'' she said. ''What're you doing with the locket?''

''Trying to find a good hiding place for it, Gussy,'' Lucy said with a frown. ''Just look at my dressing table. Have you ever seen things so out of place?''

''That I 'aven't,'' Gussy said in surprise. ''Was someone in 'ere last night?''

Lucy nodded. ''Apparently, for I awoke once and thought so, but then I went back to sleep. I haven't checked to see if any drawers have been disturbed, but I had put the locket under my pillow last night, for safety's sake,'' she said. ''I'd not be at all surprised if Lord Mortimer wanted it to give to Lord Wellington, but he's not going to get it.''

Gussy looked at her as if she was about in the head, but thought it best to say nothing.

''Can you think of a good hiding place, Gussy?'' Lucy asked as she kept looking around the chamber seeking ideas.

''That I can. There's a loose floorboard in my bedchamber beneath the chest o'drawers. Let me 'ave it for now and I'll put it there for you,'' Gussy said. ''Nobody'll think to search a servant's room for it. And stop lookin' so worried. Did you and 'is lordship 'ave another quarrel?''

Lucy sighed. ''Not really, for they say it takes two, and I said hardly a word to him. But he accused me of having looted that locket at Vitoria. You know that I didn't, Gussy, and how I felt about the ones who were looting,'' she said. ''I'd not have accepted it if I'd known what it was, but I found out too late.''

Gussy smiled and put an arm around her friend's shoulders. ''Don't take on so. I'm willing to bet you didn't set 'im straight about it, did you?''

''Why should I?'' Lucy sounded belligerent. ''If he chooses to believe the worst of me without any evidence, then let him. I want nothing further to do with him, and I intend to stay with Grandmama all day today and leave him to his own devices.''

"And speaking of Lady Amberley, I'd best get this put away, then go and get 'er ready. She's nervous enough without 'er having to rush at the last minute."

Gussy hurried out of the chamber, and now somewhat relieved, Lucy started to put on her gown. All her grand-mama's abigail would need to do when she came in would be to comb her hair into some semblance of order, which suited Lucy just fine, for she had a distinct aversion to being fussed over by the anxious old servant.

With Gussy it was different, for she was a friend and companion in whom she put her utmost confidence. She might, however, have felt some qualms had she known of the close relationship that had formed between Gussy and Lord Mortimer's former batman, Morgan, who was now his valet.

While Lucy was having the finishing touches put to her coiffure by her grandmama's maid, Gussy was having a serious talk with Morgan about her mistress's nighttime visitor.

"She's not one to imagine things," she told him. "If she thought someone was in that room, then y' can be sure she was right. And she suspected Lord Mortimer, I tell you, for she thought 'e wanted to give the locket to Lord Wellington."

Morgan shook his head and chuckled. "As if 'e'd do owt like that," he said. "I'll let 'im know, though, so as 'e can keep an eye on 'er today. She'll be safe enough with 'er family around 'er, I'm sure."

"Are you going with 'is lordship?" Gussy asked.

"Yes. I'll be riding on the box with 'is coachman and giving a 'and wherever it's needed, just like I used to do for 'im in Spain," he said proudly. "You'll be with Lady Amberley, won't you?"

"That I will," Gussy told him. "And I'd best get back inside, for the minute they finish breakfast they'll want to be off."

She went back into the house, satisfied that she had done

the best she could to help her mistress, and found that young lady in the drawing room, talking to her grandpapa and positioned on exactly the opposite side of the room from Lord Mortimer.

"Lady Amberley is all ready, so whenever y're about to leave I'll get 'er in the carriage first," she told Lucy.

"That's good, Gussy, for she would get nervous if she had to sit waiting in the carriage for long," Lucy told her. "I'll be traveling, in the Amberley coach with you, Grandmama, and Grandpapa. The others can all get into the Mortimer coach, I'm sure. Just as soon as Richard comes down, we'll be able to start out."

"I think we could get started now," Lord Amberley said firmly. "If, by the time we have Lady Amberley comfortably settled, Richard still is not down, then we'll just send someone up to get him. It seems to take him even longer, now that he has his own man, than it ever did before."

16

They had wrapped themselves in warm clothes, for Hampton Court Palace was close to the river, and though the day was bright and sunny when they left, it might easily turn cool before they were ready to start for home.

Once they were on their way, Lady Amberley's earlier fretfulness disappeared and she was quite obviously enjoying her view from the carriage window as they made their way through Knightsbridge and Kensington in a westerly direction and then turned south. Her wheelchair had been placed on the back of the carriage, and Gussy had come along to wheel her around on this her first outing since the accident.

As her nervousness left her, she turned her attention to her granddaughter. "Why are you traveling with us and not in the other carriage of young people, Lucinde? Lady Mortimer should have been in here instead of you," she said sharply.

"I wanted to make sure that you were all right," Lucy tried to explain, "and to give Gussy a hand if she needs one."

"Fustian," her grandmama said. "You've quarreled with Anthony again, I'll be bound, and don't want to be with him in such close quarters."

Lucy shrugged. "Whatever you say, Grandmama," she murmured. "But I always thought it took two to quarrel, and I've said nothing to him."

"He appeared to have plenty to say to you last night, though," the shrewd old lady went on, "and you looked none too pleased even if you didn't say anything to him. Was it something to do with the locket?"

"Grandmama, I'd rather not discuss it, if you don't mind," Lucy said firmly. "I didn't sleep very well last night, and I believe I will follow Grandpapa's lead and take a nap until we get there."

"I should have stopped the coaches and made you change places with Lady Mortimer," Lady Amberley grumbled, "for she'd be much better company than either you or your grandpapa. But it's too late now, for they passed us a little while ago and will probably be halfway there already."

Lucy had to smile then. "Not quite, Grandmama. But I was unjustifiably surly, and I'm truly sorry. Tell me what we're likely to see today."

It had been some time since Lady Amberley had been to Hampton Court, for though King George III had an aversion to it, due, she told them, to his once having had his ears boxed there by his crusty and intolerant grandfather, it was still a royal palace and one could only visit by invitation.

"So many suites have been allotted by the sovereign, in recent years, to deserving persons as grace and favor houses," she added, "that it is often called 'the Quality Poorhouse.' It is one such person who has invited us here today, with the approval, of course, of the housekeeper, who will show us around."

Lord Mortimer had misinterpreted Lucy's reason for riding with her grandparents, thinking that a guilty conscience had caused her to avoid him. And though the occupants of both coaches did not split up when they first reached Hampton Court, he made a point of remaining in the company of young Richard as they strolled around the palace and park.

They were of considerable aid to Gussy in pushing Lady Amberley's chair over some of the rougher terrain as the party visited the Old Tilt Yard, King Henry VIII's Close Tennis Court, and the Maze. Jennifer declared herself too hungry to risk getting lost behind the clipped hedges, but Lord Mortimer had brought with him a copy of the key, which he had purchased on a previous visit. Any hopes that he could persuade Lucy to try her luck at getting to the center and out again, however, had been dashed last evening.

Shortly after luncheon the gentlemen left the party and went to the paddocks to see the stud that the Prince Regent had established there in recent years.

While they were gone, the housekeeper, who had been discreetly but generously remunerated by Lord Amberley, offered to allow the ladies a glimpse of the magnificent State Apartments, and Lady Amberley insisted that the three younger ones take advantage of this while she had a comfortable cose on the ground floor with Lady Mortimer.

As they climbed into the carriages to return to Amberley House, it was agreed by all, though two voices were perhaps fainter than the others, that it had been a delightful day. The weather had remained clement, however, and though Lady Amberley was now extremely tired, she declared that she would not have missed it for anything. She added that she had begun to feel that Amberley House was a prison, but could now look forward to other, smaller expeditions.

When she tried to insist that her granddaughter change places with Lady Mortimer for the return journey, Lucinde agreed that there was plenty of room for her friend to join them, but no reason for her to change carriages. Lord Mortimer heard the interchange, and though he said nothing, he looked considerably displeased.

"You will, of course, come in and have a cup of tea before you leave, Josie?" Lady Amberley said to her friend as the coach passed through the turnpike at Hyde Park. "I told Cook we would be in need of refreshment the minute we returned."

"Very well, if you insist, my dear," Lady Mortimer agreed. "But we'll not stay long, for I'm promised to the McIntyres for cards this evening, and you need a rest before dinner."

As soon as the coaches came to a halt, Lord Mortimer jumped down and went to pick up Lady Amberley and set her in the wheelchair. Gussy then took charge of her patient, which left Lucy free to run upstairs and wash her hands before tea was brought into the drawing room, where the others had congregated.

As she hurried up the stairs, she could not help but wish that the Mortimers had gone home and taken her cousins with them, for she was tired and cross and in no mood to have to face Anthony across the tea table.

She reached the door of her bedchamber and was surprised to find it slightly ajar but assumed that the maid had not closed it properly. Giving it a slight push, she started in and stopped—then she began to scream without realizing she was doing so.

Anthony took the stairs two at a time and was by her side in less than a minute. He held her close, stroking her hair and murmuring soothingly to her as he surveyed what must have once been a very beautiful bedchamber.

The room was a complete shambles. The drawers of the escritoire and the dressing table had been taken out and tipped onto the floor, then flung against the walls, splintering the wood. The armoire doors stood wide, showing the delicate fabric of gowns ripped to shreds. Pillows had been slashed open as though with a sharp knife, and their feathers still swirled around the room. There were deep gashes in the flower-patterned fabric of the upholstered chairs and sofa near the fireplace, and the matching bed hangings had huge tears down them.

Lucy made as if to step inside, but Anthony held her back. "Don't, my dear, you might cut yourself," he said, pointing to the numerous pieces of broken glass and china on the floor.

Jennifer and Vanessa were the next upstairs, and they stood and stared at the room, but no one else ventured a step inside.

"Let me take her, my dear," Lady Mortimer said to her son, and he reluctantly released Lucinde into his mother's gentle arms.

"I think you'd better go and find Gussy," he said to Jennifer. "She'll make up a potion to calm her nerves. The person who did this was no ordinary burglar but someone who hates her."

He turned and saw Lord Amberley standing surveying the havoc wrought in the bedchamber. "I wonder where she kept the locket," the older gentleman murmured to Lord Mortimer, "for I'm sure she had nothing else of value in here. If I recall correctly, everyone who saw it last night was on our outing today, for tea had already been brought in and she did not show it to us while any servants were about."

"Perhaps she had already told others of its existence," Lord Mortimer suggested. "If she told Jennifer, then she might not have kept it as much of a secret as we thought. Or Gussy could have told someone, for they've been so close that she must have known of its existence. Would you mind if I take a good look around the chamber, my lord, to see if the culprit left anything behind?"

He had not noticed until now that Vanessa had been left standing alone in the hall, but Lord Amberley saw her at the same time.

"Come, my dear, let's go down to the drawing room and see if a good cup of tea will help," he said, steering her toward the stairs. "I'll talk to you later, Anthony."

A half-hour later Lucy was stretched out on the chaise in the sitting room off her grandmama's upstairs bedchamber, the room where she was to sleep this evening. She was quite calm now and deeply regretted the scene she had created a short time ago. Gussy's potion had achieved its purpose of calming her down, and she was more than ready to face Anthony's questions.

Gussy sat by the foot of the chaise and Lucy faced him.

"From the appearance of your bedchamber it would seem that the thief did not get what he came for—unless he did so only after he had given up looking and had started to wreak vengeance," he began, searching Lucy's face carefully as he spoke. "Have you any idea whether or not the locket is where you left it?"

"The locket is safe," Lucy said quietly.

He had thought as much, and he nodded to himself, then asked, "Does anyone else besides Gussy and those present last night in the drawing room know you have such a thing?"

"Only the person who gave it to me, I suppose," she told him.

"Then you're not still pretending it was something that your husband gave you?" he asked, unaware of the coldness that had crept into his voice.

"I never was," she suddenly snapped. "If anyone thought so, they simply jumped to conclusions."

"And you did not correct them."

It was a statement and did not call for an answer, so Lucy remained silent, though she had been unaware that anyone thought it to be a gift from Henry.

"Have you any idea who might wish to steal it or do you harm?" he asked.

"Henry's parents do not exactly love me, but I doubt that they would use such extreme measures to prove it," she said dryly.

"Was there anyone else, a cousin, brother or sister, who did not wish him to marry you?" He spoke gently again now, for he knew her to be extremely sensitive, and so it must hurt her to have anyone feeling harmful toward her.

"He told me after we were married that there was a girl at a neighboring house whom his parents wanted him to marry. If she loved him, she might wish me harm, I suppose."

His eyebrows rose, for he had not given any thought to something of that sort, but it would, of course, have been just the kind of thing Henry would have fought against. He had not been at all the sort to let his parents pick his bride for him.

"One last question, my dear, and then I'll let you rest. You said the locket was safe. Did you check?"

She shook her head. "No, I didn't. But Gussy did, and

it is safe. Aren't you going to also ask why I stole or looted it?'' There was more than a hint of sarcasm in her voice.

''You just said that someone gave it to you, so it is quite clear that I was wrong last night. And if I upset you, I sincerely apologize.'' He looked over to Gussy, who rose and quietly left the room.

Anthony took Lucy's hand in both of his. ''I'm afraid I jumped to conclusions and said some dreadful things to you last night, my love. Please forgive me, for I should have known you better than to think you would be involved in such a practice.''

''It doesn't matter,'' she said, tears springing to her eyes.

But it did matter, and he knew it. He raised her hand to his mouth, all the time watching her and noticing as his lips caressed the soft skin how the color came and went, and came again in her petal-soft cheeks.

For a moment he almost forgot himself and told her what had been in his heart for some time now, but he knew she was in a highly susceptible state and that, in any case, he should do the thing properly and first have a word with her grandfather.

''I wonder if my mama still means to go to the Warringtons' soiree this evening,'' he said. ''There is no reason why she should not go and take Jennifer along—and Vanessa, also, if she has no other plans.''

''Did you not intend to go?'' Lucy asked a little huskily. ''I feel like a fraud, for I'm perfectly all right now, though I must admit that I prefer not to attend the soiree.''

''Why don't we send them packing to the Warringtons', and then, if you still feel strong enough and Lady Amberley will invite me, I will stay to dinner and you and I can have a quiet game of piquet afterward,'' he suggested. ''I won't keep you up late, for, between the fresh air and the excitement, I believe an early night would be in order for both of us.''

''I'd like that,'' Lucy told him, still sure she could feel

his soft lips on the hand that now lay in her lap. His kindness embarrassed her a little, for this was a side of him she had rarely seen.

He rose. "Let me go and see if I can make all the arrangements, and I'll either come back or send word to let you know what everyone is doing," he said, leaning over and placing those soft lips on her forehead this time. "Don't run away, will you?"

As he left, Gussy came back inside.

"Well 'e certainly looks 'appier than when 'e left for 'Ampton Court this morning," she remarked, "and the same might be said of you, too, despite what 'appened 'ere while we were gone. Did you both come to your senses?"

"We stopped quarreling, if that's what you mean, Gussy," Lucy told her, looking a little sheepish. "It was all a misunderstanding, as might have been expected."

"Aye," Gussy said, "but now you're over the shock, who d'ye think made that mess in your bedchamber? And who came into your chamber during the night, I wonder, for I've no doubt now that you didn't make a mistake."

"It had to be a servant, listening perhaps at the door when I showed the locket to our guests last night, coming into my chamber to see if it had been left around, and then making another attempt today. You know them better than I, Gussy. Have you noticed any of them acting strangely?"

"You treat every servant in this 'ouse in the kindest possible way," Gussy told her. "I don't think there's one of 'em that would try to rob you, never mind rip up your clothes and things like that. You should've told 'is lordship that someone was in your bedroom last night."

"I suppose I should have," Lucy agreed, "but I didn't think about it. But, as I believe it was Grandpapa who said, everyone who saw the locket last night was with me on the outing today. And, in any case, I can't imagine the Mortimers or my cousins doing anything to hurt me."

"That's narrowed it down very nicely, milady, 'asn't it?" Gussy said, giving her mistress a strange look.

"I should never have told you I don't care for her," Lucy said. "Vanessa appeared to be completely disinterested in the locket last night, and she couldn't have done it, for she was with us all day."

There was a tap on the door and Lord Amberley entered. "Lord Mortimer asked me to let you know that he's taking Lady Mortimer and Vanessa home, and then he means to change and come back here. Lady Amberley invited him to have dinner with us again this evening."

He did not add that the young man had taken the opportunity to discuss with him his desire to marry his granddaughter, for she would find that out soon enough.

"You certainly seem to have made a rapid recovery from your earlier shock, Lucinde," he said, "but then, you're not one to make a Cheltenham tragedy out of anything."

"As long as I don't have to go back into that chamber until it has been put to rights, Grandpapa, I'll be fine. And it will be a comfort to know, during the night, that you're no farther away than the next room."

Lady Amberley had told Gussy to stay with her granddaughter this evening, and she would manage with Peters, and that it would be a simple family dinner.

But when Lord Mortimer returned, he had a letter with him that had just arrived from the North. He had been shown into the drawing room and served a glass of sherry while he waited, and was standing near the fireplace looking quite stern when Lucy came into the room.

She dropped him a curtsy and he took her hand in his and gently squeezed it, then he handed her the letter.

"I think you had best read this for yourself," he said softly, placing his untouched glass into her hand and going over to pour himself another.

She read the letter once and then read it again, unable to believe the contents, for it was from Lord and Lady Coldwell, stating that they had realized their folly in not recognizing their son's wife. Because of this, they had written a couple of months ago, enclosing a letter addressed to her and asking if he would do them the favor of forwarding it to her.

To Lucy this seemed incredible, but the hurt at their complete rejection of her had long since ceased to trouble her. She was sorry that their rigid stand had caused them to lose their son long before he had been killed. Had she received their letter, she would have gone to see them at once and tell them all the things they must long to know about the soldier son they knew so little about.

But they had given the letter to Lady Vanessa Langdon, they wrote, who had been on her way to London and had offered to deliver it to Lord Mortimer in person.

Now they were writing again to make sure that the original letter had been received by him. They could understand, they told him, if their son's wife no longer wished to know them, but they just wanted to be sure he had her direction and had sent it to her.

"Why do you suppose she held back the letter?" Anthony asked. "Do you think that perhaps she lost it and was afraid to tell them so?"

Lucy shook her head. "I'm much afraid that it was deliberate, Anthony. I've never been a betting person, as I believe you know, but I would lay odds that she is the young lady they wanted Henry to marry, for there's always been something most peculiar in the way she looks at me. Call it instinct, if you will, or feminine intuition, but I am quite sure that she withheld the letter deliberately."

"But what had she to gain by doing so?" Anthony asked, a little bewildered. "It was bound to come out sooner or later."

Lucy shook her head. "She might be expecting them to write to her, rather than send a second letter to you, and all she had to say was that she had met me and found that I despised them and wanted nothing further to do with them. If they had looked for her to be their daughter-in-law, she must be on familiar-enough terms with them to take her word for it."

He sighed. "I'm sure you must be right, for she has been most charming to everyone else. My mama believes her to be a delightful young lady and has even tried to steer her in my direction." A warmth came into his eyes as he looked into hers. "She has made little progress, I might add, for my affections are engaged elsewhere." He gently stroked her soft, pink cheek with a finger, and she felt that same warmth steal through her again.

"What are we to do?" she asked. "At least she cannot be the one who ransacked my chamber, for she was with us the whole time."

He nodded. "She could have an accomplice, someone she hired, but there was so much malicious damage done to your things that a hired thief would not generally stay long enough to do. I'm glad that tonight you'll be in the room next to your grandpapa, and I just hope he's a light sleeper."

She gave a little shudder. "So do I, but I don't really think anything like that will happen again. After all, whoever did it knows now that the locket is not in my chamber."

There was the sound of footsteps in the hall and she quickly whispered, "Don't tell them anything about it, please, for I don't want Grandmama worried any more than we can help."

He nodded as a footman opened the door wider and Lord Amberley pushed his wife's chair into the room.

Despite the problems they had returned to, Lady Amberley was smiling happily, for she had a nose for romance and she had been smelling the scent of it all day. She had kept her husband in her temporary bedchamber with one excuse after another for the first fifteen minutes, so that the two young people could have a little time alone together.

17

Lady Mortimer had also not failed to notice the increased warmth that appeared to have developed between her son and Lucinde, and she did not even try to tell herself that it was only sympathy on Anthony's part because of the injury done the girl. Though she liked her well enough, Lady Mortimer knew that Lucinde would never make an at all biddable wife, and with Anthony's own very definite views, a marriage between the two was certain to be extremely volatile. In her opinion, Vanessa Langdon, with her sweeter disposition, would make a far more suitable wife for her son.

She broached the subject to Anthony the next morning after his valet, Morgan, and some rather disreputable-looking men he had been speaking with in the study had left.

"I trust you did not stay too long at the Amberleys' last night, my dear, for both Lucinde and dear Lady Amberley were in need of a good night's sleep," she told him.

Anthony looked carefully at his mother and wondered what it was she had in mind, for she was not a morning person and seldom left her bedchamber before noon when she had been out the night before. She looked a little hagged, but he supposed it might be because the chair he had seated her in was in a particularly harsh morning light.

"I was fully aware of their condition and, in fact, Lord Amberley sent them both to their beds shortly after dinner. I stayed on and had a few very pleasant hours of piquet with him,'' he told her, deliberately not adding that he had been waiting until the men he had commissioned to watch the house were both on duty.

''I am sure that Lady Vanessa was hoping you might come to the Warringtons' soiree afterward, for she looked quite disappointed when you failed to appear.'' His mother's remark was accompanied by a knowing smile.

''I had already asked you to give my regrets, Mama,'' he said brusquely, ''so I find it difficult to understand why anyone would expect me to be there later.''

''Well, you do not realize, of course, what an impression you have made on that poor girl. I do believe her eyes follow you every time you move around a room,'' she said, her voice sounding a little reproachful.

Anthony looked at her as if she had windmills in her head. ''I have never given that young lady the slightest reason to look twice in my direction, and I can assure you I never will. If what you say is true, perhaps it would be a kindness to her were you to hint her elsewhere, for she has never had the remotest appeal to me.''

Having started, Lady Mortimer was not about to give in easily. ''I hope you're not becoming interested in Lucinde, my dear, for you need to father some strong sons and there is no doubt whatever in my mind that she is barren. Henry Coldwell appeared to me to be as lusty a young man as you could find, but she quite obviously never bore him a child,'' she said with a slight shrug.

This had crossed Lord Anthony's mind when he had first become interested in Lucy, and though he had posed quite a leading question to her at that time, she had adroitly avoided answering it. But as he had got to know her better, he had come to the conclusion that he had enough siblings to maintain the family name, and though he would have liked to have children of his own, he wanted Lucy much more.

''You already have two healthy grandsons, Mama, so there is no call to fear the Mortimers will become extinct. I have spoken to Lord Amberley and am now awaiting the right moment to speak to Lucy. You must regard this, however, in the strictest confidence, for if any word should get back to her before I am able to make my offer, it could seriously damage my chances. I am no longer a youngster in short pants, Mama, and I do not appreciate your only too obvious attempts at matchmaking."

Lady Mortimer had always found tears to be the best way to get what she wanted from her late husband, so it was natural for her to start by sniffing and work her way up to outright sobs. Anthony was made of stronger stuff than his father had been, however, so he simply sat back and let her get it out of her system.

When she had calmed considerably, he went over to where she sat and put an arm around her shoulders. "I've no wish to hurt you, Mama, but I am no longer a stripling in need of maternal guidance. I have fallen deeply in love with that minx, and I mean to have her, but must do it my way or she'll shy like a startled colt."

"I would not think of saying anything to anyone," Lady Mortimer said, sniffing into her kerchief. "You know that I want only the best for you, and if Lucinde is what you want, then as long as she makes you happy, I'll be well-satisfied."

He dropped a kiss on her brow, then took the chair across from her. "I have no sound reason to believe another attempt will be made to hurt Lucy, but my every instinct tells me it will. The group of men you saw in here just now are all ex-soldiers sent home with injuries. They are watching the Amberley house for me, both front and back, and will send word if anyone unusual is seen entering or leaving. I have told Jarvis they are to be shown in to me at any time, so please do not become alarmed if you hear one of them at the door."

She touched his cheek. "I hope Lucinde appreciates you. You're so very much like your papa was, for he could not abide interference in his plans, but I knew myself to be the most fortunate of women." She smiled gently. "Do what you have to do for her, and I promise that I'll tell no one until you bring her to me as your affianced."

Sir Nigel Langdon was finding his stay in London more than a little confining, but there was nothing he could do about this as long as his sister held the purse strings, for Lord Langdon kept him on what he felt was a quite meager allowance.

He had performed only one task for Vanessa thus far and found it most distasteful, for she had told him to not only search for a locket that was not there, but had insisted he also take a sharp knife with him and turn the chamber he was searching into a shambles.

Afterward, she had complimented him on the excellent job he had done, for she had seen it with her own eyes.

She was determined to have the locket, however, and he knew she would send him back again soon, probably to search a different chamber this time. If she wanted him to wreak as much havoc as before, it would cost her dearly, he decided.

He heard the faint scratch on his door before Vanessa came in and closed it silently behind her.

"Here is a sketch of the wing that houses the master suite. Don't lose it," she quietly warned, "for I would not like you to get into the wrong chamber. This is Lady Amberley's bedchamber, which Lucinde is using at the moment. There is a sitting room off it, and then Lord Amberley's chamber, but I'm told that he is a quite light sleeper, so do be sure that you don't make a sound.

"I'm convinced that she must be wearing the locket, probably in a bag around her neck or her waist. It's a pity you're so squeamish, for I'd like nothing better than for you to knock her on the head, but I can't force you to do so. Instead, what you must do is to take a rag soaked in ether and put it over her nostrils and mouth before she fully wakens. I'm sure you will enjoy stripping and searching her, though she's too small and thin for your taste, I believe. As long as you bring me the locket, you may do what you will with her for all I care."

"And what do I get for risking putting my head in a noose, dear sister?" Nigel drawled. "This time it must be more than a few paltry guineas."

"What would you say to a thousand of them?" she asked temptingly. "But you only get them if you return with the locket."

"If it's where you think, then I will get it," he promised. "But what if you're wrong? Am I to risk my neck for your mistake?"

"If I am wrong, you are to remain there until she comes around, then force her to take you to where it is. There is no danger, for you will be wearing a mask and she has never met you. A blow to her head will give you time to get away."

"How extremely bloodthirsty you are, dear sister, when someone else can take the blame for it," Sir Nigel said sarcastically, "and if, God forbid, I am caught, what then?"

"If you do not return by morning, I will come looking for you," she promised. "I can always make up an excuse, and there will be so much excitement that they will not even trouble themselves about me. But you'd best say nothing if you are caught. If I were to find that you had so much as breathed my name, I would deny everything and tell them I had been foolish enough to mention the locket to you, never dreaming you would try to make it yours."

"I've no doubt whatever that you would, my dear," Sir Nigel said smoothly, "but do you really think you would be believed? And even if you were, you would lose all chance of making the excellent match you seek, for no one would want to wed into the family of a convicted burglar. You would be forced to return home in shame."

"What complete nonsense you talk, Nigel," Vanessa said lightly. "I know you're far too clever to let yourself get caught. Don't leave before I get back tonight, for you must be sure that Lucinde is in bed and in a sound sleep before you enter her chamber."

"If you think that I intend to sit in my bedchamber all night you're much mistaken, my dear Vanessa," Sir Nigel told her. "Never fear. I will watch for a long time before making my move, and I will see you, with the locket in my hand, when I return."

She realized that he was in no mood to listen to sense, so with this Vanessa had to be satisfied, for there was no time left for further discussion. The Mortimers' coach would be at the door any moment now.

When Lady Mortimer called for Lucy and Jennifer that evening, her son was with her. He had decided, but not expressed the intent, to accompany Lucy to all evening functions for the time being.

She looked particularly lovely in a yellow lace gown that had arrived only that morning, for almost all of her gowns had been damaged beyond repair.

They were first to attend a birthday ball in honor of Lady Rutherford and then go on to a soiree at the home of Viscount and Lady Davenport, so it would, no doubt, be quite late before they finally returned home. First, however, they went to collect Vanessa from her Aunt Hermione's house.

Jennifer was all excitement, for she had met a young man a couple of times now who had appeared to be most interested in her and had sent flowers to her after each occasion. His name was Lord Christopher Townsend and he was the son of the Earl and Countess of Dartmoor.

"I told him where we would be this evening, and if he does not come, I think I will die," she moaned, enjoying the attention.

"If he does not come, there will be someone else to take his place," Lucy said practically. "You've never yet wanted for partners, and are not likely to do so for a long time."

Vanessa, who was piqued to find Anthony sitting between the other two young ladies and leaving her to sit beside Lady

Mortimer, remarked pettishly, "I'm sure things must have been very different for you when you were Jennifer's age, Lucinde."

"They most certainly were," Lucy said with a short laugh. "At Jennifer's age I had been married to Henry for almost eighteen months, and although I danced with many officers when we were in a place where a ball could be held, it was an unwritten breech of etiquette for a wife to dance more than once with any gentleman other than her husband."

Anthony gave her an amused glance. "As I recall," he said, "when you first arrived in Portugal there were so few officers' wives there, and none as pretty as you, that as a joke Henry kept a list and checked off the names at each ball so that everyone got a turn with you."

Lucy chuckled. "What an excellent memory you have. I'd forgotten about that silly list of his."

Anthony longed to take her in his arms and tell her how few things there were about her that he had forgotten, but he could not do so in front of the others and, in any case, it was not yet time to do so.

Vanessa appeared to be extremely gay tonight, and Lucy noticed that she was seldom without a smile on her face. It almost seemed as though she knew a secret and was happily hugging it to herself.

Perhaps her mood was infectious, for Lucy found that the dismals that had beset her during the day seemed to disappear and she enjoyed herself tremendously. She stood up with Anthony for the first of the two waltzes he had claimed, and felt as light as a feather as they spun around the floor, her yellow gown floating gracefully about her.

"I believe that the waltz must have been invented just for you, my dear," he murmured softly, his lips so close to her ear that she felt his warm breath, and marveled at the delightful little shivers it caused inside her. It was a long time since she had felt the sensation, and even then, it had been but momentary, unlike the feelings that continued now long after he had ceased to speak.

She sighed. "And to think that had some of the old dowagers had their way, the waltz would have been banned entirely from the dance floor," she said lightly. "It would have been a positive shame, had they succeeded."

"I was afraid that you might not feel up to attending tonight so soon after your frightening experience, and I would have been extremely disappointed." He watched with fascination as her eyelids, with their long fringe of auburn lashes, rose swiftly to reveal the intense color of her blue-green eyes, sparkling now as if with hidden laughter.

"But you surely know by now, sir, that I am not such a sickly creature as to let a thing like that prevent my enjoyment of your company."

Her voice sounded as if she were teasing, but just for a moment those lovely eyes held a feeling she had not meant to reveal. The hand that had been touching her waist so lightly strengthened its grip and her lips parted in a little gasp as she felt a sensation of longing she had never thought to feel again.

When the dance ended, and he escorted her back to where Lady Mortimer waited, she felt disappointed, as if a promise had not been fulfilled. He bowed and thanked her, and her cheeks turned a deep rose, for something in his eyes told her that he could read her thoughts.

Lady Mortimer, who was watching the two of them more than usual, realized that she had sadly mistaken things, for the romance had been progressing much more quickly than she had thought. If only Lucinde were not so outspoken in her feelings about London society, she would have welcomed the match, but perhaps her son would be able to convince the chit to keep her odd ideas to herself, once they were wed.

She had best keep a sharper eye now on Jennifer, she decided, for should anything untoward occur there, she would lose the friendship of one of her very oldest bosom bows. She need not worry tonight, however, for Richard and some of his friends were here, and of late the boy had become very protective of his younger sister and had developed an almost sixth sense as to who was suitable for her to dance with and who was not.

That left only Vanessa, and Lady Mortimer could now see exactly why her son had no interest in the girl. She had a decided smugness about her tonight and was flirting outrageously with one young rake right under Anthony's nose, as if she foolishly thought to make him jealous. Well, the girl would find out soon enough that his feelings were most decidedly engaged elsewhere.

They were in the supper room nibbling on oyster patties and slivers of smoked salmon, among other delicacies, when Lucy noticed a strange name on her dance card. Fortunately, Anthony, who was sitting by her side, saw her frowning as she looked at it.

"Something appears to be puzzling you, my dear," he remarked softly. "Can I be of service?"

"There is someone's name written down that I do not recall. This one, the third one after supper," she said, handing the card to him and pointing out the name. "Do you know anyone by the name of Gardener?"

"Perhaps you're not reading it correctly. Let me take a closer look," he requested, then he smiled and said quietly, "Ah, yes, quite so. The name, my dear, is not Gardener but Gardenroom, and I'm quite sure, because I put it there myself. When everyone else is dancing the cotillion, I intend to meet you in the garden room, which is just two doors beyond the ladies' retiring room."

He looked with equanimity at the puzzled frown on her face, then said, "If you know me at all, my dear, you will be quite sure that I have no intention of ravishing you amid the orange and lemon trees."

It was well-planned, for she could slip out as if going to the ladies' room; then, when no one was near, she could move quietly past and into the garden room. A thought occurred to her and she smiled impishly.

"Now what is it?" he asked, trying not to look smug.

"I was just wondering what you would do if you found another couple there ahead of you," she told him.

"There won't be," he said firmly.

"How do you know? Someone else could have had the same idea," she persisted.

He grinned at her, looking for all the world like a naughty schoolboy, then he leaned forward and whispered in her ear, "Because the door is locked and I have the key in my pocket."

Lucy abandoned all attempts to appear ladylike and laughed aloud, causing everyone near to turn around and wonder what on earth had got into her. But nothing could persuade her to say what she was laughing about, and once again they decided that Lady Lucinde Coldwell's behavior was not always as becoming as it might be. From the far end of the long table, Lady Mortimer raised a disapproving eyebrow, but neither Lucy nor her son took the least notice.

Lucinde was so excited she could scarcely remember the steps of the next two dances, and when they were over, she excused herself at once from Lady Mortimer, who was intently watching Jennifer and did not even notice that her son was nowhere in sight.

It was a simple matter from then on for Lucy to pause to adjust a slipper until the coast was clear, then go quickly through the door Anthony had indicated.

She heard a key turn in the lock behind her and swung around, eyebrows raised.

"Just to keep others out, my dear, not to keep you inside against your will," he said gently, pointing to the lock, which still held the key.

He took her hand and led her to a small bench in front of a flowering orange tree.

"I have secured your grandfather's permission to speak to you, my love, and to ask if you would do me the very great honor of becoming my wife. I feel as though I have always loved you, but these last months it has strengthened and matured to a point where I cannot envision a future without you."

She had known when he suggested the secret meeting that this was the reason, and had welcomed it, but now she began to tremble. Tears filled her eyes and spilled over and she swallowed hard.

Anthony looked gravely concerned. "If you need more time," he began, but she put a finger to his lips to stop him.

"I never cry," she told him between sniffs, "but now you've seen me crying twice in as many days. But this time it's from happiness."

She could get no further before his arms came around her and he crushed her to his chest. "I think I just aged five years in five minutes," he murmured, producing his own larger kerchief for her use.

With the utmost tenderness he placed a finger beneath her chin and tilted her face so that he could see the love shining from her eyes. It was his undoing. He had not meant to do more in the privacy of the garden room than to ask her to be his wife, but now that was not enough. He had to taste her soft, rosy lips, to see if they might fulfill the promise in her eyes.

The touch of his lips on Lucy's hand had made her warm before, but it was as nothing to the heat that rose inside her as his mouth descended slowly on hers. She could no longer think, for the gentle pressure had induced a warm lassitude that spread quickly throughout her body. She was glad of his supporting arms, for she felt she might easily have slipped to the floor without them.

His lips moved, tasting hers with increased intensity, and suddenly she felt more alive than ever before. It was as if her body had lain dormant after Henry died, though she had not realized it, and now suddenly all the familiar feelings had wakened inside of her, but now they were stronger than before.

She wanted much more than Anthony's kisses, for she had

not been a cold wife to Henry, but had soon learned to please him as much as he pleased her.

Anthony felt her reaction both in her warm lips and in the way her body had seemed to respond without actually moving, and he inwardly rejoiced. But this was not the time or the place to explore further, so he gently released her.

"You have made me the happiest of men, my dear, and I now regret even more that we must return to the ballroom before my mama sends out a search party for us," he said as he checked her appearance, tucking a straying curl into place before turning the key in the lock.

"I believe it would be best if you return to the ballroom now, for I have no wish to damage your reputation at this point. I will follow a little later, but first, give me your hand," he requested as he reached into a pocket.

Lucy gasped as he placed the most beautiful emerald ring she had ever seen upon the third finger of her left hand. Then he raised the hand to his lips for just a moment before turning her around and pushing her through the garden-room door and into the deserted hall.

She found her next partner just inside the ballroom door, impatiently waiting for her, and as she danced by, she saw Lady Mortimer's sigh of relief and wondered if Anthony would give his mother any explanation unless the beautiful ring on her finger was noticed.

But, of course, it was noticed at once by Jennifer, so that everyone within several yards started to wish her happy and to congratulate Anthony. Their hostess, Lady Rutherford, surprised at the commotion, begged to make the announcement and they had no option but to give their consent.

Vanessa did not bother to convey her good wishes to Lucy, for she was sure the chit would not notice whether she did or not in the excitement. Now all she hoped was that her brother was still at her aunt's when she got back, for she had an urge to snatch that ring off Lucy's finger and wanted to make sure that Nigel took it from her tonight, as well as the locket.

Amid a generous burst of applause, Lucy and Anthony waltzed once around the floor before others joined them. Then they were constantly besieged by friends wishing to be among the first to convey their best wishes to the happy couple.

The good news reached the Davenports before they did, and Lucy was most embarrassed to walk into the room and receive a hug from her hostess and more applause as waiters went around with trays of champagne with which to toast them. Lady Davenport confessed she could not have been more pleased, for the betrothal announcement had turned her party into the event of the Little Season.

18

The considerable excitement that had started with the announcement at the ball and followed them to the Davenports' soiree was completely absent when they reached Amberley House, for both Lord and Lady Amberley were already abed and Richard had gone with a good friend to one of his clubs.

"I'm afraid my news must wait until the morrow," Lucy told her cousin, who was sorely disappointed, for she had partaken of two small glasses of champagne and was eager to taste some more. "In any case, I doubt that they will be surprised, for Grandpapa had already given his permission for Anthony to address me."

"I must confess," Jennifer started to tell her, "that when I first met Anthony I—"

Lucinde interrupted her, for she was fully aware that her cousin had developed a *tendre* for Anthony, and was not in the mood for champagne-induced girlish confidences that might very well be regretted if remembered in the morning.

"It's late, Jennifer, and I'm really quite tired, so I think we should go quietly to our beds and break the good news in the morning," she said firmly, picking up a branch of candles to help light their way.

She steered her cousin up the stairs and to her chamber; then, putting her in the hands of the waiting maid, she proceeded to her grandmother's room, which was now her bedroom. To her complete astonishment, she found Gussy waiting with one of Cook's rolling pins in her hand.

"My goodness, Gussy, you gave me quite a start. Please put that thing down before you do any damage with it," she scolded, "and tell me what this is all about."

Gussy put the rolling pin on a chest near the door and went over to help her mistress out of her gown. "Morgan, Lord Mortimer's man that took us to the ship, told me that they're keeping watch outside tonight in case that scoundrel 'as another try."

"But his master did not tell me anything about it, and I was with him most of the evening," Lucy protested.

"I s'pose 'e didn't want to frighten you, milady, for they're supposed to catch 'im afore 'e gets inside," Gussy said, "but I thought I'd best stay in 'ere with this just in case they miss 'im."

From where he waited, Sir Nigel could hear the voices but could not distinguish the words. The first thing he must do when he finally got into the chamber, he decided, was to lock the maid in her small room and hope that she was a sound sleeper.

He stood in a patch of shadow in case anyone else on the floor might leave their room for any reason, and he watched for the light under the door to go out. Once it did and a slight click of a door being closed could be heard, he waited another fifteen more minutes to allow them time to fall asleep.

Moving closer, he grasped the knob and silently turned it, then slowly pushed the door open—not too wide, for there was still a small light burning in the hall and he did not want it to shine in the girl's eyes and waken her. Without making a sound, he stepped inside and closed the door behind him.

He turned as he heard a faint rustle, but he was too late, for something hard made contact with his head and he knew nothing more.

As soon as she heard the thud of Gussy's rolling pin, Lucy jumped quickly out of bed and relit the branch of candles she had left on the night table. Then she picked it up and took it over to where Gussy still stood near the door, watching for any movement from the dark figure on the floor at her feet.

She lit a single candle and handed it to the maid. "Did you knock him out?" she asked.

"Seems as if I did, milady," Gussy said gleefully, bending over him to make sure. "Go and wave them candles at the window to let Morgan know we 'ave him, while I tie 'is 'ands up in case 'e comes 'round."

Lucy did as she was bade, then came back to see if she recognized the man, but before she could even bend down to take a look, she saw Gussy's grim face. The maid held out to her a pad of cloth.

"Just you take a faint smell of this, milady, and tell me if y'think the same as I do," she said grimly.

"Ugh." Lucy shook her head. "It's ether, Gussy, so he must have meant to put me to sleep this time." A thought struck her. "Do you suppose he was going to kidnap me?"

"It looks like it t'me. We'll see what Morgan thinks when 'e gets 'ere."

"Aren't you going down to let him in?" Lucy asked.

Gussy nodded. "Aye, when I 'ave this one tied up so as 'e can't get at you," she said, fastening a heavy cord around his ankles.

While Gussy went downstairs, Lucy bent over the man and looked hard, but though there was something familiar about him, she did not believe she had ever met him. She was a little surprised to find that he was dressed like a gentleman.

Gussy, with Morgan and his colleague, came up the stairs and into the chamber just as the door to the sitting room and Lord Amberley's chamber opened and his lordship stepped through, clad in a deep-burgundy dressing gown.

"What on earth is going on here?" he asked, peering at the person on the floor, then looking at the two rough-looking men who had followed Gussy into the chamber.

"We had another visitor, Grandpapa, probably the same one, I should think," Lucy told him calmly.

The young man was starting to come around, cursing softly to himself as he found that he was bound hand and foot.

"Who are you?" the old man asked. "What are you doing here in my house?"

"Dashed sorry, sir, must have got into the wrong house," Sir Nigel said. "After a drink or two these houses are all alike."

"I asked who you are?" Lord Amberley repeated sternly.

Sir Nigel had complete control of his senses now and realized what a mess he was in. "Darned if I know who I am, sir," he said, looking quite bewildered. "Remember wondering why the front door was open and coming up the stairs. I count doors, y'know. Sometimes it's the only way to find the right one if you've been imbibing a little, as I did tonight. I suppose this harridan here thought I was after her mistress and knocked me on the head when I came in by mistake."

He rambled on quite cleverly while the others stood watching him but not believing anything he said.

There was a sound from below and Richard came up the stairs, just returning from a club he had joined.

"What happened?" he asked. "Surely not another try for that locket, Lucy?"

Before he could answer, however, Jennifer appeared, white-faced and wrapped completely in a huge dressing gown. She peered over her brother's shoulder, then murmured, "Oh, no."

" 'Twas no accident, milord," Gussy said to Lord Amberley. "This dropped out of 'is 'ands as 'e fell." She showed him the ether-filled pad.

"We've come to a sorry state," Lord Amberley said, "when a man can't enjoy the comforts of his own home without having people come to rob and plunder the minute his back is turned. I suppose you hit him with that, Gussy?" he asked, pointing to the rolling pin, and when she nodded, he murmured, "Good girl! Nice bit of work!"

Footsteps could be heard in the hall and the murmur of voices as Lord Mortimer came up the stairs. He was still in his evening clothes, for he had not yet retired when one of the men had come for him.

Sir Nigel tried again. "Ah, someone sensible at last. You've got to believe me, my lord. It was an accident. I just came into the wrong house. Had a few drinks at the club and thought this was where I was staying." He tried to laugh. "Right door, wrong house, that's what it is. You see, these houses are all alike and I count the doors as I walk along the corridor to be sure I get my own."

"And what club was it where you had these drinks?" Anthony asked.

"Do you know, sir, I cannot recall either the club or my name? It was the knock on the head did it, I'm sure. Ought to prosecute her for it," he blustered, then his voice wavered as he realized that not one of them believed his story.

"If you like, sir, I'll have my men get him out of here. They can carry him downstairs and then I'll take him to the nearest jail for the night. He should come before the magistrate in the morning, but I'll have it put as far back as possible to give us time to discuss what we want to do with him first." All the while he was speaking to Lord Amberley, Anthony kept glancing over to Lucy to make sure she also was in agreement.

Not until Morgan and another man had carried Sir Nigel out did Lucy say a word, then she spoke to the maid. "Show Lord Mortimer the cloth he carried, if you please, Gussy, for I cannot help but wonder just what he intended to do to me."

Gussy took the cloth to Anthony and he took a sniff and looked grim.

"He most certainly meant to render you unconscious, my dear, but to what purpose we may never know. He could hardly hope to take you from the premises, so I would think he simply wanted you silent. I would recommend you try to get some sleep now, perhaps with the aid of a sleeping draft. We'll find out more about that young man in the morning,'' he assured her; then, at Lord Amberley's command, he followed the old man into his room.

At the slightly unfashionable hour of ten o'clock the following morning, Lady Vanessa Langdon called to see her dear friend, Jennifer. The latter did not invite her friend up to her bedchamber, however, as she usually did, but sent word for her to wait in the drawing room.

With her hot chocolate that morning had come a note from her grandpapa instructing her not to receive any visitors without either Lucinde or Richard present. Though she could not think that dear Vanessa had anything to do with the incident last night, Jennifer knew better than to disobey Lord Amberley, so she went along to Lucy's room when she was ready, and the two young ladies went downstairs together.

''We were just about to have breakfast, Vanessa,'' Jennifer told her friend. ''Won't you join us?''

''A cup of coffee, perhaps,'' Vanessa agreed, ''and a sweet roll if you have one.'' She glanced at Lucy as they took their places at table. ''You look a little under the weather, my dear Lucinde. Did you not sleep well last night?''

''It was rather a late evening,'' Lucy told her, thinking the same thing about their guest but politely refraining from saying so.

There was no doubt but that Vanessa was agitated, and Lucy longed to ask her why she had come at such an early hour, but she restrained herself and waited.

''I know I don't seem quite myself today, but the fact of the matter is that my young brother has been staying with me and has got himself in with a quite shocking set. Last night he did not come home and I'm so worried,'' she told them, pressing a kerchief to her eyes, though Lucy had not yet seen a single tear.

''What kind of a shocking set?'' Lucy asked.

''Thieves, by the sound of it. I saw a piece of jewelry in

his bedroom that he couldn't possibly have bought himself, and he absolutely refused to tell me where he got it."

Lucy was facing both Vanessa and the door, and she tried not to register surprise when Anthony walked in quietly and stood behind their guest, listening to her agitated words for a moment before taking a seat beside Lucy and asking, "Would he, by any chance, be a little taller than you are, and with your coloring, my lady?"

Vanessa had swung around when he entered, startled to see him there at that hour. She inclined her head. "I suppose so. His hair is more dark brown than black. Why do you ask, my lord? Have you seen him?"

"A well-dressed young man answering your description is at present locked up in jail. He will appear before the magistrate around the noon hour. He has refused to give his name, or the reason for entering Lady Lucinde's bedchamber early this morning," Lord Mortimer informed her, watching her face all the while he spoke.

An insinuating smile flickered across Vanessa's face. "Perhaps you have a rival, my lord, but I was unaware that my brother was acquainted with Lucinde."

"Or perhaps he was following the instructions of an older sister who was too cowardly to do her own dirty deeds," Lord Mortimer thundered, furious that she would make insinuations against Lucy. "He'll not stay silent long, however, for when the magistrate sends him to his guards for questioning they'll get everything out of him in no time at all. They have interesting ways of making people talk."

Vanessa believed him, and her eyes widened with horror, for she knew her parents would never forgive her if their dear Nigel was hurt in any way.

"You must not let them touch him," she said, her voice rising hysterically. "He was only trying to help me, for that locket Lucinde has is really mine and I want it back. Henry showed it to me before he ever met her and told me it would be mine. Then she came along and bewitched him into marrying her instead."

Once she started, it seemed as though she could not stop. "She killed him. She stole him from me and took him back to the wars," Vanessa went on, her voice now almost to screaming pitch.

Jennifer was staring wide-eyed and openmouthed at the girl she had thought a friend.

Lucy had heard enough. She got slowly to her feet, and as Vanessa screamed imprecations against her, she slapped the girl hard across her face.

There was a momentary silence in the room, then Vanessa put her head in her hands and started to sob quietly.

Gussy and Morgan, who had apparently been waiting outside the door, entered then and helped Vanessa to her feet and out of the room. Then Lord Amberley and Richard came in and closed the door behind them.

"What happens now?" Lucy asked, a little shakily.

"I think Lord Amberley will agree with me that it is now up to you, my dear," Anthony said. "Although your grandparents sustained damage, the real intent was to rob and harm you."

She looked across at her grandpapa's stern face, and he nodded his agreement, then she turned back to Anthony.

"I believe she is deranged and could not help herself, and she probably exerted much financial and other influence upon a younger brother to make him do her bidding. Thanks to Gussy, I was not hurt," she said quietly.

"Do you want to press charges against them? If you wish it, either I or your grandfather will act on your behalf," Anthony advised her.

She shivered at the thought of that jail and shook her head. "I don't think they should be let loose on society with not even a slap on the hand, but I have no wish to see them thrown in jail or transported. Perhaps their parents . . ." she hesitated, not knowing quite how to put it.

For the first time since he entered the room, Anthony smiled and its warmth took away her sudden chill.

"I believe I can secure a statement from the magistrate,

whom I know quite well, telling Lord and Lady Langdon what they must do as a condition of the release, for they are both still under age. And I will see them both safely into their parents' hands," he told her.

Lucy looked worried. "You will take someone with you, in case . . ." she began, but he stopped her by placing a hand upon hers.

"I will most certainly take someone with me, my love, and I will return as quickly as I can," he said huskily, for she was looking at him in a way that made him wish the others were not in the room.

There was a sound of commotion in the hall and then an outraged Lady Amberley was wheeled into the room by her abigail.

"It would seem that I am the last person in this house to find out what is going on." The old lady was in a rare temper. "I am not an invalid any longer, for things to be kept from, and it looks to me as though I should have been included in what seems to be a family conference, for I assume that you, Anthony, are about to become one of us."

Chuckling to herself, Lucy jumped up and took the handles of the wheelchair, dismissing the abigail and instructing her to close the door behind her. She placed her left hand on her grandmama's lap to show her the ring.

Lady Amberley was immediately mollified. "Excellent taste, Anthony. Just the thing for a redhead like this one," she said, smiling happily.

He came over to kiss her cheek, then asked, "May I steal my fiancée for just a moment, for I have something private to say to her before I must leave. The others will, I know, tell you all about the events of last night."

Before the old lady could tell him it was not fitting, he had grasped Lucy's hand and pulled her out of the room and into the empty study.

"I hate to leave you so soon, but I have a favor to ask," he said, taking her into his arms and holding her close. "If I get a special license, would you be willing to forgo a grand wedding and just have something simple in two weeks' time? I feel as though I have waited long enough for you already."

"Of course," Lucy agreed at once. "You know I don't want a big fuss, and Grandmama's not up to it yet anyway. I'll miss you."

He bent his head and captured her lips, and Lucy closed her eyes as the room began to spin. There was no hesitation in her response, for she was hungry for his love, and her fingers stroked his hair, then curled around his ears and his cheeks.

Somehow he had always known she would be like that, as honest in her love as in everything else, and now he hated all the more to leave her, but he had no alternative.

They drew apart. "If I don't leave now, I'll not be able to," he said raggedly. "I will stop and see Lord and Lady Coldwell while I'm in the north, and explain everything to them."

"Tell them I will come to see them as soon as we are settled, for I want to talk to them about Henry and let them know he missed them as much as they missed him," she said softly. "Take care, love."

He dropped a last kiss on her forehead, then opened the door, to find Jennifer waiting on the other side.

"Grandmama told me to come after you," she explained, "but I decided I was best out here."

"Good girl," Anthony said, spinning her around and planting a brotherly kiss upon her cheek, "you're learning." Then he hurried out to the waiting carriage.